WRONGFUL DEATH

Books by L.J. Sellers

WRONGFUL DEATH

A DETECTIVE JACKSON MYSTERY

L.J. SELLERS

Published by Thomas & Mercer, Seattle
www.apub.com

Amazon, the Amazon logo, and Thomas & Mercer are trademarks of Amazon.com, Inc., or its affiliates.

ISBN-13: 9781477822180
ISBN-10: 1477822186

Cover design by Paul Barrett

Library of Congress Control Number: 2014951152

Printed in the United States of America

This story is dedicated to all the compassionate people around the world working to reduce homelessness and improve the lives of those who live on the streets. In addition, I'm dedicating a monthly portion of the royalties from *Wrongful Death* to my foundation, Housing Help. I started the charity with a goal of keeping families from becoming homeless, typically as a result of a short-term financial setback. Last year, we helped one family a month stay in their homes. This year, we hope to double that. Please visit the website and make a contribution if you can: www.housinghelpfoundation.com.

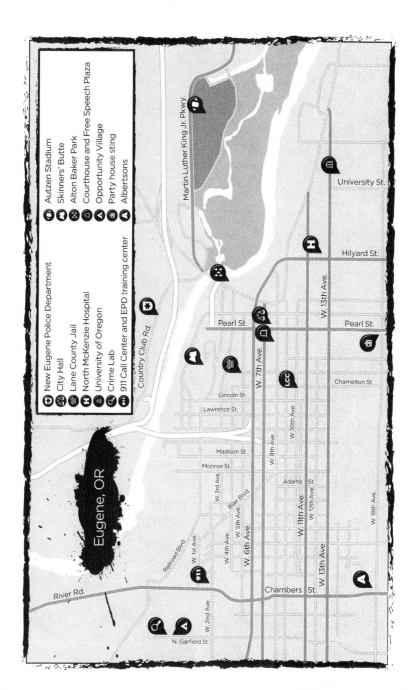

Eugene, OR

New Eugene Police Department
City Hall
Lane County Jail
North McKenzie Hospital
University of Oregon
Crime Lab
911 Call Center and EPD training center

Autzen Stadium
Skinners' Butte
Alton Baker Park
Courthouse and Free Speech Plaza
Opportunity Village
Party house sting
Albertsons

Martin Luther King Jr. Pkwy.

University St.

Hilyard St.

Pearl St.   Pearl St.

Country Club Rd.

W. 13th Ave.

Chamelton St.

Lincoln St.

Lawrence St.

W. 10th Ave.

W. 8th Ave.

Madison St.

Monroe St.

Adams   St.

Railroad Blvd.

W. 1st Ave.

W. 3rd Ave.

W. 4th Ave.

W. 5th Ave.

Blair Blvd.

W. 6th Ave.

W. 11th Ave.

W. 12th Ave.

W. 13th Ave.

W. 18th Ave.

W. 7th Ave.

LCC

River Rd.

Chambers   St.

W. 2nd Ave.

N. Garfield St.

Cast of Characters

Wade Jackson: detective, Violent Crimes Unit
Katie Jackson: Detective Jackson's daughter
Derrick Jackson: Detective Jackson's brother
Kera Kollmorgan: Detective Jackson's girlfriend / nurse
Lara Evans: detective / task force member
Rob Schakowski (Schak): detective / task force member
Michael Quince: detective / task force member
Denise Lammers: Detective Jackson's supervisor / sergeant
Sophie Speranza: newspaper reporter
Rich Gunderson: medical examiner (attends crime scenes)
Rudolph Konrad: pathologist (performs autopsies)
Jasmine Parker: evidence technician
Joe Berloni: evidence technician
Victor Slonecker: district attorney
Dan Thompson: slain police officer / Schak's cousin
Donna Thompson: Officer Thompson's mother / Schak's aunt
Kurt Thompson: Officer Thompson's brother / Schak's cousin
Trisha Weber: Officer Thompson's girlfriend
Gene Burns: Trisha's ex-boyfriend / murder suspect
Jacob and Henry Walsh: homeless twins / suspects
Pete Scully: homeless man / suspect
Ashley Devonshire: sexual assault and suicide victim
Daren Sorenson: Ashley's friend / suspect
Mara Andrade: sexual assault victim
Grace Marston: sexual assault victim

WRONGFUL DEATH

CHAPTER 1

Friday, November 21, 7:45 a.m.

YOUR DAUGHTER IS A WHORE. Clare Devonshire drew in a sharp breath. The phone pinged again, and a second text landed. No message this time, just an attached video. Fear pulsed through her torso. Paralyzed, she stared at the device. A third ping signaled another text. If Ashley was in some kind of trouble, she had to know. Bracing for the worst, she clicked it open. The message was brief: *The video will go viral unless you pay me $15,000 to destroy it. You have until five today to get the cash. If you call the police, I'll post it everywhere. I'll text with instructions soon.*

Oh god. What had her daughter done? Clare tried not to think about the money. They had just cashed out a retirement fund to pay their portion of her husband's second round of leukemia treatment. And they'd maxed out their credit cards long ago. With a shaking hand, she plugged her phone into her laptop, downloaded the file, and clicked it open. In a low-lit room,

Ashley lay on a mattress, naked, with her eyes closed. The bed was pushed up against a wall, covered with only a wrinkled white sheet. The camera focused on her daughter's face, then zoomed in on her pubic area. A hand came into the picture, covered by an elbow-length dark-leather glove. The bastard began to fondle Ashley's genitals. Her daughter didn't move. She was unconscious! Coffee soured in Clare's stomach. The man began to probe Ashley's vagina, and Clare moved to shut it off.

But not fast enough.

"What are you watching?" Her daughter rushed into her small office and leaned over her shoulder. "Was that me? Turn it back on!"

The look on her daughter's face hurt Clare's heart. "You don't need to see it." She stood and tried to take Ashley into her arms.

Her daughter pushed her away. "Where did that come from?"

"It was texted to me." Clare didn't want Ashley to know about the blackmail. "But don't worry, we'll handle it."

"How?" Ashley shrieked. "It's a video. It's probably online already!" She burst into tears. "If people see it, I can't go back to school."

The outburst brought her husband into the room, his pale, gaunt face pinched with concern. "What's going on?"

Clare would have preferred not to burden him with more stress. He'd been through so much recently just to stay alive. "Let's all sit down and be calm," she said. "We have to figure out what happened, then decide our next move."

Jay's eyes darted back and forth between the two, but he didn't sit. "What is this about?"

"Read the text." Clare handed him her phone.

"What does it say?" Ashley demanded. "I have a right to know."

Clare couldn't hold back a sigh. "He wants money to destroy the video."

"How much?" Ashley started to cry. "I'm so sorry."

Through clenched teeth, her husband said, "We have to call the police."

Clare knew he was right. But Ashley cried out, "No! I'm not talking to the cops. I'm not getting a rape kit. I'll kill myself first." She was sixteen and fully developed but emotionally still a kid.

"Sit down, Ashley!" Clare had to take charge before her daughter lost control. The girl was high-strung and probably needed a prescription, but they'd tried to teach her meditation and self-calming techniques instead. Clare didn't trust antidepressants, or any mental health drugs for that matter. "Take three deep breaths and visualize yourself at the beach with all this in the past. You'll get there soon."

Ashley started to breathe in, then ran to the hall bathroom, where they heard her vomiting.

Jay squeezed Clare's hand. "Did you watch the video?"

"Only the first minute. Ashley is naked and unconscious and being sexually molested."

Jay let out a guttural sound, then jumped up and swore like a bouncer at a biker rally. He paced the room, shouting questions. "How did this happen? Where was she? Did you ask her?"

"Not yet. She got hysterical."

"I'm calling the police."

"Wait. Let's find out what we can from Ashley first. Maybe we can handle this."

"We don't have that kind of money anymore. We should call the police."

"He said he would post the video if we did." Clare heard her own voice rise in pitch. "What are the cops going to do? They'll never find him in time to help us."

Ashley came back into the room, her face chalk white and damp from being splashed with water. "Don't do anything! Don't call the police and don't pay him. This is my fault."

"Who is he?" Clare finally asked. "Do you know him?"

"No!" Her daughter's eyes were wild with pain. "I was at a party, and I must have blacked out. I woke up in front of the house after midnight, and I knew I'd been raped."

"When did this happen?" Her husband's voice had a tortured quality—as if he knew the answer would hurt.

And it did.

"Wednesday. The last night you were in the hospital." Ashley glanced over at Clare. "Mom was out with friends."

Guilt ripped at her guts, and Clare lashed out. "Goddammit! One fucking night to cut loose and be a person, instead of a nursemaid or a mother or housekeeper. And now we all have to pay for it!"

Her husband and daughter both looked stunned—Jay with his mouth open, and Ashley with tight, angry lips.

"I'm sorry." Clare met her daughter's eyes. "This isn't your fault. You were victimized. But you need to tell us everything about the party. What house? Who was there? Who did you talk to?"

"I can't! My friends will hate me." Ashley spun and fled the room.

Clare turned to Jay, her jaw aching with tension. "Should we just borrow the money and pay him?"

Her mild-mannered husband slammed a fist into the back of a chair, making her jump. "Even if we could get a bank loan, it'll take a week." His face twisted into a derisive sneer. "Do you want to ask your mother for it?"

"You know I can't. What do we do?"

"I don't know yet." Her husband's voice was so tight, he sounded like a stranger.

Clare's cell phone pinged again. "That's him, texting with instructions."

"Tell him we need more time."

. . .

Friday, November 21, 5:25 p.m.

Officer Dan Thompson recoiled at the man's smell—booze, piss, and a splash of vomit. But he handed the homeless guy a blanket and a pair of wool socks. Everyone had a story, and some people's bad luck started early in life. "Find shelter and stay warm tonight." The old man thanked him and headed back toward the camp, a hodgepodge of ragged tents and cardboard lean-tos. It wasn't a sponsored, supervised site like Opportunity Village or the rest stops, but those sleeping areas were limited in how many they could accept. This camp was farther from the town's center than usual, but his fellow officers routinely rousted the campers, forcing them to keep moving.

Only a few more people lined up near the back of his truck, where he handed out jackets, blankets, and whatever warm items the community had donated over the last week. He did the giveaway every year when the temperature dropped down. It was always on his own time, but he'd kept his uniform on to help build goodwill with the homeless community. His weapon was locked in the truck for the same reason.

A woman with a young child stepped up. "Do you have a jacket for my daughter?" The mother was still in her twenties, but even in the fading light he could tell she'd been homeless long enough for her facial skin to develop a protective thickness.

"I'm sorry, but I gave away the children's coats at Shelter Care." The complex where homeless families with young children could stay temporarily had been his first stop. But why wasn't this woman in a shelter? This camp wasn't safe for children. He handed her a blanket and a sweater. "This is the only clothing I have left."

"Thanks, officer."

"Where are you sleeping tonight?"

"In a tent here with a friend."

"It's freezing, and your daughter should be in a shelter."

"I know." Her face crumpled with anguish. "But I missed my intake appointment because I had a job interview. Then I didn't get the job." Tears rolled down her face.

Thompson dug for his wallet and held out a couple of twenties, all he had left. "Go get a motel room for tonight, then show up at Shelter Care first thing tomorrow morning and talk to Gayle."

The woman hesitated for a brief second, then grabbed the cash and stuffed it into her front jeans pocket. "Thank you so much." The woman and child hurried away, heading back toward Sixth Avenue, where they could find a cheap room rental.

Thompson handed his last blanket to the next man in line, thirty-something with a full beard, but clean and—based on his eye contact—sober too.

Thompson looked at two men in line behind him. "I'm sorry, but I'm out of stuff." No matter how much he collected, it was never enough.

"Do you have more money?" one of the men asked, stepping toward him.

Thompson recognized him and his brother. Twins who'd been a part of Eugene's street scene for as long as he could remember. Henry and Jacob. But he could never tell them apart.

"No. I'm done here. Sorry." Thompson closed the tailgate and climbed into his truck. There was nothing more he could do for the homeless tonight. Engaging with the mentally ill brothers would be a waste of time.

He sat for a moment, watching the camp a half block away. This one didn't have sponsors, stability, or a portable toilet like several others in town did. It was chaotic and messy, with an ever-changing population. The drunks and crazies stayed here because they weren't welcome—at least for long—in the other camps, and most had been banned from the Mission. But they were still people, and he slept better at night knowing they wouldn't freeze to death on his watch. The cold had come early this year, and the warming centers weren't open yet, so people on the street were vulnerable.

Thompson reached for his keys, ready to go home, pour a shot of bourbon, and unwind. If he could. He had a lot on his mind and tough choices to make. A knock on the passenger's window startled him, and he turned. *Now what?*

CHAPTER 2

Saturday, November 22, 7:45 a.m.

Wade Jackson opened the newspaper to the real estate section and scanned for house rentals. At the counter, Kera made coffee with her usual efficient grace. An overwhelming love and gratitude filled his heart. She was beautiful, even first thing in the morning. Wide cheeks, full lips, and a smile you could see from a mile away. But it was the size of her heart that made him lucky to have her in his life.

She set a tall cup of java on the table near him, and he patted her butt, which she pretended to ignore. He was enjoying their time alone. He'd spent a rare night with her, and their toddlers were still sleeping.

She leaned over his shoulder, glancing at the paper. "What are you looking for?"

"A four-bedroom rental." Jackson looked up and grinned.

"You really think you're ready?" Her green eyes were both hopeful and skeptical.

"It's time. I'm tired of shuffling back and forth between houses. And now that Derrick is home all the time, and Benjie is with us, the old house feels too small." His brother, Derrick, had been a long-haul truck driver when Jackson and his daughter moved into the old family home, so they'd had the place mostly to themselves. Then Derrick had switched jobs, and Jackson had brought Benjie home after finding him at a crime scene.

Kera gave him a mock scowl. "You were supposed to say something sweet about how you can't stand to be away from me."

"That too." He stood and pulled her in for a hug. "Let's do this. I want you in my life every day, even if only for a few minutes when I have those long investigation days."

"What's the plan? Sell both houses?"

"Let's call an agent and put them on the market." They had discussed it a few times since Benjie had come into his life and Danette, Kera's daughter-in-law, had left hers, but always in a vague, someday way. "Derrick and I planned all along to sell our folks' house, and you . . ." He trailed off, not wanting to remind her of her grief.

"I know. I should get out of here."

Kera's only son had died in Iraq at the age of eighteen. But Nate had fathered a child before he left. Then the boy's mother, who'd lived with Kera since the baby was born, had died in a car accident recently. Now Kera was raising little Micah in a big house filled with painful memories.

"We'll rent a place for now and start looking to buy something together down the road." Had he gone too far? Was that what he really wanted?

"What about Katie? She just moved back in with you. I'm afraid to disrupt her again."

Jackson had worried so much about his fifteen-year-old daughter over the previous year that he'd developed some emotional scar tissue. "Now that she's pregnant, she's in a different mental space. She'll come along." He grabbed Kera's hands. "It's our time to be together."

"I love the sound of that." Kera kissed him deeply, but their moment was interrupted by a tug on Jackson's pant leg.

He reluctantly pulled back and reached down to touch Benjie's head. "Good morning."

"I have to pee."

"You know where the bathroom is." Jackson walked him there anyway. Like Jackson, Benjie had lost his mother, a homicide victim with no family. The little boy had clung to him at the crime scene, and Jackson had taken him home and eventually filed for custody. The hearing was set for next week, and he was eager to get beyond it.

As they came back up the hall, he heard his phone ring. Tension filled his body. On an early Saturday morning, it could only be one person.

He stepped into the kitchen, and Kera handed him the cell. "It's Sergeant Lammers. You'd better take it." She kept her face impassive, but he knew she was disappointed.

Reluctantly, he put the phone to his ear and walked away. "What have we got?"

"Officer Dan Thompson was killed near a homeless camp last night." Her gruff voice broke at the end. "You have to take this one, Jackson," she pleaded. "We need the killer in custody ASAP. The whole department will be chaotic until we've made an arrest."

Grief, fear, and stress seized him, and for a moment, he couldn't speak. Thompson was one of the good guys. A cop with a big heart and a moral code he never compromised. He was also Detective Rob Schakowski's cousin. "Does Schak know?"

"Not yet. Do you want to tell him, or should I?"

Jackson didn't have the heart. Schak might break down and cry, and he wouldn't want Jackson to witness it. "Will you tell him, please? And don't let him come out to the scene."

"Of course not." Lammers' gruffness was back. "Thompson was found this morning by a college student on her way to do some research at the new camp. He was in the grass near West Fifth Avenue, with his truck parked nearby. It's a short chunk of street off West First, then Wallis."

Jackson visualized the industrial area, surrounded by wetlands. "How did he die?"

"Multiple stab wounds."

"I'm on my way."

. . .

The early-morning drive across town was quiet, with crisp, cold air and dark, leafless trees lining the streets. Eugene, Oregon, was prettier in the summer, but Jackson loved it year-round and had never lived anywhere else. He probably never would. Tucked in between the mountains and the ocean, it never suffered the extreme weather going on everywhere else. On a cultural level, it was just big enough to be interesting. As a law enforcement jurisdiction, they were facing the highest annual murder rate they'd ever had. Violent, inexplicable homicides had sucked up their time and left the unit members shaking their heads, but they had all been resolved.

He hoped that would be the case with this one as well. What had Dan Thompson been doing near the camp? It had to be charity. For the previous seven winters, Thompson had collected blankets and warm clothing at the first sign of freezing temperatures to give to needy individuals. The early onset of cold weather had set the campaign in motion a few weeks ago, so Thompson had likely been handing out goods. Had a drunk, psychotic hobo killed him? It was easy to jump to that conclusion, even though Thompson would be the first to counter that kind of thinking. Dan had advocated for the homeless among his peers, but his message had gone largely unheard. For most officers, street people were a pain in the ass. A problem that continued to grow as the city council kept making Eugene more attractive to those in need.

He turned on Wallis and saw three squad cars at the end of the block. Beyond them, in the clearing, was the homeless camp. He drove toward them, passing small businesses operating out of metal buildings. As he turned onto Fifth Avenue, he spotted another patrol car parked on the street behind a red pickup. He climbed out of his city-issued sedan, and the quiet morning erupted in shouts. Jackson spun toward the ruckus. Uniformed officers tore through the camp, ripping down tents and kicking cardboard boxes. The shouting grew louder.

"Get up!"

"Put your hands in the air!"

"Move, scumbag!"

They were searching everyone, and Jackson knew it had to be done. If a suspect in the camp still had the murder weapon, they needed to find it right away. But the anger and aggression could backfire, and more people could be hurt. He grabbed his phone and called Lammers. "You need to get down here. Maybe Sergeant Bruckner too. We've got angry officers tearing the camp apart. But I need to focus on the crime scene and can't babysit them."

In the distance, a man cried out in pain. Jackson hung up and ran toward the camp, touching the Sig Sauer under his jacket out of habit. The patrol officers carried batons and Tasers to deal with unruly citizens, but he didn't. Yet he wasn't afraid for himself. He feared for the vagrants—and for the department, if this scene got out of control and lawsuits followed. They didn't need another scandal.

He charged past an officer talking to two handcuffed men seated near a makeshift lean-to and into the center of the camp. Another officer, a big man he didn't know, shouted at a ragged camper who was on his knees. "Take off your coat now!" The officer raised his baton.

The homeless man cringed but clung tightly to his jacket. The air was freezing, and the coat was probably his only possession.

"It can wait until the command unit gets here," Jackson said, stepping up. The big mobile bus would arrive soon and serve as an interview room. "What's your name?" He locked eyes with the officer.

"Greg Bremmer." The uniformed man bristled with anger. "One of our own is dead, and I *will* search everyone in this camp."

"Just do it respectfully. This man could be a witness, and no one is leaving the area until I've talked to them."

"Respectfully?" Bremmer rolled his eyes in disgust. "Give me a fuckin' break."

"You took an oath. Respect that, at least."

More shouting and cries of pain came from inside a nearby tent. Jackson rushed to the opening. Inside, an officer was kneeling on a man's back.

"No one gets hurt here!"

The officer popped to his feet and spun to face him. Keith Markham. They'd worked patrol together long ago. "Jackson. You're handling this case?"

"I am. And I want cooperative witnesses."

"I'm just trying to help you out. This scumbag had a weapon." With a bare hand, Markham held out a small, closed pocketknife.

"Slip it in my jacket. My gloves and evidence bags are still in my car."

The officer complied. Below him, the homeless man rolled over to face them. He looked seventy, with brown weathered skin and a gray scraggly beard, but he could be closer to fifty.

Jackson kneeled down. "What's your name?"

"Ricky Jones." He had watery eyes and a voice ragged from smoking unfiltereds and drinking rotgut. "Why did you take my knife?"

"Who did you stab with it?"

The old man looked startled. "No one. I'm not a fighter."

"Did you see anyone get stabbed last night?"

He shook his head, and spit dribbled off his lip.

Jackson would ask a lot more questions later, but he had to see the slain officer first. He turned to Officer Markham. "Keep him here until we can start questioning. But no rough stuff."

Jackson jogged back toward the side street, worried the crime scene had been contaminated. Another patrol unit screamed down the road, siren wailing. The entire morning shift of officers was now on the scene, and more were probably being called in. He grabbed his shoulder bag from his car and headed toward Thompson's red truck. A female officer stood on the road nearby.

As Jackson reached the vehicle, he heard another engine behind him and turned. Schak parked near the patrol unit blocking the street and jumped out. "Where's Danny?" Voice tight, his partner charged toward him, his barrel-shaped body moving faster than it seemed capable.

"Near here somewhere." Jackson hoped Schak would stay out of the crime scene once he had processed and accepted his cousin's death. Jackson pulled gloves from his shoulder bag and slipped them on. "I'm sorry about Dan. I know you were close."

"He's like a brother. We grew up together. He even stayed with us for a while." Schak scanned the wetlands, his pupils dark pinpoints, a man holding in a cauldron of emotions.

"He was a good man," Jackson said, touching his partner's shoulder. "We'll get the perp who did this."

Schak was silent.

The female officer stepped toward them and pointed. "He's by that clump of shrubs near the tree." Officer Gardner. New to the force, she'd taken Jackson's crime scene class recently.

"Where's the student who called it in?" Jackson strode toward the officer.

"I checked her ID and let her go." Gardner shifted her feet. "The witness was upset and crying, and it was obvious the victim had been dead for a while."

"What's her story?"

"She was biking to the camp to do research for a school paper. She saw a rabbit and watched it run into the brush, then spotted the body. She called 911, and I was the first to arrive." Gardner handed him a page from her notebook. "Sabra Yokum. Here's her phone number and address. I hope I did the right thing."

"You did fine." Behind her, Jackson spotted a homeless person at the end of the short street. "Go question that guy, then send him back the way he came and block that path." He hated public crime scenes. They were difficult to manage.

Schak was already moving across the rain-soaked grass toward the body, which was faceup near a wild rose bush. Jackson followed, nearly bumping into his partner as he stopped short a few feet back. Jackson moved past him, pulling out his camera. He had learned to look at bodies through the lens first, creating a sense of surreality and distance. When the victim was a woman or a child—or in this case, a fellow officer—it helped him push past an emotional reaction.

Behind him, Schak's primal gasp of anguish was like a punch in the gut. This wasn't just another victim. Dan Thompson was a brother to them all. Jackson turned to his partner. "You shouldn't be here."

"I had to see him."

"I get that. Now you need to go."

"What else am I going to do?"

"You can notify his family. Ask a few questions." Normally, Jackson would do it, but Schak would be contacting them anyway.

"I already called Danny's ex-wife," Schak said. "I feel so bad for his kids."

"Is she here in town?"

"Harrisburg. The boys are usually with him on weekends though."

"What about Thompson's parents and siblings?"

"His mother, my aunt, lives not far from me. She and Kurt will be devastated."

"Go be with them."

"You can't kick me off this case."

Jackson was torn. Schak was a tenacious and dedicated investigator and could be useful. But not here. Not right now. "It's not my call, and Lammers didn't want you at the scene. She's on her way here."

After a pause, Schak turned and walked away. Jackson snapped photos, forcing himself to focus on the process. Take pictures of the scene, the position of the body, and the wallet lying next to it. Then close-ups of the wounds. Check the hands for defensive nicks and bruises. Search the area for trace evidence and debris the killer might have dropped.

The stab wounds gave him pause. A jagged gash low across his throat and another just above the belt on his left side. Wide, angry openings that had formed congealed pools of blood. These weren't knife wounds. He'd seen something similar only once before, when a man had been attacked with a broken bottle in a bar fight. In the earlier case, the assailant had aimed for the chest, and his victim had survived. Had this killer gone for the throat on purpose? But why? Thompson had been a friend to the homeless community.

"Oh god." Detective Lara Evans walked up and kneeled beside him. "This is brutal. Like someone crazed on meth." Her heart-shaped face tightened with disgust.

"It was done with something big, jagged, and sharp. Like a broken bottle."

"Probably someone from the camp. Or a transient passing through." Evans stood and looked around. "What was Thompson doing in this area? He's in uniform, but not in a patrol unit. He must have been off duty."

"I think he was passing out blankets. He'd been collecting them again."

"Right. I saw his poster at the department. But why twenty feet from his vehicle?"

It bothered Jackson too. Still on his knees, he picked up the wallet, noting that it had no cash or bank cards. "The perp robbed him."

"I'm not surprised." Evans was searching the immediate area on the other side of the body. "What about his weapon?"

"I haven't seen it. Maybe it's in the truck or his locker at work." Jackson dug through the victim's pockets, finding only car keys in his jacket. No cell phone. The killer had probably taken it too. And Thompson's jacket was open. Why hadn't it been zipped? The temperature was in the mid-thirties. Last night had been even colder.

Jackson stood, feeling a familiar pinch in his gut. Was it time to start taking the prednisone again? "We need to find the weapon." He started to scan the tall grass, but the position of the body caught his attention. Thompson's feet pointed toward the road, so he'd likely been facing that direction. It seemed odd. He would have expected to find him facing the brush, as if looking for someone or something. Had Thompson tried to stop an altercation between two other men? The medical examiner and crime scene techs would arrive any moment and begin to collect trace evidence. Eventually, they'd have answers.

"We need to round up every transient in the area and check for stains," Evans said. "Whoever did this probably has Thompson's blood on their clothes."

The task seemed monumental, but if a street person had killed him, at least they hadn't gone home and washed their clothes. "We'll get a volunteer team out here to comb the wider area for discarded clothing."

They both squatted and began to search the immediate area, looking for anything sharp. The flat ground was covered mostly with tall grass, with a few shrubs. In the distance, the land sloped uphill into a thicket of trees. On the other side of the thicket were more industry and retail shops. Jackson searched the clump near the body, finding only a faded and weathered food wrapper.

He heard an engine and looked up to see the medical examiner's white van drive over the grass to get around the police cars blocking the end of the street. A moment later, Jackson found a broken bottle of Colt 45 about ten feet from the body on the west side. What looked like dried blood covered a sharp protrusion.

"I think I've got it," he called to Evans. Jackson looked over to where Officer Gardner was talking to the transient. Had the killer gone down the dirt path through the open wetlands? He assumed it came out on West Seventh, another short chunk of road that connected two other main streets.

Jackson pulled out two large evidence bags and slid one inside the other to form a thick seal. Grabbing the sharp end, he slipped the potential weapon inside, hoping to preserve any fingerprints that might be on the bottle's neck. When the mobile command arrived, they would print everyone at the camp. He felt a glimmer of hope that this investigation might not be as challenging as he'd first thought.

The medical examiner and two crime scene techs climbed from the van, burdened by equipment. Time to step away from the body and interview potential witnesses and suspects. Where was the command unit?

Jackson greeted the death crew, who he'd worked with for years. Rich Gunderson, the ME, looked the part in all black. "I can't believe we lost another one," he said. "Fucking mental illness." Gunderson set down his gear and pulled on protective booties.

Thompson was the fourth Eugene cop to die in three years. A patrol officer had been shot after pulling over a woman with schizophrenia, and more recently, a community service officer had killed himself. Two years earlier, an officer had died from an accidental gun discharge at a shooting range. But the murders hit the department the hardest.

Gunderson reached for the evidence bag and shook his head. "Nasty weapon."

An engine rumbled, and Jackson turned to the main street. A white vehicle that looked like a cross between a bus and a mobile home parked in the intersection of the two dead-end streets. It looked like Detective Michael Quince was driving. "I'll be in the command unit conducting interviews," Jackson said. "Please send a tech over with the time of death as soon as you know."

"Give me a minute, and I'll get his body temp." Gunderson squatted next to the corpse.

Jackson turned to Evans. "We need to print everyone in the camp. Bring them to the command unit two at a time, but have Quince do the prints. You start the questioning. I'll be there in a bit."

"I'm on it." Evans jogged off, moving at her usual high-energy pace. The only woman in their fourteen-person unit, she was also the youngest. But Jackson had mentored her from her first day in Violent Crimes, and she'd never let him down. She was also the only female in the SWAT unit and the smallest person to have passed the rigorous physical test. Some of the SWAT guys were rooting for her to fail, but Jackson would never bet against her.

Typically, three or four detectives would be assigned to each task force, but because the victim was one of their own, Jackson might end up with seven or eight people working the case—if it dragged on. He hoped not. They needed to find a fingerprint match or an eyewitness this morning and arrest someone before nightfall. Officer abuse of the homeless could get ugly if they failed.

While the medical examiner probed Thompson's hip with a thermometer, Jackson scanned the area across the street. All industrial. No houses with potential witnesses who might have seen or heard something that would help pinpoint the time the officer was killed.

Gunderson mumbled something about temperatures, then said, "He likely died between five and eight last night."

Thompson had come here after work to hand out blankets in the dark. Grief squeezed Jackson's heart. Why did the good ones die so young? His own parents had been murdered too, when his daughter was just a baby. He tried to shake it off. "I'll do a quick search of his vehicle, then I'll be down the street if you find anything I need to know."

"You already said that." Gunderson gestured for him to move along.

Jackson headed toward the red truck, a late-model Tundra. Still wearing gloves, he reached for the handle on the driver's side. Unlocked. Thompson hadn't planned on being gone from his vehicle for long—or maybe he jumped out in a hurry. The interior was spotless. No blood, no fast food wrappers or receipts to indicate where he'd been. Searching under the seat, Jackson found a flask that felt empty. He opened it and sniffed. Whiskey? Had Thompson had a drinking problem?

He found a flashlight under the seat too and used it to probe further. Jumper cables, an ice scraper, and an oil rag. Standard vehicle stuff. The glove box held the usual paperwork, but no weapon. Some officers took their weapons home when they clocked out, and others left them in their lockers at the department. He didn't know Thompson's pattern. Maybe Schak did. But why hadn't Thompson locked his truck? Because he didn't plan to walk away from it? Or had he finished off the bourbon in the flask and been stupid drunk?

Jackson ran his hand along the crease in the back of the bench seat and bumped into something solid. He pulled out a mini digital recorder, a little surprised by the find. Detectives used them, but patrol officers typically did not. Was it a personal organizer? Jackson clicked it on and saw it held six files. He pressed Play and heard Thompson's voice say, "Don't forget to pick up your prescription." A personal note. But what medication? He slipped the recorder into his carryall, closed the truck door, and started toward the big rig.

From behind him, a technician called, "Wait! I want you to see this."

Jackson hurried over to where Jasmine Parker stood, about halfway between the vehicle and the body.

"See those marks on the grass?" she said, pointing.

Jackson squatted next to her. In a small area where the vegetation was shorter—more clover than grass—parallel indentations were visible.

"Drag marks," Parker explained. "I saw grass stains on the edge of the victim's heels and wondered how they got there. I think the killer dragged him away from the road."

CHAPTER 3

Inside the command unit, Michael Quince had set up a fingerprint station and was inking a young man with a full beard, shaved head, and tattooed hands. Jackson pulled out a folding chair and sat next to them. Before he could ask a question, the suspect looked over and said, "The only reason I agreed to do this was to get the cuffs off. I had nothing to do with the cop. I didn't take any blankets from him or see him last night. I was out on a day labor job yesterday and didn't get back to the camp until late. I've never been to jail, and I'm not going today. My homeless situation is temporary. I'm just having trouble finding a full-time job."

The calm, articulate statement surprised him. "How do you know the police officer was at the camp last night?"

"I saw a dude with a thick blanket and asked where he got it."

"What's the dude's name?"

"Gabe. That's all I know about him. Except he's a Vietnam vet."

"Is he around this morning?"

"He's sitting out there on the curb with his hands cuffed, just like I was."

"What day labor did you do yesterday?"

"I helped build a fence at some farm out of town. Call Labor Ready and ask them."

He would check it out. "What's your name?"

"Dave Kirkland. But I already told him." He pointed at Quince.

Quince, who looked more like a movie star than a cop, nodded. "He showed me his state-issued ID."

"Did you run him in the database?"

"He's never been arrested in Oregon, and he's not in CODIS."

Jackson looked him over. No blood on his jacket. No cuts on his hands. He nodded at the man. "You're free to go. Unless your prints match the weapon."

"They won't." The guy hustled out of the rig.

Evans stepped out of a small room in the back. "This witness says the twins were the last people in line to get blankets from Thompson."

The twins were familiar street people and could be seen walking and talking anywhere in central or West Eugene. Albertsons on Eighteenth had big restrooms in the front, and the twins were known to wash up there. "Did you see them in the camp?"

"No. I think they sleep at the Mission."

"Let's go get them. If they're not there, we'll put out an attempt-to-locate."

Jackson checked his watch: 9:32. The Mission made everyone leave during the day after they did a morning chore, but he didn't know the schedule. They would find the twins. Eugene was their home, so they weren't likely to run even if they had committed the murder. And they didn't have the mental ability or resources to hide for long.

"How many have you printed?" he asked Quince.

"Three. Dave Kirkland, the guy who just left. Suri Baylor, the woman in back with Evans. And some drunk with no ID. He was so out of it he couldn't talk. He's outside sleeping now."

Jackson hadn't seen him on the way in, so he stuck his head out and looked around. A patrol officer was headed their way with another handcuffed camper, but no one was on the ground. He stepped back inside. "I think the drunk gave you the slip."

"Damn. Sorry."

"Write down his details so we can pick him up again."

Evans asked, "What about the witness? Should I let her go?"

"Do you believe her about the twins?"

"I think so. Plus, she's tiny. I can't imagine her taking Thompson down."

"It's hard to think anyone could." Thompson had been built like Schak, with a barrel chest and massive arms, but was still in his early forties.

Heavy footsteps on the stairs made them all turn. Lammers stepped into the rig, and the room shrunk a little. She was Jackson's height and weight, but she made it look bulky. "Have you made an arrest yet?"

"Not quite." Jackson gave her a tight smile.

She grimaced. "Keeping patrol officers from using excessive force during this investigation will be impossible. We need to lock this one down ASAP."

"Evans and I are heading over to the Mission now, hoping to find the street twins. They were the last to see Thompson last night."

"Good. But be careful," their boss cautioned. "They're probably mentally ill and unpredictable."

"I plan to take them into the department and use the interrogation rooms."

"Let's meet this afternoon at four and update," Lammers said. "I don't want Schak on this case, so I'll work it with you until Peterson is available to step in."

Surprised, Jackson opened his mouth to speak, then stopped.

"What do you need me to do?" Lammers asked.

So he *was* still running the case. This would be weird, giving tasks to Lammers. "Will you call in some volunteers to search this whole area for discarded clothes? We think the killer used a broken bottle and likely got blood on their jacket." He gestured at the interview room. "Then question everyone Quince fingerprints from the camp. There's another five or six, at least."

"Yes, sir." She gave him a mock salute.

Jackson held back a smile, but Evans choked on a laugh.

"See you at four." He headed out, with Evans following.

• • •

Jackson spotted the two identical men on Garfield, moving toward them and away from the Mission. Tall, skinny men in their mid-thirties with sandy hair, they talked nonstop as they walked, gesturing with their gloved hands, their spirits seemingly unfazed by the cold. Where were their shopping carts? He pulled over, catching sight in his rearview mirror of Evans doing the same. The men didn't notice him until he stepped onto the sidewalk in front of them.

"Detective Jackson, Eugene Police." He showed his badge, something he rarely did, but he wanted this encounter to go smoothly. Evans stepped up next to him. "And this is Detective Evans. We need to talk to you about last night. And we'd like you to come with us to the department."

They blinked in surprise, a synchronistic response. The one in the green jacket said, "We don't make trouble. We have to go." He grabbed his brother's arm and tried to turn him around.

The other twin, in black fleece, resisted. "Mom always said don't run."

Green Twin countered, "But Willow says we're citizens and have the right to sleep."

They spoke rapidly, with surprising passion, their narrow faces animated. Jackson let them argue for a moment while he scanned their jackets. Because the fleece was black, he couldn't tell if it was stained. The coat had a tear on the right sleeve that looked recent though. He studied the green polyester as best he could from the side angle. Was that brown spot on the shoulder blood? And could he confiscate the jacket without a warrant?

Evans eased herself onto the curb, where she could move in either direction. He was glad for her presence. She could out-run anyone, so they would at least take one of the suspects into custody.

"We just want to talk," he cut in. "If you come voluntarily, we won't cuff you." He held out his hand. "Show me your ID." He needed their names, but he didn't trust them to be honest. Street people tended to lie about their identity, a protective instinct.

The man in the green jacket reached for a wallet, and Jackson tensed.

"I'm Henry Walsh. He's Jacob Walsh, but I call him Jake."

The state card confirmed his identification and that he was thirty-three. The address listed belonged to White Bird, a chari-table medical facility that let homeless people pick up mail at its downtown clinic.

His brother reluctantly produced his ID as well. "We didn't do anything wrong."

"Then come with me, tell us where you were last night, and clear yourself of suspicion."

"But we have to get our carts and pick up cans. This is recycling day in the Friendly Street neighborhood."

They had routes? "This won't take long," Jackson lied, handing back his card.

"I'll give you some cash to make up for the cans," Evans offered.

Jackson gently reached for Henry's arm. He seemed to be the more dominant one. "Just come talk to us." He didn't want to cuff either of them. If they came willingly, without restraint, he didn't have to advise them of their rights.

Henry muttered what sounded like a prayer and let Jackson lead him to the car. He heard the other twin chatting up Evans as she searched him for weapons. With any luck, they would quickly connect the twins to the crime scene and maybe get a confession.

CHAPTER 4

Saturday, November 22, 9:40 a.m.

Rob Schakowski rested his head against the steering wheel and fought for control. Seeing Danny's body torn open and lifeless had been harder than he expected. But blubbering all over himself wouldn't help Danny. He needed to get his shit together and function like a detective. And a solid family member that others could count on. He started the car and cranked the heat, shivering for the first time since he was a kid.

He pulled onto the street as the command unit passed with Quince at the wheel. A warm, comfortable place to question the scumbag suspects. A goddamn bum had killed the nicest guy on the planet, probably right after Danny handed him a blanket. What the fuck was wrong with people? The voice of the department's sensitivity trainer tried to break into his thoughts, but he shoved it away. *Fuck that!* Danny was dead, and he didn't have to be politically correct. Not today. He pulled back off the street and called his wife.

"What's wrong?" Tracy said, without a greeting, sounding a little breathless.

He'd been in a restaurant having Saturday breakfast with his son when they'd gotten the call and had come straight to the scene. "Danny is dead. Stabbed by a transient."

"No!" She gasped and let out a shocked cry.

"I just saw his body. Somebody gutted him." Grief cut into his words, and Schak fought for control.

"When?"

"Probably sometime last night, after he handed out the stuff he'd collected."

"Oh my god. That's horrible." A pause while the TV in the background shut off. "Why are you at the scene? Lammers didn't call you out for it, did she?"

"No. Brad got called in when we were having breakfast." His son had surprised him by joining the department six months earlier, following his example, the way Danny had. Schak was proud of his son, but now more worried than ever.

"But you're working too?" A hint of anger. "You should be with Danny's family."

"I'm headed there now."

"Give Donna a hug for me."

"Okay." He knew he wouldn't.

"And, Rob," she warned, her voice a familiar nag, "don't use this as an excuse to keep drinking. I love you, but I'm serious about you quitting."

Irritated now and still in shock, he hung up without responding. And immediately regretted it. If he knew how to text, he would have sent a quick apology. But he wasn't calling her back and risking more emotional fallout.

He drove across town, watching the neighborhoods improve as he headed south and uphill. His aunt lived on College Hill, a dense older neighborhood with nice views but missing the fir trees that thicketed the South Hills. He hoped to find Donna home on a Saturday morning. As a surgeon and board member of various organizations, she kept busy, and Sunday nights seemed to be the only time she had available for family gatherings. He'd seen her, Danny, and Kurt for dinner at the Oregon Electric Station a few weeks ago.

Schak parked in front of her home on Lawrence and sat for a moment. His aunt's car wasn't in the driveway, but she always kept it in the garage, and he noticed a light on in the foyer. She was home, and he was rehearsing what he would say. Telling Danny's ex-wife hadn't been too bad. They had divorced two years ago and were both dating again, so the news hadn't been that devastating to her. But telling Danny's mother that her son was dead would be rough. He wished he had a shot of whiskey to take the edge off. The thought jarred him. It wasn't even noon yet. Maybe his wife was right about his drinking. She'd given him an ultimatum the day before—quit drinking or she was leaving. The timing couldn't have been worse.

Schak climbed out and trudged up the walkway, and a light snow began to fall. Donna opened the door before he reached the landing.

"Rob. It's nice to see you. But what's going on?" A look of mild alarm flashed across her face, which had recently been tightened. Her blonde hairstyle was perfectly smooth, as was her tailored clothing.

His own mother, Donna's older sister, had gone a little plump and frazzled, but the resemblance would always be there. "I have some bad news. Let's go inside."

She froze in the doorway.

"Please," Schak said. "Let's go in. And if Kurt is here, go get him." His younger cousin finally had his own place, but because he only worked part-time as an IT guy for the county, he still spent a lot of time with his mother. As they walked into the living room, Kurt rolled his wheelchair in from the kitchen. "Hey, Rob." Danny's half brother gave a small smile, worried eyes contrasting with his handsome face. As a child, Kurt had been injured in a shooting accident and had remained disabled despite years of physical therapy. Danny, only eleven, had been holding the revolver. The accident had shaken the whole family, but in time, Donna had come to terms with her feelings, and they'd all recovered emotionally. For the most part.

Schak greeted him with a fist bump. "Are you okay?"

Kurt nodded. "It's just one of my painful days."

Schak took a seat on one of the couches, and Donna sat across from him, clutching a sweater in her hands. He hated what he had to tell them and prayed he wouldn't cry. "It's about Danny. He was handing out blankets last night at a homeless camp, like he does every year." Schak stalled, giving them time to brace themselves. "And someone killed him. Cut him open pretty badly. I'm sorry. I loved him too."

"No!" Donna argued, as if he'd just lied to her. "He's a cop. He carries a gun. How could he get stabbed?"

"We don't know yet how it happened, but we'll get the guy."

Tears welled in Donna's eyes, but she steeled herself and suppressed them.

Kurt made choking sounds, like someone trying to swallow his grief. Donna moved to his side and squeezed his shoulder. Kurt finally managed to say, "I worried about him for years after he became a cop. Then a few years ago, I kind of stopped. I was wrong."

"This shouldn't have happened." Schak didn't know what else to say. He'd known these people his whole life, but he didn't know how to comfort them. He would ease his own pain by working to find the perp.

"Did a street person kill him?" Donna asked, her voice trembling. "I worried about his contact with the homeless. Many of them are mentally ill."

"Most likely, but we'll look into all possibilities." Schak's investigative instincts kicked in. "Was Danny in any kind of trouble?"

They both looked surprised.

"What do you mean?" Donna stiffened. "He was a good man, a straight shooter. You know that."

Guilt made Schak hunch forward. He should have let someone else do this. "I mean, was there anyone who had a reason to want him dead?"

"You should be looking at his case files," Donna said. "He dealt with criminals all the time."

"We'll do that, of course. But I had to ask. Even cops have personal lives."

Kurt spoke up. "Have you talked to Trisha? She might know more than we do."

Schak had met Danny's new girlfriend, a forty-year-old medical assistant, but he didn't really know her. She was pretty, but she had two kids in high school and seemed a bit flaky—not right for Danny. "Do you know how to contact her?"

"She works at the Crescent Clinic." Kurt abruptly began to cry.

Schak couldn't bear to witness it. If he stayed, he'd start crying too. He and Danny had been Cub Scouts together, had spent weekends at each other's houses, and had taken road trips as teenagers. Years younger, Kurt had tagged along whenever he could. As adults with jobs and families of their own, Schak and Danny had less time, but had still gotten together for monthly restaurant meals and occasional fishing trips. The "boys," as their mothers had referred to them, would never all be together again.

"I never wanted him to become a cop." Donna's voice held bitterness. "But he worshipped you and did everything you did."

Schak had always suspected she felt that way, but it still stung. "I have to go help find the killer." He gave his aunt a quick, one-armed hug, which she shrugged off, then he locked forearms with Kurt the way they had since childhood. "I'll be here for you as much as I can." Schak vowed to spend more time with his younger cousin. The wheelchair made it challenging, but Danny had never let it stop him from trying to include Kurt in everything.

. . .

He drove back to the crime scene, hoping the body would be gone so he could focus better. The ME was loading Danny into the van, so Schak trotted up to the command unit instead. Quince and Lammers were inside questioning people from the camp. His boss excused herself from the man she was talking to and said, "Let's step outside."

He knew the tone and braced himself as he went back out.

"You can't work this case." Lammers pressed her hands to her hips. "I know you think you have to, but I'm ordering you to stay out of it."

"This is bullshit! Jackson worked his ex-wife's kidnapping."

"They'd been separated for years. And the FBI was in charge. It was their call." Lammers touched his shoulder—a rare gesture. "I have another assignment for you."

Frustration and relief flooded him at the same time. He hated being dismissed from the task force, but at least she was giving him something. It was better than being sent home. That would have made him crazy. And driven him straight to his bourbon stash. "What's the case?"

"A teenage suicide. Her parents just called it in, and they say she was sexually assaulted recently."

Oh shit. He hated working sex crimes. "Why isn't Vice taking it?"

"Because they're swamped, and the case involves blackmail. Plus a young girl is dead." Lammers handed him a slip of notebook paper. "That's the information I have. Go find out what's going on."

Schak glanced at the details: *Clare and Jay Devonshire, 2345 Brookview Drive. Daughter: Ashley Devonshire, 16. Found dead, likely overdose of sleeping pills.*

Dead young girls were hard to take too, but at least he wouldn't have to think about Danny or worry about bursting into tears. "Will do." He started to walk away, then turned back. "Tell Jackson that Danny's girlfriend is Trisha Weber, and she works at the Crescent Clinic. She's probably worth talking to."

CHAPTER 5

Saturday, November 22, 12:05 p.m.

The Devonshire home was in a new upscale neighborhood not far from the Valley River mall. Big houses on tiny lots, with masonry exteriors and lush landscaping. Most were in the floodplain of the river, but the West Coast's drought would probably keep them safe.

Not a single patrol car was on the scene—because they were all at the homeless camp, along with the medical examiner. So the girl's body would likely not be examined or picked up until late this afternoon. No wonder Lammers had sent him—the rest of the department was focused on Danny. He knocked on the front door, and a woman opened it. Mid-thirties, slender, with eyes swollen from crying. A day of grief for everyone. He made up his mind to have a shot of bourbon tonight, because he'd earned it. His wife would just have to deal with it.

"Clare Devonshire? I'm Detective Schakowski, EPD." He displayed his badge, then slipped it back into his pocket.

She motioned him in. "Why did it take so long for someone to get here?"

"A police officer was murdered, and everyone on duty is looking for his killer."

"Oh god. I'm sorry." She blinked back fresh tears.

"I'm sorry for your loss too." He hesitated. This was a new scenario for him. "Can I see your daughter?"

"This way." She moved toward a hallway, and he followed.

A man came out of the kitchen. Schak paused while he walked over and introduced himself. "Jay Devonshire. Thanks for coming." He was all bones, with thinning hair and sagging facial skin.

The wife gestured to an open bedroom door, and Schak entered the room. Everything was purple and black, including the pajamas on the poor dead girl. She lay on top of the bedspread, hands folded on her chest the way a body in a coffin would. Pale lifeless skin, eyes closed, but a look of sadness frozen in her expression.

"When did you find her?"

"About an hour ago," Clare said. "I knocked and called out to get her up because it seemed so late, even for a weekend. I finally opened the door, and when I saw her like that—" The mother took a long breath that sounded painful. "I knew she was dead. I knew she'd killed herself." Clare picked up a piece of lavender paper from the desk and handed it to him. "She left a suicide note."

Schak noticed a small, clear-plastic pouch on the desk next to where the note had been. But first he read Ashley's words. The message was handwritten in pretty cursive: *I can't bear the shame and guilt. How can I ever look at my friends again? Or at you, now that you've seen me that way? I'm sorry I let this happen. Love, Ashley.*

Poor girl. Why did they always blame themselves? Schak folded the note and slipped it into an evidence bag. "You're certain this is your daughter's handwriting?"

"Yes." Clare frowned. "Why do you ask?"

"Just part of the investigation. I'd like to see her phone and computer, but let me take some photos first." He pulled out his camera and took several shots of the corpse—photos he would probably never look at again, because he didn't have any doubt this girl had committed suicide. He moved in and took a couple close-ups of a plastic bag with a trace of white coating on the inside. He turned to the parents, who were still huddled in the doorway. "Do you know what she took?"

Clare choked back a sob. "I think some of my prescription sleeping pills are gone."

"I'm not sure that would be enough."

Mr. Devonshire stepped forward. "I have cancer, and I've taken a lot of pain pills over the last few months. Ashley could have stolen a bunch from me, taking a few at a time."

"You think she planned this for a while?"

"I don't know." Anguish made the father's voice ragged. "She was emotional and sometimes threatened to kill herself."

Clare cut in. "I didn't want her to even know about the video. But she walked into my office just as I opened it." Another round of tears.

Schak waited her out. "I need to see the blackmailer's message."

The father spun around, as if he couldn't leave fast enough, but Clare walked over to the bed and stroked her daughter's dark hair. As she walked out, she said, "I can't just act like she's not here anymore."

Schak followed them to a small office near the front of the house. Clare grabbed a phone from her desk and handed it to him so he could read the text: *The video will go viral unless you pay me $15,000 to destroy it. You have until five today to get the cash. If you call the police, I'll post it everywhere. I'll text with instructions soon.*

The assailant/blackmailer was articulate but not greedy, which surprised him. "Did he text you again?"

Mr. Devonshire nodded. "We asked for a couple days to get the money together."

"What did he say?"

"He said no." Mr. Devonshire clenched his fists. "We tried to explain that we had to cash out the rest of an IRA and that it would take time, but he posted the video last night anyway."

"Can I take the phone with me? We need to trace these messages."

Clare blinked, then stammered, "Is that necessary? I run my business with this phone. Can't you just write down his number?"

Schak nodded, annoyed. Yet he knew he would be nearly dysfunctional if someone took his cell phone. He noted the number and took photos of the messages, so he would have the exact wording if he needed it. "I'll see if I can engage him and trace the phone he's using." But Schak wasn't optimistic. The perp had probably used a cheap prepaid phone and tossed it when the Devonshires didn't cooperate. "Please forward the text with the attachment to my email at the department."

Clare bit her lip. "Do you really need to watch the video?"

He cringed. "I'd rather not, but there may be information we can use. Plus, our tech team may be able to locate where the video was taken. Especially if he filmed it with a smartphone."

"He uploaded it to a site called Young and Hot," Clare said through gritted teeth. "And he posted the link on several of her friends' Facebook pages."

The prick. "We'll do what we can to trace the source." Schak pulled out his notepad. "Tell me about the night the assault happened. Where was Ashley?"

"She went to a party but wouldn't tell us where," Clare said. "I'm sorry. We tried to find out, but she shut down and wouldn't talk to us."

Someone knew where Ashley had been. "Give me the names of her closest friends."

"Anna Sorenson and Taylor Crenshaw," Clare said. "The girls all go to Riverside High School."

Schak made notes and wondered how he could cut through the schoolgirl drama. "Does Ashley have a Facebook page?"

"Yes. We looked at it this morning, but she hadn't friended us, so we can't see her posts." Clare answered his questions while her husband paced the room.

"I'll need to take her computer with me. Maybe our tech guy can hack into her account and check her Facebook messages." Schak hated to ask, but he had to. "Did Ashley have a boyfriend? Was she sexually active?"

Mr. Devonshire spun and shouted, "No! She was assaulted. This is not her fault."

Oh boy, he'd stepped in it big-time. "I'm not suggesting she's to blame. I just need to know if she had regular contact with a boyfriend or guys at school. Most young women who are sexually assaulted know their assailant." Yet the blackmail was highly unusual and indicated the perp might be older. He would explore that angle as well.

Clare drew in a long breath, but it didn't help. Her husband put his arm around her as she cried.

Her pain reminded Schak of his own loss, and he struggled not to be pulled in by it. Maybe he shouldn't have taken the case.

Maybe he needed a vacation instead. That would make his wife happy.

When the grieving mother was calmer, he asked, "Did Ashley have a license? Did she drive herself to the party?"

"She could drive but didn't have her own car," Clare said. "She left here around six thirty on Wednesday to go study with Anna. She lives about a half mile away, and Ashley always walked there."

"How did she get home?"

"Ashley didn't remember. She said she woke up on the sidewalk around midnight." Mr. Devonshire sounded sad and defensive. "Neither of us was home. I was in the hospital, and Clare was out with friends."

It had been cold that night, but not freezing yet. "Give me Anna's address." Schak resigned himself to questioning several teenage girls. "Did Anna throw parties at her house?"

"Not that we know of."

"Do you know any of her friends who might have?"

Clare reached for a tissue on her desk. "The girls had slumber parties, but they were small gatherings, and parents were always home."

Yeah, right. Schak nodded. "I need to search Ashley's room, then take her computer to the department." He started for the hallway. "And I need her cell phone. Her assailant could have contacted her directly."

"Her phone is on her dresser," Mr. Devonshire said. "We looked to see who had called her, but didn't see anyone we didn't know."

Clare blinked back more tears. "What about Ashley?"

"The medical examiner will be here later to process her body." Oh boy, wrong thing to say to parents. But he couldn't fix it. "Please stay out of her room until he's done. And call me if you hear from the blackmailer again." Schak handed them a card and got back to work.

CHAPTER 6

Saturday, November 22, 1:27 p.m.

Jackson and Evans put the twins into the two interrogation rooms, ignoring their distress at being separated, then stepped back out into the open space to confer.

"I wonder if they've ever spent time apart," Evans said. "I've never heard anyone say they saw them individually."

Did they have a mental health evaluation on record somewhere? "I'm more concerned about the spot on Henry's jacket that looks like blood."

"We need to get both coats to the crime lab." Evans snapped her fingers. "Let's turn up the heat in the rooms and force them to take off a layer."

Jackson was skeptical. Long-term street people tended to wear everything they owned, even in the summer. "Let's get one of the clerks to run over to Walmart and buy them new jackets and gloves."

Evans' brow creased. "Do we tell them why? Will they under-stand what's going on?"

"I don't know their mental capabilities. Just keep saying we're trying to clear them." Jackson ignored a pang of concern. As long as the suspects handed over the coats willingly, it was legal and moral to process the evidence. And as long as they weren't under arrest or in custody—meaning physically confined in any way—everything they said could be used in court without reading them their rights. Still, he worried about how a judge would view it. "While you get someone to go to the store, I'll chat briefly with Jacob, then switch to Henry when you get back. And I'll make sure they understand their presence here is voluntary."

Jackson stepped toward the opposite door. Their new build-ing had more space than the department needed, but the inter-rogation rooms that had been added during the remodel were purposefully small. He took a deep breath, went inside, and sat down.

"Where is my brother?" Jacob Walsh rocked forward, hands in his lap.

Jackson had second thoughts about leaving the twins uncuffed. Their mental illness made them potentially danger-ous. But it also meant that confinement might be so stressful that they'd become incoherent. He needed information. "Henry is in the room next door. You can see him in a few minutes." He clicked on his recorder and set it on the table. "I'm recording our conversation, and I appreciate you coming here voluntarily to answer questions."

"We always cooperate." His eyes were a bit too close together and sharply distrustful. "What do you want to know?"

"About last night. A witness says you spoke to Officer Thompson near the camp at the end of Wallis Street."

"We wanted blankets, but he didn't have any more."

"Did that make you mad?"

"No. But he could have given us money." A little frustration in his tone. "But we never beg."

That threw him a little. "Why would you expect Officer Thompson to do that?"

"He gave the lady with the kid money. But we were last in line. It's a long walk to the new camp." The suspect's shoulders twitched. "Can I have a sandwich? It must be lunchtime."

"In a minute." Why had Thompson given away cash? "Do you know the woman with the kid?"

Jacob shook his head. "I never saw her before."

"What happened after the officer told you he was out of blankets and money?"

"We left." More twitching.

"Where did you go?"

"To the shed where we sleep."

"Where is that?"

"In Ella's side yard. It's on Monroe Street. Why?" Abruptly, he jumped up.

Jackson did too, reaching for the cuffs he had ready in his pocket. "Please sit down."

"We just wanted a new blanket!"

"We're getting you a new blanket. And a new coat too. Please sit down." Jackson started softly but ended with a command.

Evans stepped into the room. "Ready?"

Jackson turned to her. "Almost. Let's get them new blankets too, since they missed out on the giveaway last night."

"I'm on it." She trotted back out, and he heard her making a call.

Jacob finally sat, so Jackson asked, "What's Ella's address?"

"It's near Third and Monroe. I don't know the numbers."

He would find it. Jackson excused himself and met Evans out in the foyer. "I'll question Henry now and see if he tells the same story. We also need an address for the shed they sleep in at night."

"I'll get Jacob to give us permission to search it."

"That's my thinking." Jackson stepped into the small, dark room next door. It was much like the one in the previous building, only this time, they had a metal table and modern technology. But he wasn't videotaping these interviews. Not yet. He put his personal recorder out, clicked into a new file, and repeated his cover phrase. "Thanks for waiting, Henry. I appreciate your coming here to voluntarily answer questions."

"Did you talk to Jacob?"

Where his brother had twitched, Henry vibrated. "I did. And he told me you were mad when Officer Thompson ran out of blankets and didn't give you one."

"I sometimes sound mad when I'm not."

"Did you hurt Officer Thompson?"

"No." Henry looked away.

To hide his guilt? "What happened after he told you there were no more blankets?"

"Jacob asked for money. He said he didn't have any." Vibrating and rocking now. "So we went to our special place."

"The shed where you sleep?"

The suspect made a surprised sound. "No, that's just a shed. Our special place is in the trees."

Had his brother forgotten or lied? "What did you do there?"

A long pause. "We made a campfire and sang. Like we used to with Daddy." He jumped up like Jacob had. "Why do you ask these questions? We don't make trouble and no one bothers us."

"Sit down. Officer Thompson is dead. Do you know what happened?"

He complied, but his eyes blinked rapidly and he let out a moan. "We liked him. He didn't hurt people like the other cops do."

Jackson experienced a flush of shame for the department brutes who used excessive force on street people. "Do you know who hurt Officer Thompson?"

"No." His wide-open eyes didn't look away, but he shifted constantly in his chair.

Jackson didn't know if he believed him. "You're going to be in here for a little while longer. But we'll give you a new jacket and a blanket soon."

"What about lunch?"

"That too."

Another twenty minutes of questions produced nothing useful except that the Walsh twins had met Ella, the owner of their sleeping shed, at the community outreach day at the fairgrounds, where homeless people could get free services such as haircuts and dental exams. They were only allowed in the shed at night, and they could never bring anyone else with them. They liked it better than sleeping at the Mission because they didn't have a curfew and didn't have to listen to "God talk." But they still went to the Mission for breakfast.

A knock on the door gave him a sense of relief. A desk clerk stood outside with large plastic shopping sacks. "I bought two shades of blue. I hope that's okay."

"It's perfect. Thanks." Jackson took the bags, noticing she'd bought warm, stylish jackets with lots of zippered pockets. "I'll reimburse petty cash with my expense account." He knocked on the other interrogation room and stepped in. "Hey, Jacob. I have some new things for you. Why don't you try on this jacket?" Since the man was wearing black, Jackson held out the dark-blue one but didn't let go. "Please hand me the one you're wearing."

"Why? I want both."

"I'd like to check yours. That way I can clear you of suspicion in Officer Thompson's death."

"You suspect me?" Confusion made Jacob look like he was about to cry.

"We have to question everyone who was near the camp. We have to check the clothes of everyone who talked to the officer. This is how we do our job." Jackson used his best we're-all-in-this-together voice. "Officer Thompson was a good man, and we need to find his killer. We need to make the streets safe for everyone. You want to help us, don't you?"

Jacob took a moment to process the information, then finally pulled off his jacket and handed it to Jackson while reaching for the new one.

"Thank you. You can have this too." Jackson pulled a thick plaid lap blanket from the second bag. "I'll give Henry one too."

Jacob put the blanket on his chair, zipped the new jacket, and checked out the pockets. "I like this, but I hate the smell."

Jackson smiled. Only a homeless person would hate the smell of new clothes.

Evans spoke up. "You were just telling me about someone who threatened Officer Thompson."

"No." Jacob shook his head. "Boxer just hates all cops."

"Why?"

"Because they like to beat him." Anger tightened his already pinched face. "Some will hit you if you don't move fast enough. And Boxer is slow. He's injured from the war."

Jackson tapped Evans' shoulder, signaling that they would have Boxer picked up, then stepped out. He knew the abuse happened, and he hated it, and he decided to talk to the chief about it later. For now, he couldn't let it distract him. A street person had likely stabbed a fellow officer in the throat and gut with a broken beer bottle, and he had to find that killer. He couldn't let unrelated compassion derail this investigation.

Outside the confined space, he stuffed Jacob's jacket into a large paper evidence bag. They didn't use plastic for clothing, especially if it was damp or bloody. When he entered the other room, Henry was standing again. Jackson tensed, put his bags on the floor, and kept his distance. He'd searched the suspect for weapons before putting him in the car, but the man wore so many layers of clothes that he could easily hide a knife in the folds. The talk about Boxer's hatred for uniformed officers had made Jackson wary. He held out the other new jacket and gave Henry the same spiel about clearing him and helping find the killer. Henry peeled off his stained green jacket and made the trade before Jackson finished his plea. The suspect pulled on the new one. "It's warmer."

"It looks good too. Please sit down. I want to show you something."

"I'm hungry."

"I know. I'll bring you a sandwich in just a minute."

Henry sat.

Jackson reached for his carryall. "Do you ever get into fights?"

"No."

"Did you ever hear anyone threaten Officer Thompson?"

"No."

Interesting that he didn't mention Boxer. Jackson put the evidence bag with the broken beer bottle on the table. "Have you—"

He didn't get a chance to finish. Henry started wailing, a high-pitched sound of distress unlike anything Jackson had ever heard. He retracted the weapon and tried to calm him, but Henry ran for the door and pounded.

What now? Take him to jail, where a doctor could sedate him? It would be hours before he got medication, and the intake process would only make his mental state worse. But Jackson couldn't let him back out on the street. His reaction to the bloody weapon made him a viable suspect. They had to hold him until they could process the fingerprints they'd taken and see if the stain on his jacket was blood. The DNA analysis would take days beyond that.

"Please sit down. I'll go get some food."

Pounding started on the wall between the interrogation rooms, and his brother called out Henry's name.

Oh boy. They were both agitated now. Jackson grabbed his carryall and the evidence bag and moved toward the door. "Step aside!"

Henry continued wailing and pounding.

Crap! He had a Taser in his car, but he would never use it in this situation anyway. He wasn't being threatened. Jackson gently pushed Henry aside, stepped out, and closed the door. Maybe food would help.

Evans came out of the second interrogation room, shaking her head. "What now?"

"Let's get them some sandwiches."

"What about giving them some booze? Maybe they're in withdrawal."

He hated the idea, but if it produced information, he would go along. He stepped back into the room and tried to catch Henry's attention. "Would you like a beer? Would that calm you down?"

"It's too early," Henry shouted. "We don't drink during the day."

Surprised, Jackson said, "You could make an exception."

"Mom said one beer, after dinner. No exceptions." Henry went back to pacing and talking to himself.

Jackson stepped out of the room and saw a desk clerk coming down the stairs. "Sidney Willow is here," the clerk said. "She claims to represent the twins and wants to see them immediately."

Evans cursed, but Jackson held his tongue. This situation was a potential public relations fiasco. Willow, as she called herself, was a law student and a self-appointed spokesperson for the homeless. She talked to the media and gave speeches to the city council. She was not only a voice for street people but an organizer too. Ever since the Occupy movement, Willow had encouraged the homeless to camp in public places, defying ordinances against it, and she'd finally won the city's approval for designated supervised camping sites. The department had been treading lightly around the whole issue.

"We can't let her hear them wailing like that," Jackson finally said. "But we don't have a reason to book them."

Evans gave an emphatic head shake. "You can't let them go until the lab processes their fingerprints."

Jackson turned to the desk clerk. "Tell Ms. Willow that the twins have not asked to see a lawyer, so she can leave." To Evans, he said, "Get them sandwiches and soda and play some mellow music. I'll take everything to the lab."

"So we're stalling."

"At least until the task force meets." He gave her a tight smile. "Will you write a subpoena too? We need to get their DNA."

The desk clerk hadn't moved. "You need to talk to Willow. She's pretty insistent, and I think she'll just ignore me."

Resigned to the confrontation, Jackson headed upstairs.

Willow stood in the middle of the bright lobby, a petite woman with a big picket sign that read "Sleep Is a Right." Did she carry that everywhere? She had a pageboy haircut and wore a brown tunic that came to her knees, making her look like an extra in *Game of Thrones*.

Jackson approached her and introduced himself.

"I'm Willow. I represent Henry and Jacob Walsh, and I want to be present during their questioning." Despite her size, her voice was throaty and powerful.

"The twins haven't asked for a lawyer, so I'm not letting you see them until they do."

"They're not fully capable of understanding their situation or their rights. You have to let me see them."

"No. I have to investigate a murder, and the twins were the last people to see Officer Thompson alive."

"They didn't kill anyone!" Almost a shout.

"Then the evidence will prove that. We have to do our jobs, and your presence here is interfering."

"I'm not leaving until I get to see them."

The thing that had been nagging at him surfaced. "How did you know they were here?"

"The homeless community looks out for each other. Someone at the Mission saw you pick them up and called me. I want to see them."

"Not until they ask for you."

"You're taking advantage of their diminished capacity, and it's not right. I'm calling the media. And the citizens' advisory board."

She meant well, but at that moment he hated her. "I have to get back to work." Jackson headed for the front door, wondering if she was right. But that was their job—to exploit any opportunity to solve crimes.

"Did you read them their rights?" Willow called after him.

He ignored her and jogged to his car. He had to get the coats and the weapon to the lab and get them processed before this case turned into a public relations nightmare.

CHAPTER 7

Saturday, November 22, 3:05 p.m.

At the crime lab, Jackson learned that a technician had found the broken bottom half of the beer bottle and intended to piece it back together and dust it for prints. After he dropped off the jackets, Jackson rushed back to the department. In the conference room, he checked the monitors to see how the twins were doing. Jacob had his head on the table and seemed to be napping, but Henry paced the other room, talking to himself. A sandwich lay on the table, half eaten. They weren't hurting themselves or making any noise, and that was all he cared about for now.

Jackson stopped at his desk, opened a Word document, and started a file of case notes. But that was all he had time for. The task force meeting was about to start.

As he hurried toward the conference room, his phone rang. He glanced at the ID: *Kera*. If he took it, he would be late to the task force meeting. If he ignored her, he would feel guilty. She was taking care of Benjie for him, so he owed her the consideration. The toddlers could be exhausting. He knew from taking his own solo shifts.

"Hi, Kera. Is everything all right?"

"More or less. Benjie's having a bad day and wants to talk to you. You're usually with him on weekends, and I think he's worried you're not coming back."

"Put him on, but it has to be quick. I have a task force meeting starting now." He wondered how long it would take Benjie to forget the trauma of his mother's death and trust Jackson not to disappear on him too.

"Daddy?"

"Hey, Benjie. Are you having fun with Micah?"

"Are you coming back?" Straight to the heart.

"Of course. But I have to work all day. I'll call you later though."

"Okay. Read a bedtime story later too."

Another stab of guilt. He might not make it home that early. Homicide cases required nearly round-the-clock focus for the first few days. "Kera can read to you."

"No, you have to."

"I'll call before bedtime, I promise. I have to go." He hung up, realizing he should have talked to Kera again.

"You're going soft, old man." Evans walked up and smacked his shoulder. "And you're late. Come on."

They crossed the open space outside their cubes and entered the conference room. Lammers and Quince were already seated. Where was Schak?

"I assigned Schak to another case," Lammers reminded him, as if reading his thoughts.

"What does he have?" Jackson took a seat near the whiteboard on the wall.

"Sexual assault, blackmail, and suicide. A young female victim."

A squeeze in his guts. "How tragic." Thank goodness he hadn't been given that one. Dead young women unnerved him because they made him think of his daughter. "But shouldn't Schak be on leave?"

Lammers gave him a furrowed brow. "Would you stay home under the circumstances?"

"Good point." He opened his notebook, dismayed at the lack of detail. "Let's get started."

Evans stood. "I'll take the board."

"Let's hope we don't need it," Lammers said. She wore a beige pantsuit that blended with the wall behind her and seemed less intimidating than usual. "What did you get out of the twins?"

"Nothing solid, but I took their jackets and prints to the lab. None of the technicians usually work Sunday, so we may not get confirmation until Monday."

Lammers made a disgusted noise. "That's unacceptable for a fellow officer. I'll make a call. Are the suspects still in custody?"

"Yes." Jackson paused while Evans wrote the two names on the board. "But I don't know how long we can hold them here. They need mental health supervision."

Lammers raised an eyebrow. "What's going on?"

"Henry started shrieking when I showed him the bloody weapon. Then his twin got worked up too. They don't like to be separated."

"Too bad," Lammers said. "A reaction to a bloody weapon is a classic sign of guilt."

"Maybe one of the shelters will take them," Evans offered. "With an officer keeping watch, of course."

"We'd have to pull someone off the search for bloody clothes," Lammers said. "So let's wait and see how they do."

Jackson spoke to Evans and gestured at the board. "Henry was the one in the green jacket and has a small mole on his neck." As Evans made notes, he turned to Quince. "What else did we get from all the interviews out there today?"

"Not much." Quince glanced at his notes. "Everyone saw Thompson passing out blankets, but afterward, they went back to the camp to be near the fire. One man, who came late, said he saw Thompson sitting in his truck. He doesn't know what time it was, but he says it had been dark for a while."

That was odd. "So he was there after he handed out blankets."

"That's what it seems like. But the guy is not exactly a reliable witness."

"Was he sober when you interviewed him?"

"I don't think he's ever sober."

It didn't matter, Jackson told himself. They had the twins in custody. "Did we get anything from the search party?"

"Not yet," Lammers said. "But we'll get a canine unit out there tomorrow."

"We still need a door-to-door sweep. I know there are only businesses in that area, but some of those shops may serve as apartments too, and we have to talk to every possible witness. I need you and Evans to start after our dinner break."

Quince started to say something, then stopped and started over. "I have something I have to do later, but I'll get out there for a while."

That surprised Jackson. Before he could say anything, Quince added, "It's personal. And financial."

Evans jotted a name on the board. "I also need to find a homeless vet named Boxer and bring him in. He supposedly hates cops and may have threatened Thompson."

"Do you know where to look?" Jackson asked.

"Jacob says he sleeps at the Mission most of the time when it's cold."

"I can put out an attempt-to-locate," Jackson offered, knowing it wasn't much good without a description. "We do have to look at other suspects. Thompson's credit cards and phone were gone, but the twins didn't have either. Still, one of them could have killed him, then they panicked and fled. Someone else could have come along after he was dead and picked up the valuables." Jackson remembered the shed they'd mentioned. "They sleep in a shed that belongs to a woman named Ella. Near the corner of Third and Monroe. I'll track it down and do a search."

"What have you got for me?" Lammers asked.

He hesitated, not wanting to annoy her with a crappy assignment. The payback could be rough. "Will you look into Thompson's financial records?"

"Sure. But it's Saturday, so it could be slow getting access." She made a note on her yellow pad, then looked up abruptly. "That reminds me. Schak said Thompson was dating a woman named Trisha Weber, who works at the Crescent Medical Clinic."

"Thanks. I'll track her down. Maybe she can help us trace his last days."

Lammers added, "Thompson worked a shift yesterday and left around four. I'll access his log and see who he interacted with."

Jackson's phone rang, and he glanced at the ID: *Schak*. He had to take it. He signaled to the others, then stepped away from the conference table. They would still hear his side of the conversation, but it wouldn't be in their faces. "Hey, Schak. Are you doing okay?"

"Sort of. I know the task force is meeting. What have you got?"

"The street twins, Henry and Jacob Walsh, are in custody. They interacted with Thompson right before he died, but we don't have anything solid yet."

"That's better than I expected to hear." A pause. "Do they have a history of violence?"

"Nothing recent. But they were incarcerated briefly as teenagers for assaulting a caregiver."

"Lammers gave me a case to work, so I'm keeping busy, but leave me a message if anything develops."

"I will. Take care."

Jackson turned back to the task force. "You heard what I said about the twins' record?"

Evans was already writing the information on the case board.

From below, a loud wailing came from the interrogation rooms. The pain in their cries made Jackson's nerves ping.

Lammers said, "If we can hear them, Willow can too. And she's probably calling the media. Let's go talk to the chief about how he wants to handle this."

Jackson stood. "We'll meet back here in the morning—unless something breaks."

. . .

Chief Warner looked like a man having a bad day. His shirt had a stain, his face shimmered with sweat, and his jaw was clenched. "I just got off the phone with the head of the citizens' review board," Warner said, not inviting them to sit. "He wants to meet right now to talk about how we're treating the homeless during this investigation. Apparently, that damn activist is already complaining to everyone who will listen."

"You mean Sidney Willow?" Lammers asked. "She's here in the building."

"What?" Warner's eyes twitched in panic. "Please tell me you have a suspect in custody."

"We have two suspects," Jackson said. "The street twins. Can't you hear them?"

The chief's forehead crinkled and he cocked his head. "I thought that was the heating system. It's noisy in this corner, and my hearing is shot."

"The activist is demanding their release, unless we charge them and process them," Lammers added. "And if we don't do something, she'll stage a protest right in our parking lot, with media cameras and all."

"Oh fuck." The chief rubbed his face. "Do we have anything on them?"

"Just proximity so far," Jackson said. "But we think we have the weapon, and we're waiting for the crime lab to process the twins' prints."

"Then let them go. But put an officer on them until we know more."

"Thank you, sir." Lammers turned and headed out.

Relieved, Jackson followed. At least now if things went south, the chief would take the heat for it. On the walk back to their corner of the building, he said, "I'll call the crime lab and see what they have on the prints." The second floor of the building was spacious and quiet, and Jackson was reminded of how nice it was compared to the old headquarters.

Yet below them, the twins were still making a ruckus.

"Let's get them out of here, one way or another," Lammers grumbled, then ducked into her enclosed office.

Jackson stepped into his cubicle and called Joe Berloni, who picked up after a long series of rings. "Hey, Jackson."

"Anything on the prints from the broken bottle yet?"

"Come on, you just dropped it off. And I'm on my way to another death scene."

"I know. Any idea when you'll get to it?"

"Maybe tomorrow, if I can get the overtime approved."

"Thanks. Keep me updated." Jackson started to hang up.

"Wait," Joe called out. "I did look at it, and there aren't any prints on the neck of the bottle, where you would grip it to use as a weapon."

Had it been wiped? "What about the rest of the bottle?"

"I'm still working on it."

"Thanks." Jackson hung up and headed for the conference room, his mind on the bottle neck. Would a street person know to wipe his prints off the weapon? And if he was that careful, why leave it near the scene?

Then it hit him. Gloves. It was cold out there, and Thompson had been handing out gloves and socks, along with blankets. They weren't going to get prints off the weapon because the killer had been wearing gloves. *Crap.*

Jackson found Evans in the conference room, watching the twins on the monitor. They were talking to each other through the wall—shouting, actually, to be heard.

"The chief wants to release them," Jackson said.

"I knew it." She turned to face him. "Should I tail them?"

"We'll put a patrol officer on them. I need you with the investigation."

• • •

Released from the interrogation rooms, the brothers clasped hands for a moment in a silent gesture of reassurance, then started talking in rapid fire, some of it directed to each other and some at Jackson.

"When do we get our other coats back?"

"What time is it?"

"Can we still get to the diner?"

"Is Willow here?"

They seemed almost childlike. Was either really capable of a violent murder?

Jackson led them into the lobby, where Willow waited with two other women. One was Sophie Speranza, a reporter from the *Willamette News*. What a pain in the butt she could be. But at least the TV people and their cameras weren't present. Jackson spun around and disappeared down the hall. He had no intention of speaking to any of them.

After the group left the building, he went back to the desk officer. "Which sergeant is on patrol command?"

"Bruckner. But Sergeant Lammers already notified him. Officer Bremmer is following your suspects now."

Bremmer? Wasn't he the one who'd used a baton on suspects at the camp that morning? "Does Bremmer know to contact me first if anything happens?"

"I'll radio and remind him."

"Tell him I said to keep his hands off the twins."

CHAPTER 8

Saturday, November 22, 2:07 p.m.

Sophie's desk phone rang, startling her. Almost all her calls came on her cell phone, and it was Saturday. Not many people called the newspaper on the weekend. This was a new shift for her. She picked up. "Sophie Speranza."

"Hi. It's Willow. We met at a city council meeting once."

"I remember. You founded the Sleep Is a Right Association." Known as SIRA, the group advocated for homeless people.

"I've got a story for you."

A shot of adrenaline made Sophie sit up. "What is it?"

"A police officer was killed last night, and they're holding the street twins. They won't let me see them or give them counsel."

What the hell? "What officer? When did this happen?"

"Dan Thompson, the one who collected blankets and jackets every year and passed them out."

"That's tragic." Why hadn't the police department told her when she called for the morning update? "When did he die, and how did you find out?"

"I don't know exactly when, but today a SIRA member called and told me the police had picked up the twins."

"What twins?"

"The homeless brothers who've been on the streets of Eugene forever. You've never seen them?"

"No. Sorry." Sophie had moved to Eugene to attend college, so she'd only been in the area about eight years. It had never been her intention to stay, but newspapers and magazines across the nation had started laying off thousands right after she got the job at the *Willamette News*, so she'd been more or less stuck.

"Henry and Jacob Walsh, age thirty-three, with mild mental handicaps and personality disorders. Their parents died in a freak accident when they were thirteen. They lived with an uncle for a while then ran away and have been on their own since."

A profile story by themselves. "Who's handling the investigation?"

"Detective Jackson. Do you know him?"

"We have a working relationship." Meaning, Jackson tolerated her because he found her useful sometimes. "He's also a decent man. He won't abuse the twins to get information."

"But he will take advantage of their naïveté. Any cop would. I need to get in there and make them understand their right not to incriminate themselves."

"Could they have committed the murder? Jackson must think so."

"No." Willow raised her voice. "They were just in the wrong place at the wrong time."

"What do you want from me?"

"Come to the department and start asking questions. The fear of bad press might pressure them into doing the right thing."

"I'll do that." She would call Jackson first and see what he had to say. "Let's stay in touch." Sophie started to hang up, then remembered she was on a landline. "What's your number so I can contact you?"

They exchanged information, including emails. Sophie closed out the article she was working on—an update on a murder trial in which a young man was accused of killing his ex-girlfriend with a baseball bat. It was the third murder trial in Eugene in as many months. This time, meth hadn't been to blame. The guy was just a control-freak asshole who'd killed the woman he loved rather than let her date someone else.

Sophie headed for the break room to make a cup of tea. The office was quiet on Saturday, with only a few sportswriters, her, and a copy editor in house. An intern from the University of Oregon was supposed to show up today and start shadowing her. The interns made everyone nervous, Sophie included. Management had been shifting experienced reporters into crappy positions, such as obituaries or covering Springfield, their sister city. Or, in one case, writing entertainment reviews they weren't qualified to do. Eventually, the stress or the bad performance reports forced the old-timers to quit or be fired, then the paper hired an intern at half the wages and benefits.

She'd felt protected, having only been employed for five years and earning well under the top of the pay scale. But recently, management had shifted her to working weekends and hired an intern for the crime-and-court beat. Sophie knew she was next to go, and it broke her heart. No, Jasmine had broken her heart by dumping her. This was just a job, she reminded herself. A job she loved! And was damn good at.

Back at her desk, she sipped her tea and decided to call Jasmine. Maybe her ex-lover would give her another scoop—out of guilt. It couldn't hurt to ask. Jasmine's phone went unanswered. The crime scene technician was probably working the new homicide. Sophie left a message: "Hey, gorgeous. I heard that an officer was murdered. Can you tell me anything? I'm hanging on to my job by a thread here, and insider details are all that make me look better than the intern they brought in to replace me. Thanks. Call me."

She tried Jackson next and left him a message too, but with less personal pleading. Her next call was to Brian, the crime-beat photographer, and she asked him to meet her at the police department if he could. Sophie shut down her computer and grabbed her big red shoulder bag, which contained her own camera. She needed to get down to the department and cover the story about the twins and the officer's murder. The intern would get by without her for half a day.

But on her way out, she ran into the young woman, as she clumped up the stairs to the second level, where the whole staff was now crammed in.

"Hi, Sophie." A big friendly smile. With a volleyball player's body, Zee towered over her. She was pretty too. Men still ran newsrooms.

"Hey, I was headed out," Sophie said. "Sorry we didn't connect today."

The intern's happy face fell. "Is it a new story? Can I go with you? I want to learn."

Shit on a stick. How could she say no to another upcoming journalist? How could she not help another woman who was trying to launch a career? Sophie hated management even more for putting her in this position—training the person who would push her out. How fucked up was that?

"Sure," she finally said. "I'm headed to the police department." Sophie passed Zee on the steps and kept moving. "It's a breaking story about a murdered officer and the suspects they're holding."

Zee pounded down after her. "Suspects? More than one person killed the cop? That's horrible."

Sophie made another decision she knew she would regret. "Why don't you ride over with me, and I'll fill you in on the way."

• • •

It snowed for a few minutes on the drive over, and Sophie cursed the weather. She also complained about the location of the EPD's new building on Country Club Road. It seemed wrong for the community that neither the newspaper nor the police department were downtown anymore.

Willow stood in the lobby with the sign that she seemed to carry everywhere. The activist was about Sophie's age and claimed to be a U. of O. law student. But Willow showed up everywhere, and Sophie didn't understand how she had time to attend classes and study.

An officer entered the space, so Sophie stopped ten feet back and took a photo of Willow with the uniformed man in the background. It would make a nice shot—if she didn't get one with the twin suspects.

"Any update?" she asked as Willow approached her. Sophie took out her recorder and clicked it on. Zee quickly did the same.

"Detective Jackson won't let me see them unless they ask for me. They know they can call me if they have issues about where they're going to sleep, but we never talked about what to do if they were arrested."

"Do they have a diminished capacity?"

"Somewhat. But they also have mental health issues. I'm very worried for them."

"Should you try for a court order?"

"One of my associates is working on that now."

"You mean someone from SIRA?" Beside her, Zee used her cell phone to take photos of Willow talking.

"A lawyer who does pro bono work for us."

Sophie wanted case details. "What do you know about the murder? Or the police officer?"

"His name's Dan Thompson, and he was a great guy. He advocated for the homeless community within the police department and conducted the annual drive to gather and distribute warm items to those in need." Willow finally put down her sign. "His death is very disturbing to me. Especially if a street person killed him. And I just heard that he was murdered near the new camp out on West Fifth. Apparently, the twins were the last people in line to get blankets."

"Is that why Jackson picked them up? Is that all the police have to go on?"

Willow's brave face collapsed. "I don't know. I don't believe the twins killed him, but if they were in the vicinity, the evidence might look bad for them."

A barrage of footsteps caught their attention. Detective Jackson was in front of the group. A well-built, attractive man with dark hair and even darker irises. Sophie loved the little scar above his left eye. He was too old to be her type, but now that she was dating a man again, she found herself more attracted to all of them.

Behind Jackson were two men in their early thirties—tall, skinny guys with matching faces, both wearing new jackets. They looked at each other as they talked—rapid-fire dialogue about where they would go next. Sophie started toward Jackson, hoping to ask him a question, but he turned and strode away.

Chicken.

The twins rushed to Willow. They expressed thanks but didn't hug her. Sophie took photos as the three talked, getting close-ups as well as distance shots that showed the police department counter behind them. Willow introduced Sophie and Zee as "observers" and "truth tellers," then suggested they all go outside. The five of them moved toward the doors.

While Willow made a call to the pro bono lawyer, Sophie interrupted the twins to ask a question. "Do you know what happened to Officer Thompson last night?" Recorder still in hand, she clicked it on.

"They say he was killed," Henry, in the lighter-blue jacket, responded.

"Do you know who did it?"

They both shook their heads.

"Did you see anything unusual? Did you see Officer Thompson talk to anyone after he stopped handing out blankets?"

"In the truck, yes," Henry said.

"Who was it?"

They both shrugged.

"We're hungry." Jacob touched his stomach. "Will you take us to the diner?"

Sophie wanted to ask more questions, but she'd lost their attention, and they were chatting with each other again. She clicked off the recorder, wondering if Jackson knew someone had been in Thompson's truck with him before he died.

CHAPTER 9

Saturday, November 22, 3:35 p.m.

The Sorensons' home looked much like the Devonshires'. Red-brick trim, beige paint, and a lush green yard, even in November. But at this house a small bicycle lay near the front step, and the trash bins had been left on the curb—the only signs of disarray in the whole upscale neighborhood.

Schak stopped on the street, noting that the driveway held three vehicles, parked at an angle to fit them all in. Pleased to find occupants home on a late weekend afternoon, he knocked on the door. Music from inside the house pulsed through the walls. Rap crap. Why were the parents putting up with it?

No one answered, so he pounded on the door. After a long wait, he turned the knob, leaned in, and shouted, "Eugene Police!"

A moment later, someone yelled, "Turn that off! Someone is here!"

A middle-aged woman came to the door and gave him a nervous smile. Her baggy black clothes and makeup-free face made him wonder if she was in mourning.

When the music cut out, Schak introduced himself. "Detective Schakowski, EPD. I'd like to ask a few questions."

"Sorry about the music. I was wearing headphones and didn't realize Daren had it that loud." She didn't move to let him in.

"This isn't about the noise. I need to talk to Anna Sorenson. Is she your daughter?"

The woman's eyes widened for a quick second, then she stepped back and let him in. "What's this about?"

"Ashley Devonshire. And a party they both attended."

"Were they drinking?"

"Yes, but that's not the issue." Schak realized there were several teenagers in the house. "How old is Daren?"

"Eighteen."

"I'll need to talk to him as well. But Anna first."

"Have a seat in the living room. I'll get her." Mrs. Sorenson started up the stairs, moving slowly, as if in pain.

It seemed everyone over forty had something wrong. He'd had a heart attack a few years back and lived with the constant worry that it would happen again. He remained standing and looked around. The home was nicely appointed but had suffered some abuse. A dark stain on the area rug, a tear in the arm of the leather couch, and a layer of dust everywhere.

A teenage girl came down the stairs a minute later. She had her mother's cheerful but forgettable face and the body of a gymnast. Her mother followed her into the living room.

"I'd like to speak to Anna alone for a moment." Teenagers never confessed anything in front of their parents—even knowing they would find out later.

Mrs. Sorenson hesitated, staring at her daughter.

Anna said, "It's okay, Mom."

The mother retreated into a bedroom on the first floor. Schak thought she might do that a lot, especially if she was raising the kids alone. He gestured for the girl to sit, and she curled herself into one end of the couch. Schak perched on the opposite arm. "Where did you and Ashley Devonshire go last Wednesday?"

"What do you mean? We worked on our science project." She looked at him with innocent eyes, then chewed on a hangnail.

"You went to a party. I want to know where." Schak softened his voice. "I'm not here to cite you for underage drinking. But I have to know the location and who Ashley talked to that evening."

"Brian Carter's. He's a friend of my brother."

"Did Daren drive you there?"

"No, I have my own car."

She looked fourteen. "How old are you?"

"I'll be seventeen in January."

"But your brother was at the party too?"

"Yes."

"Who did Ashley leave with?"

The girl squirmed and tucked her feet under herself. "I don't know. I left after an hour, but she wanted to stay."

How many kids would he have to talk to? "Who was she with when you left?"

"No one, really. She was doing shots and dancing."

"Were any boys hitting on her?"

"The usual." Anna suddenly sat upright. "What is this about? Did something happen to Ashley?"

"She didn't tell you?"

"Tell me what?" A high-pitched panic.

He really didn't want to have the next part of the conversation. "Ashley was sexually assaulted and dropped off in her yard. Any idea who could have done that to her?"

"Oh god. I shouldn't have left her." Anna pulled up her legs and wrapped her arms around them. "No wonder she didn't come to school Friday."

"Answer my question. Do you know who could have assaulted her?"

"No." The girl was near tears. "I don't think she's the first one."

A shock wave kicked through his chest. "What do you mean?"

"I heard a rumor that Mara Andrade was raped last year. She's a senior at Riverside, but I don't really know her."

Schak wrote down the name, worried that he'd spelled it wrong. "Do you have her phone number? Or know her parents' names?"

"No, but I can ask around and see."

The family might even be in the phonebook. "Does your brother, Daren, know Mara?"

The girl's eyes shifted from puzzled to nervous. "Yeah, so? We all go to the same school."

"I need you to make a list of everyone you knew at the party."

"Is Ashley all right?"

He wasn't going to break the news of another death. Not today. It wasn't his responsibility. "No, she's not. But I'm not answering questions. Go make that list."

She scampered toward a drawer in the kitchen, chewing the hangnail again.

Schak went to the stairs and yelled for Daren to come down. When the teenager didn't respond or show his face, Schak trotted upstairs to search. He opened the doors on both sides and found two empty bedrooms. Daren wasn't in the bathroom either. *Well shit.* The kid had bolted. Schak went to find the mother to get permission to search her son's room. The idiot should have stayed and answered questions. Just one piece of incriminating evidence, and he would put out an attempt-to-locate. Daren Sorenson wouldn't get far.

CHAPTER 10

Saturday, November 22, 5:05 p.m.

Without a last name for Ella, Jackson decided to drive to the corner of Third and Monroe and look for a house with an accessible shed. Daylight was fading fast, and he wished he'd gotten out earlier. The homes in the Whiteaker neighborhood had been built in the fifties, so they were smaller than those in the new subdivisions. They had mature landscaping and overgrown trees with red and gold leaves still clinging to the branches.

After a minute of walking around, he spotted a cottage with a green metal shed in the side yard. The name on the mailbox: Ella Fitzroy. No one answered his knock, so he entered the side gate and jogged up the path to the shed. A shopping cart handle stuck out behind the metal structure, and beyond it, a tall hedge separated the side yard from the backyard. A padlock held the sliding doors closed, so Jackson scooted back to look at the shopping cart. He found two. Various soda cans and empty beer bottles filled the bottom of both carts. Piled on top were items of clothing, a back-pack for each, and an odd collection of that day's findings: a ratty stuffed elephant, a dying houseplant, and a pink yo-yo.

Jackson rummaged through the clothes, but none seemed to have blood spatter. Then he noticed the label on the brown bottles. Colt 45. The same brand as the jagged weapon at the crime scene. He took pictures of the bottles, hoping the flash on his camera would produce a decent picture in the dim light. A sliding metal sound made him pause.

"What are you doing back there?" The woman's voice startled him, and he spun around.

Shaped like a funnel, with linebacker shoulders and skinny ankles, the older woman stood in a doorway on the side of the house.

"Police work." Jackson smiled and introduced himself. "I knocked on your door and nobody answered."

"So you thought you'd just enter my property?" Her mouth pulled into a grim line, and she looked as if she'd just woken up.

"I'm sorry. But a police officer has been killed, and the home-less men who sleep in your shed are prime suspects."

"Oh no!" Her hand flew to her mouth. "I can't believe the twins would hurt someone."

"Can I come in? I'd like to ask some questions."

"I don't know anything that would help you. The twins come and go independently."

Jackson stepped toward her and pulled out his notepad. "What time did they show up here last night?"

"I don't know. But I heard them arguing around ten."

"Did you see them or talk to them?"

"No. That's part of our deal. We don't interact much."

"How do you know them?"

"They attend my church. I didn't know they were homeless until I saw them at a service event at the fairgrounds. I offered them a safe place to sleep."

Jackson didn't think it was smart or safe to offer shelter to mentally ill street people, but he kept that to himself. "When you heard them argue, were they just arriving?"

"I don't know." She pulled her sweater tight, bracing against the cold. "I'd like you to leave, please."

He didn't understand her attitude. "I need permission to search the shed. As I said, a police officer has been murdered."

"You'll have to ask the twins. I won't invade their privacy."

"Do you have a key?"

"Somewhere. But you're wrong about them. Please leave." She started to close the door.

"I'll be back with a search warrant."

She ignored him, and he heard the door lock. Jackson went back to his car, wondering if she would go so far as to hide evidence after he'd left. Was she more connected to the twins than she was willing to admit?

· · ·

Jackson drove to the department and updated his case notes. His stomach growled, and he checked his watch. He'd missed lunch, and it was time to pick up Benjie and go home for dinner. But he wanted to contact Trisha Weber before she left the clinic. Was it too late? He called Crescent and asked to speak to her, but was informed she'd left for the day.

"When is she scheduled again?"

"I can't give you that information. But if you're the guy that keeps harassing her, I'm calling the cops."

A bad vibe flashed through his head. "I'm Detective Jackson, Eugene Police. Who is the guy who keeps harassing Trisha?"

"Her ex. I don't know his name."

"Will you give me Trisha's phone number? I need to talk to her."

"I can't do that. But she'll be here tomorrow morning at ten. Our urgent care clinic is open until three tomorrow." The receptionist hung up before he could ask another question.

Jackson googled Trisha Weber but didn't find anything but an old newspaper article in which she was mentioned as someone who'd been helped by Womenspace, a local shelter for battered women. How violent was her ex? A sense of urgency tugged at Jackson to find the man. But Trisha didn't have a Facebook page or a criminal record. He finally found her in a case file from two years earlier. She'd been assaulted by Gene Burns, who'd gone to prison and was now out on parole. Jackson would check with the Parole and Probation office in the morning to see if they had an address for Burns, then he would visit the clinic to talk to Trisha. What if her ex had been jealous of Trisha's new boyfriend, Dan Thompson, and come after him?

CHAPTER 11

Saturday, November 22, 4:40 p.m.

Schak questioned Mrs. Sorenson about Daren, but she became uncooperative, insisting her son couldn't possibly be a sexual predator. No one wanted to believe the worst of their children. He would have said the same if someone had suggested Brad was a rapist. The mother reluctantly gave him a photo of Daren, but refused to let Schak search his room or turn on his computer.

He went to his car, turned on the heat, and compared the names on Anna's list with the contacts in Ashley's phone. Two overlaps came up. Taylor Crenshaw, who was already in his notes as a best friend, and Daren Sorenson, the brother whose friend held the party. As much as he wanted to go home, put up his feet, and toss back a shot of bourbon with a Miller chaser, he decided to check out the party house first. If he kept working, he wouldn't be sad about Danny, or think about all the violent assholes who lived in Eugene, or worry about his son getting shot in the head during a traffic stop—all of which made him want to get numb-drunk. If he wanted to stay married, he had to stay sober.

He called Tracy—relieved when she didn't pick up—and left her a message that he had to work late. Feeling hungry, he picked up a small cheeseburger, because he really needed a moment of pleasure in this bleak day. In the dark parking lot, he ate in his car, sipping coffee and wishing it were beer. Danny kept floating into his brain. All the camping trips they'd taken together, with their mothers when they were young, then on their own as teenagers. Drinking beer around a campfire and speculating about their futures. Danny had no future now. The realization overwhelmed him, and rather than let himself be paralyzed by it, Schak started the car and moved on.

The address where the party had taken place was in a neighborhood near campus, so he crossed the downtown area, noticing that the teenagers who hung out near the bus station and library had gone home—or wherever they went at night. Many were sofa-surfers, who lived out of a backpack and slept in a different house every night so they wouldn't wear out their welcome anywhere. Technically, they were part of the Eugene homeless population, but he didn't think they got counted.

The party house on Lawrence, just outside the university area, was a ranch-style home built in the sixties that had become a rental as people bought newer homes farther out. The lawn hadn't been mowed before winter set in, and the paint on the house didn't match in places. Cool fingers of worry tickled down his neck. Gang members had likely tagged the home, and the residents had painted over the graffiti. Schak called dispatch to let them know where he was. "It's just routine questioning," he added. "But send a patrol unit around if they're not busy."

He climbed out and strode up the edge of the driveway, noting that both cars were silver Toyotas—the most frequently stolen vehicle in the state. Before he reached the cement landing, a young man stepped out and closed the door behind him, cheerfully calling out, "Hey, what can I do for you?"

The kid obviously had something to hide and didn't want a guy in a dark suit and crew cut poking around. "Detective Rob Schakowski, EPD. You had a party here last Wednesday."

"What about it?"

Schak took mental notes. Early twenties, stocky build, and shaggy hair. Hazel eyes and freckles. "First, what's your name?"

The young man hesitated.

"Lying to a police officer is punishable by up to six months in jail and a twenty-five-hundred-dollar fine."

He swallowed hard. "Brian Carter."

Schak jotted it down. "I want a list of all the men who attended the party."

"Whoa. That could be tough. I have roommates, and they invited people. And those people have friends." He nodded his head in an exaggerated gesture of uncertainty. "So a lot of people came and went. And I only know a few."

Schak wanted to go inside, but he suspected he would need a warrant. This kid was cagey. "Do you know Ashley Devonshire?"

"I think I met her at the party. A friend of a friend. Why?"

"Did you get her drunk?"

"No."

"Who gave her alcohol?"

Carter shrugged. "Maybe she brought her own."

"Who did you see her with?"

"She spent time with Daren Sorenson."

The best friend's brother. "Did she leave with him?"

"I don't know. Someone called the cops, and after the officer showed up, all the minors ran."

That threw him off. Had the assault happened here in the house? Or had someone grabbed Ashley as she left? "What time did the party break up?"

"Around ten thirty. It was a bummer."

"I'd like to come in and look around while you make that list. And talk to your roommates."

Silence while he shifted his feet and worked up his courage. "I can't let you do that without a warrant."

Schak was tempted to pretend he smelled someone smoking pot in the house as an excuse to go in. But he changed his mind. It wasn't even a crime anymore, and if he found the assault room, he needed his search to hold up in court. "I need to talk to your roommates."

"They're not here."

Bullshit. Two cars were in the driveway. "I want that list of guys who attended. And their phone numbers." Schak handed him a piece of notepaper and a pen.

Carter scribbled for fifteen seconds and handed it back. Four names and two phone numbers. It was something, but Schak also needed a search warrant and subpoenas to compel testimony. He handed Carter a business card. "A young girl was sexually assaulted during or after your party. Be a good citizen and help me with this investigation."

"Right. I will." The young man's body relaxed with obvious relief.

Schak took his picture and several more of the house just to make the guy nervous again. He also sat in his car out front for a few minutes, just for good measure.

Still hungry on the drive back, he stopped for another burger at the Sixth Street Grill—an old habit from when the department was located downtown. When the waitress asked him if he wanted to start with something to drink, he hesitated, then thought, *Fuck that.* His cousin had died, and he was grieving. Tracy couldn't expect him to stop drinking today, of all days. So he ordered a pint and a bacon cheeseburger, which would also piss her off. But he needed something to make him feel better.

While he ate, he planned his next moves. First, run the names of the men at the party through the database and see if any had criminal records, particularly sexual crimes. Then, if it wasn't too late, visit Mara Andrade and see if she had been victimized by the same person. He hoped she would provide more detail. Schak changed his mind and decided to visit Mara first. The more he knew about the predator's MO, the better chance he had of finding him in the files.

• • •

The Andrade house was dark, and no one answered the door, so he drove back to the department. Typical. So much of his time was wasted driving around trying to find people who were constantly on the move and often didn't want to be found. He sometimes called in advance to set up appointments, but in sensitive situations like this—in which a young girl had been sexually assaulted and no one had reported the crime—it was better to show up for a face-to-face and catch them off guard. People who didn't report crimes either feared the police or had something to hide. In this case, they were likely trying to keep their daughter's degradation private. He didn't understand why anyone would protect such a predator, but he didn't have a daughter. Thank god. Drama drove him crazy.

At his desk, he keyed in the names from both witnesses' lists. The only person with a criminal record was Brian Carter himself. He had a drug conviction for possession of cocaine, plus a harassment complaint. The charge had been dropped when his accuser failed to show up in court. What kind of harassment? If it was sexual, Schak might be able to get a search warrant for Carter's computer and cell phone.

The case file revealed that Sasha Kapoor's complaint was that Brian Carter had called and texted her with insults and minor threats, once even showing up at her apartment to berate her in person. Nothing sexual, but still worth asking about. If the guy liked degrading women, then his deviancy could have worsened in the two years since he went after Kapoor.

Schak dialed her number, but it was no longer in service. The file contained her last known address, and he added it to his notebook. A search of the phone directory produced only one listing for Kapoor, and he tried it. A woman answered in a soft Indian accent. He introduced himself and asked to speak to Sasha.

"She doesn't live here. Can I help you with something?"

"I'd like her phone number."

"What is this about?" Her soft voice tightened a little.

"I'm investigating a series of assaults, and I think she might have been the first victim."

A pause. "You mean Brian Carter. That was long ago."

"Did he sexually assault Sasha?"

A little gasp. "I don't know. Sasha didn't tell us about the harassment until it was over."

"Please give me her number."

"She's going to school in Portland now, and it would be best for her not to talk about the incident."

That wasn't his concern, but he did his best to care. "I'm trying to keep other young girls from being victimized."

"Let me look in my phone for it." After a pause, she gave him the number.

Schak added it to his file of contacts, thanked her, and hung up. Sasha didn't answer, so he left a message, emphasizing the need to protect other students from assault or harassment. He pulled up an e-form and worked on a search warrant for Carter's personal electronics. He had diddly-squat so far, and a judge wouldn't sign the paper as is, but he had to be ready. So much had changed in the decades he'd been in law enforcement—everything was on a computer now, and he was the world's worst typist. Sometimes it overwhelmed him, and he thought about quitting. But he didn't want to be one of those guys who retired too early and died at sixty out of boredom and regret.

. . .

Tracy hugged him when he walked in the door, something she rarely did anymore. He squeezed back, liking the unexpected closeness. But he pulled away before she could kiss him, not wanting her to smell the beer on his breath.

"Are you doing all right?" she asked, searching his eyes.

"I'm fine." He pulled off his jacket and weapon, dropping them on the couch. "As long as I keep busy," he added. "If I think about Danny, I get mad. Stabbed by some goddamned lowlife who probably took a blanket from him twenty minutes earlier. The homeless problem here is out of control." He went straight to the fridge and yanked it open. But his beer was gone. *Hell's bells.* He turned to Tracy. "What did you do with my last two brews?"

"I dumped them out." A quiet tone laced with confidence. "You said you were going to quit."

"Goddammit! You had no right to do that. It's my decision." He spun toward the pantry and searched for the half bottle of Wild Turkey left over from his last camping trip with Danny. Gone. White-hot, need-fueled anger gripped him, and he wanted to punch the nearest wall. But it was covered with shelves and canned goods, and he wasn't that kind of guy.

"I'm going out to pick up a six-pack," he said, walking past Tracy. He pulled his weapon and coat back on. "My cousin and best friend just died. I'm not quitting drinking until I get through this."

Tracy pressed her lips together, staring at him the way she did when she wanted him to read her mind. As he walked out, she called after him, "Grief is forever. This is just another way of stalling."

Schak kept going. He just needed a little more time.

CHAPTER 12

Saturday, November 22, 6:07 p.m.

Jackson drove up McLean Street to Kera's lovely home with the stunning view. As he walked along the path, he couldn't believe he'd asked her to sell it and move in with him. Two separate issues, but both significant. She would be making the greater sacrifice, as always. He knocked on the door, waited a minute, then opened it. "Hey, I'm here."

A cacophony of laughter from the family room gave him a jolt of joy. What better sound to soothe his nerves after a day of grief and stress. So far, patrol units hadn't found Gene Burns, and the lab had yet to compare fingerprints. He stepped inside, called out again, then headed to the back of the house.

Kera and the two little boys sat on the floor, building a crazy fort-like structure with colorful blocks. Only Kera looked up when he came in.

"That looks like fun," Jackson said.

Benjie jumped up and ran to him. Jackson scooped the boy up in a tight hug. "I missed you."

"I'm here." Benjie's standard response to affection. His mother must have said it to him.

Micah, a little younger, hugged his legs. Kera's grandson was warming up to him now that his mother was gone too.

"How was your day?" he asked.

Kera kissed his cheek. "Hectic and fun. With occasional moments of sadness."

He hugged her around the shoulders but didn't comment. She would always grieve for her son, and there was nothing he could do or say to make it better. But he worried that taking care of the boys was too much to ask of her. Or maybe it was exactly what she needed. "Thanks for watching Benjie." Pangs of guilt as he braced for her reaction to his next comment. "Why don't you take a break while I'm here?"

Kera gave him a look. "You're not staying for dinner?"

"I can't. I need to spend time with Katie, drop off Benjie, then get back to work. This is the most important case I've ever handled."

"Any leads you can tell me about?"

"A couple of viable suspects, but we're waiting on forensics."

"I'll take you up on that break." She gestured at the blocks on the floor. "We were building forts. But they think the best part is tearing them down. You have to do it quickly, with lots of gusto, for maximum effect."

"I can do that." Jackson sat down cross-legged, pushed everything from his mind, and focused on the toddlers, letting himself remember the joy of play.

· · ·

He ended up staying longer than he'd planned to, but Kera had made him a cup of coffee and persuaded him to hang out with her for a few minutes while the boys watched a cartoon. Now he felt anxious, late for his standing dinner date with his daughter and behind on the investigation. As he drove across town, a dark, free-floating dread crept in, pushing out the good vibe from Kera and the boys.

What if the Walsh twins hopped on a train and disappeared? Then tomorrow, the lab called with one of their fingerprints matching the weapon? The department's scorn would be palpable. He'd forever be the idiot/asshole who let a cop killer go. Gene Burns was still out there too, and he might have already left town. His jealousy motive seemed more viable than one of the twins snapping because he didn't get a blanket.

Worry wormed its way into his gut, where he'd had surgery the year before. The scar tissue and the fibrosis worked together to cause him pain, but there was little he could do. He cycled on and off prednisone to keep the retroperitoneal fibrosis at bay, and he was currently off. Narcotic pain meds weren't an option; he needed to function at 100 percent. Jackson reached for his naproxen sodium and swallowed two with the dredges of that morning's thermos of cold coffee.

He pulled up to the home he shared with his brother and fifteen-year-old daughter. He'd grown up here, moved out as a young man, then moved back in after his divorce forced him to sell the home Katie had grown up in. His parents had been murdered in the interim, and living here was an odd mix of nostalgia and grief. He'd be glad to move on and find a place without any painful memories of lost loved ones. Derrick's vehicle was gone, and he was glad for a dinner alone with just himself, Benjie, and Katie. Or so he thought until he went inside.

His daughter was rummaging through the refrigerator in the kitchen and turned to yell at him. "Where have you been? There's nothing to eat in this house. And I thought having dinner together every night was a big deal to you." In that moment, she reminded him of his ex-wife. Dark curly hair and delicate features, plus a tendency to blame him for everything.

Because she was nearly five months pregnant, he let it go, took a deep breath, and said, "Sorry I'm late. I've been working all day."

"I played with Micah," Benjie said. The boy copied nearly everything Jackson did and said. Another huge responsibility. Sometimes, the commitment terrified him, especially when he thought about helping to raise his grandchild too. And Kera's grandchild.

Katie turned to him. "You could let me have the keys to the GTO, so I'm not trapped here."

Not a chance in hell. And they'd had this conversation before. "It's too valuable. We'll find you an inexpensive car that I won't worry about." He'd spent years restoring the midnight-blue '69 GTO and might never let her drive it. He also owned a three-wheeled motorcycle that he and Katie had built together, but she had no interest in driving that. Thank goodness.

"Why are you working on Saturday?"

"I was called out to a homicide scene this morning."

"I know what you do is important, but it's also creepy. Who's dead, by the way?"

"A police officer named Dan Thompson."

Shame washed over her face. "I'm sorry. Was he a friend?"

Jackson hadn't really known him well. "He's Schak's cousin, the guy who does the donation drive for the homeless every year."

"Now I'm going to cry." And she did.

Teenage hormones and pregnancy had turned his daughter into an unpredictable bundle of emotions. Jackson hugged her, uncomfortable with the small bulge of her belly. Benjie rested his head against Katie's legs in support. The two had bonded quickly, and for that, Jackson was grateful.

Katie stepped back and said, "I still hate the gun hugs."

Since he planned to work at home, he would take the weapon off. "Give me ten minutes, then we'll cook. There's leftover spaghetti sauce in the freezer."

. . .

After dinner and a game of Uno with the kids, Jackson left them while they continued playing and went to his desk. He pulled Thompson's recorder from his shoulder bag and clicked it on. He wished he had the man's cell phone to search, but at least he had something to get him started. Tomorrow, he would search Thompson's house, but he wasn't optimistic that it would produce any useful leads. After Benjie went to bed, Jackson would make a quick trip to the department to check in with the search team. Now that Katie was pregnant, she'd quit drinking and running around, and was good about watching her little brother. He was starting to think the baby might be a good thing.

His cell phone rang, and he looked at the ID. Joe Berloni, the crime scene technician. "What have you got for me?"

"I pieced together the broken part of the bottle and got a print. It matches Henry Walsh."

The news should have elated him, but it didn't. A sense of relief, yes, but prosecuting the mentally ill was not rewarding. "Thanks, Joe. I appreciate you working late on a Saturday night."

"Dan Thompson was a great guy. It's the least I could do."

Jackson called the front desk at the department. "We need to bring the Walsh twins back in. Will you check with Bremmer, get their location, and call me right back?"

"Sure." A hint of excitement from the desk officer. "Do we have new evidence?"

"A fingerprint match on the broken bottle found near the body."

"Good news. I'll get right back to you."

Jackson texted Evans with the update. She might want to be there for the arrest.

In the kitchen, he gave Katie the news that he had to go back to work and asked her to watch Benjie.

"What if I had plans?" she said, a playful smile on her face.

"You mean like a yoga class for preggos?" He grinned back.

"Hey, I still have a social life." But her expression turned sad. "If you count Facebook."

Her boyfriend had dumped her, and Katie was talking about giving up the baby for adoption. Jackson tried not to influence her. Either choice would last a lifetime.

"I have to go. I'll text you later." He kissed Benjie good night, pleased that the boy didn't seem bothered by his leaving again.

Jackson strapped on his weapon, grabbed his jacket, and hurried out. As he started the car, he pushed away the guilt. He'd been home with the kids every night for months. He only worked crazy hours like this when he'd been assigned a homicide. The Violent Crimes Unit handled other types of assaults, but Lammers always gave him the tough murder cases. He put in his earpiece and drove out.

A moment later, the desk clerk called to say that Bremmer and the twins were at the Albertsons on Eighteenth and Chambers. About twelve minutes away. Most everything in Eugene was less than a twenty-minute drive. He called Evans and relayed the location.

"I'll be there in fifteen," she said. "We haven't found a single witness, and I just sent Quince home. He said he had something to take care of."

They hung up, and Jackson stepped on the gas. The dark streets were empty, and he felt pressed to get there before Bremmer arrested Henry.

. . .

A few minutes later, he turned into the Albertsons parking lot and drove back to the area where the bottle-return machines were located. A man with a shopping cart full of recyclables and another cart with all his worldly possessions cursed at a machine that had quit working. But he wasn't one of the twins. Jackson spotted a patrol car near the front entrance of the grocery store, but Bremmer wasn't in it. He drove up, parked behind it, and jumped out. Not seeing Bremmer or the twins in the parking lot, he rushed into the store. Loud voices to his right made him turn. Jacob Walsh, still wearing the dark-blue coat, burst out of the bathroom door.

"Henry's hurt! I need help! Call Willow."

Jacob didn't even notice him. The twin charged around the corner and toward the customer service station, still yelling. A knot of dread gathered in his guts. Jackson pushed open the bathroom door.

Henry lay on the floor near the sink, bleeding from his head. Officer Bremmer kneeled next to him, talking into the radio he wore on his shoulder and asking for an ambulance.

"What the hell happened?"

Bremmer looked up, his eyes jumpy and his voice defiant. "He came at me, so I tasered him. He hit his head on the sink when he went down."

"Goddammit! I asked you to wait for me." Jackson pulled off his sport coat. "Get out of my way."

Bremmer stood and stepped back against the wall. For a store restroom, it was bigger than most, but it was still a confined space for three men. Jackson kneeled next to Henry and wrapped his jacket around the bleeding man's head, keeping pressure on the wound. Turning back to Bremmer, he asked, "What the hell were you doing in this bathroom?"

"Checking on them, like I was supposed to." Bremmer shook his head, his expression a sneer. "You're wasting your time and jacket. He's dying and good riddance. The bastard murdered Dan Thompson. Why the fuck are you trying to save him?"

Rage burned in Jackson's throat. "This investigation isn't over. I have another suspect!"

The door opened and a store clerk peeked in. Before Jackson could tell her to leave, she backed out.

"You get out too!" he yelled at Bremmer. The officer left, muttering "Liberal asshole" under his breath.

Jackson glanced down at the wounded man. Blood no longer seeped into the jacket around his head. He touched two fingers to the man's neck and found no pulse.

CHAPTER 13

Sunday, November 23, 6:55 a.m.

Schak woke to the jarring noise of the alarm, head pounding and throat dry. Why the alarm? What day was it? He staggered over to the dresser and slammed the clock. The quiet, traffic-less morning made him realize it was Sunday. But he was working a case; that's why he'd set the alarm. He'd also drank more than he intended, which was why he felt so crappy. The smell of coffee made him aware that Tracy was awake and hadn't left him. He crossed himself, a reflex, and got in the shower.

His wife didn't come into the kitchen to talk as he ate the breakfast she'd cooked for him, so he knew she was mad. He didn't blame her, but they would get through this. He would limit himself to an after-work beer or two until after Danny's funeral service—and after his killer was caught. Then he would quit.

Schak rinsed his plate and stuck his head into Tracy's craft room. "Thanks for breakfast. I have to work today, but I'll try to be home for dinner."

For a long moment, she didn't look up. Finally, she said, "Be safe," her usual farewell as he left for work. She still cared about him. Heart lighter, he hurried out of the house, hoping to reach the Andrade home before they left for church or whatever they had planned for the day.

• • •

The Andrades lived on the other side of the expressway from the Sorensons, in the Cal Young area, where the homes were older, but just as large and with more property. He noticed a new-model car in the driveway and suspected the three-car garage held another high-end vehicle. If this case was related, the perp was targeting rich families. And if so, the crimes had to be as much about blackmailing for cash as they were about sexual perversion. But he didn't know yet if Mara's family had been targeted.

Relieved someone was home, Schak rang the bell and heard a small dog barking behind the door. The man who answered the door surprised him. A tall white guy with blond hair going gray and a slight European accent.

Schak introduced himself, then asked, "Are you Mr. Andrade?"

"Yes, but call me John."

"Is Mara Andrade available? I'd like to speak to her."

"What do you want with my daughter?"

"I'd like to ask about a possible assault earlier this year."

The man's eyes narrowed, and his shoulders tensed. For a long moment, he was silent. Finally, he asked, "Why now? We didn't officially report it at the time."

"There's been another victim."

A quick squeeze of his eyes. "I worried there might be. Please come in."

Schak waited in the foyer while Andrade went upstairs. Muted voices engaged in a heated discussion, but eventually Andrade came back down, followed by a teenage girl.

Schak stared, mesmerized by her doll-like appearance. Huge eyes like a Disney princess, flawless mocha skin, and perfectly straight brownish-black hair. The girl didn't quite seem real until she spoke.

"I really don't want to talk about this, but I understand why I have to. Let's make it fast, please."

The father and daughter sat across from him at a formal dining table that looked as if it had never been used. Schak took out his notepad and recorder. Sometimes he couldn't read his own handwriting and had to go back to the source. He struggled with how to begin. This wasn't an easy subject for two men to discuss. "Please tell me what happened when you were assaulted. Start with the exact date, if you remember."

"May seventeenth. I'll never forget. It was Saturday, and I went to a party with some friends."

The girl stopped, so he prompted her. "Where was the party?"

"At Alex Crenshaw's house. He's a friend who graduated last year."

Schak cut in. "Taylor Crenshaw's brother?" The name had been in the suicide victim's contact list.

"Yes, but like I said, he's my friend. He didn't assault me."

"Who else lives with him?"

"Tristan Channing. He's a university student. And gay. So it wasn't him either."

Schak wrote down the names. How would he keep all these young people and connections straight? "I still have to question both men."

"I never confronted them," her father said, sounding a little ashamed. "Because it could have been anyone at the party, and I didn't want to risk the video going viral. Especially after I'd paid the extortion."

So this one had been about money too. "How much?"

"Ten thousand."

The perp had gotten greedier. "What's the address?" He really hoped to get lucky and find some overlap between the crimes.

"It's on the corner of Eighteenth and Patterson."

Only a half mile from the more-recent assault. But the whole neighborhood was party central.

Mara spoke up. "The last thing I remember is doing tequila shots with Alex, then my mother was waking me up, and I was on the sidewalk in front of our house."

Did the perp drug the girls? "Any flashes of what happened in between?"

"No." She glanced away.

Was she lying or just ashamed? Schak was starting to think both victims had been drugged. "Did he record the assault?"

"He sent us a video," Mr. Andrade said, struggling to keep his voice even. "It showed Mara on a bed with her eyes closed, and he was—" The man paused, searching for a word he could live with. "Probing her."

"With his hand?"

"Yes. He wore a white latex glove." Mr. Andrade was still talking for his daughter.

Were the gloves hiding a scar or a tattoo? Or was he just being extra careful?

"He texted us and said he would post the file online if we didn't pay him ten thousand dollars within five hours." Mr. Andrade rubbed his forehead, his face anguished. "I know we should have gone to the police, but Mara was terribly upset, and her mother was horrified, and they just wanted to give him the money. So I did."

"Where and how did you pay him?"

"He had us put the money in a pouch that was hanging off the back of a disabled woman's wheelchair," Mr. Andrade explained. "She was waiting to board a Mobile Source van, which showed up moments after we dropped it in."

Weird, but clever. "Did she know she was a courier?"

"I doubt it. I walked by and slipped the cash in, and she never seemed to notice."

"What location?"

"Lincoln and Twenty-Third."

Did the perp live nearby? Or drive past the pickup site on his way to work? He had to know about the disabled woman's schedule somehow. And where had the perp picked up the money? Schak scribbled a note to check with Mobile Source. "Did the blackmailer keep his word?"

"We never heard from him again, and the video was never shared. That we know of."

"Do you have a copy?"

"No!" Mara sounded mortified. "I couldn't even watch it."

Schak shifted in his chair. How was he supposed to ask this? He looked at the father. "Tell me about the actual assault. I need to know what he did, so I can look for similar crimes in the database."

"I can't listen to this." Mara scrambled out of her chair and ran upstairs.

Mr. Andrade closed his eyes. "He penetrated her with his fingers, then with a dildo. That was all he recorded. But he also raped her, because she got pregnant." A pained intake of breath. "And had an abortion. Her mother is still upset about it, but Mara wanted to terminate the pregnancy, so I took her."

Mara's assault had happened in May, and Ashley's in November. Had there been more in between? Or some before?

"Rape is rape," Mr. Andrade added. "I'm glad Mara was unconscious. She's still depressed about the abortion and ashamed of what happened. But she's not traumatized. Not like she would be if he had dragged her behind a bush with her eyes open."

Some consolation. "Did you keep the texts the blackmailer sent?"

"For a while, then I couldn't bear to have them on my phone. But I wrote down the number before I deleted them, and I know it from memory."

Schak let him have the notepad. "I need to know more about the party. Can you get Mara back in here?"

Schak spent another ten minutes with the girl and came away with a list of five people she'd known at the party, two only by first names. He needed help with this case, but with Danny dead and everyone focused on finding his killer, he might not get any backup for a while.

He needed to know how the perp targeted and accessed his prey. "Is there anything else you can tell me, particularly about the party?" Schak glanced back and forth between the father and daughter.

"I don't think so." Mr. Andrade stood. "I'm sorry there's another victim, but I'm glad you're investigating. I feel better now than I have in six months."

Mr. Andrade was done talking. Schak shook his hand, gave both his business card, and headed out. When he was halfway down the sidewalk, the door behind him opened and Mara called out, "Wait."

He turned, eager to finally hear from the girl out of her father's earshot.

Mara glided toward him, her voice soft. "I think I was already pregnant when he assaulted me. But I let my parents believe—" She looked down, then finally met his eyes again. "It was easier for them to support my decision that way."

He wished it didn't matter, but it did. "Are you saying the assailant didn't actually penetrate you?"

"He didn't—" Again she struggled to express herself. "He didn't ejaculate in me. And he may not have put his penis inside me." Her face hardened. "But it's still rape."

He didn't know the legal distinction between rape and assault, but he wanted to say the right thing. "Either way, we'll find him and send him to prison."

Mara nodded. "I also remembered something else. One of my friends told me the cops broke up the party. When she said it, I had a dreamlike flash of an officer helping me."

The other party had been busted too. Was the sexual predator and extortionist a police officer?

CHAPTER 14

Sunday, November 23, 7:05 a.m.

Jackson made breakfast for the kids, then disappointed them both by announcing he had to work for a while. "But I promise to take time off as soon as I have some level of resolution for Officer Thompson's case," he said, getting up.

"What exactly does that mean?" Katie asked. "You've said it takes months to build a murder case against a suspect who doesn't confess."

That, of all things, she remembered. "What I mean is that once we know for sure we have the right perp, we can slow down and collect every piece of possible evidence. And I can take a day off before that phase begins."

"Are you close?"

"Sort of." The truth was much messier. A viable, but unconfirmed, suspect was dead, and a second suspect had yet to be located.

"What's a perp?" Benjie asked, with a mouthful of banana.

"The bad guy," Katie answered. "Dad catches bad guys, in case you didn't know."

"I know." His little voice had a note of seriousness. "He saved me from the bad man."

They were all quiet for a moment. Benjie's first father had threatened both of Jackson's kids—the worst day of all their lives. Katie patted her belly and broke the mood. "I think the baby wants another waffle."

"You'll have to make it yourself." Jackson grabbed the stack of mail on the table. "I have to see what bills I haven't paid, then get moving." He wanted to be at the clinic when it opened to question Thompson's girlfriend. After that, he had to go into the department and give his statement about the tragic incident at Albertsons. There wasn't much to tell. He'd arrived too late to prevent Henry's death. His brother had been inconsolable. Jackson had called CAHOOTS—Crisis Assistance Helping Out on the Streets—a mobile social service that dealt with situations that involved people who were intoxicated, irrational, or self-destructive. Bremmer had argued for arresting Jacob, but Jackson had pulled rank and refused to let him. Mental health assistance at the jail would have taken hours, or days, to be administered, and he didn't want another death on his conscience. Especially if the twins weren't guilty. He wasn't yet convinced they were.

He focused on the mail, sorting the junk from the stuff that looked important. A letter from the county court gave him pause. He opened it and scanned the top paragraph. Another person had filed for custody of Benjie and both petitions would be heard next week. Stress gripped his gut and gave a twist. Who could it be? He'd traveled to Utah to search for relatives. Jackson scanned the letter and found the name: Caprice Arlen. She didn't match Benjie's mother's name, and he had no idea of the woman's

relationship to the boy. He remembered receiving an earlier letter from the court about Benjie's great-grandmother's estate going
into probate. Was this about money? Had some relative come out
of the woodwork to claim the boy's inheritance? He would gladly
pay her to go away if that's all she wanted. He made a note to call
his custody lawyer in the morning.

His phone rang, and it was Lammers. Jackson grabbed his
coffee and headed to his desk, away from the kids.

"Jackson here."

"The chief wants to meet with us this afternoon." Lammers
wasn't known for small talk.

The big boss didn't come into the department on Sundays—
unless all hell had broken loose. "When? I've got leads to check
out." He'd have to call Evans and ask her to search Thompson's
house.

"At noon. It's about Henry and Jacob Walsh. Sidney Willow
has the homeless community all stirred up, and they're gathering
on the courthouse plaza."

"They know about Henry's death?"

"Of course. You let Jacob go, and CAHOOTS medicated him,
then released him to Willow."

His fellow officers would blame him for this. Could he diffuse
it? "County or old federal courthouse?" The two plazas were only
a block apart, but both were popular protest sites.

"Both. It's not just the homeless but their supporters. This
could be huge."

Damn! "I told Bremmer not to arrest Henry, to wait for me.
This could have been avoided."

"Bremmer is on paid leave, if that helps at all."

"Not really. I'll see you at noon."

. . .

Crescent was a midsize clinic on the outskirts of town. The parking lot was nearly empty, and he was hopeful they wouldn't be busy dealing with urgent care patients. As cold as it was, few people were willing to venture out this Sunday morning. He expected a minimal staff and hoped Trisha Weber would make time to talk to him.

Inside, only two patients waited in the chairs along the wall. They both looked like flu victims.

"How can I help you?" The receptionist was young, pretty, and tan—for November in Oregon.

"I'm looking for Trisha Weber."

"She's with a patient. Can you wait a few minutes?"

At least she was here. Jackson showed his badge. "This is important."

The receptionist swallowed hard, said, "I'll get her," then went to retrieve the medical assistant.

A few minutes later, a tall woman in purple scrubs hurried out of the back area, a nervous smile playing on her face. "I'm Trisha Weber. What's this about?"

Jackson's heart sank. She didn't seem to know her boyfriend was dead. "Can we go somewhere private and talk?"

The pretty woman's lower lip trembled. "Sure."

She led him to an alcove in the waiting room, and they sat on facing chairs. Jackson dreaded the conversation. How to start? "Did you know Officer Dan Thompson?"

Her hands flew to her mouth. "What happened?"

He noticed the tattoos covering her entire left arm. "I'm afraid I have bad news."

"Just fucking tell me."

Jackson braced for hysteria. "Dan was killed Friday night." He started to mention the homeless camp, then stopped. He wanted to see what conclusions she jumped to. Everyone was still a suspect.

"Oh, fuck me!" She slammed a fist into the padded chair. "I knew better than to date a cop."

Her coarseness surprised him, perhaps because of the medical setting. He wanted to acknowledge her loss, but he had to press forward. "How long had you known Dan?"

"About three months." She kept looking at her hands and twisting a ring back and forth.

Had Thompson given it to her? "Where did you meet him?"

"In a bar." Her head jerked up. "How did he die?"

"He was stabbed."

She burst into tears. After a brief, noisy cry, she said, "My ex-boyfriend threatened to hurt Danny. But I didn't think he would kill him." She slumped back in the chair, arms crossed. "Gene had it in his head that we would get back together when he got out of jail, but that's not gonna happen."

"Where can I find Burns?"

"He's staying with his brother in Springfield."

"Can you be more specific?"

"Greg and Jolene Burns. Near the corner of Twentieth and Main. That's all I know." A tear rolled down her cheek. "Did you tell Danny's mother and brother? He was close to them."

"Another officer did." Now for the tough questions. "When did you last see Dan?"

She sat forward again. "Wednesday night. We had dinner at that new steakhouse at the mall. Why?"

"I'm trying to trace his last days." Jackson jotted down her answer. "How did he seem to you? Was he worried or stressed about anything?"

She squinted. "He'd been kind of depressed and had something on his mind, but it was probably work related."

Typical for a police officer. Jackson had to ask. "Where were you Friday night between five and nine?"

"You're shittin' me. You think I could have killed him?" She shook her head. "Fuck you."

A real charmer. He wondered how Thompson had ended up with her. She was pretty, no doubt, with nice breasts and long legs. But the scenario with her ex should have made Thompson wary. "Tell me where you were Friday night."

She glared. "I left here after work to go visit my niece in a treatment center in Corvallis. It's called Milestones. You can call them."

He heard the front door open on the other side of the wall, and a man's voice demanded, "Where is Trisha? I want her to see this."

Jackson leapt to his feet and so did Trisha.

"That's Gene!" Eyes wide with uncertainty.

The receptionist's response was meek. "I don't think she's here."

"I see her fucking car out there! And I'm gonna torch it."

"No!" Trisha Weber ran for the front.

Jackson charged after her, hand reaching for his weapon. In the lobby, he yelled, "Call 911! I need backup."

The front door slammed as Trisha scurried out to the parking lot. Jackson glanced out the window and didn't see either of them. He pushed past a patient and bolted outside.

A man in a denim jacket was at the end of the lot, pouring gas on a small red car. Burns didn't have a weapon that he could see, so Jackson didn't want to draw his Sig Sauer. Instead, he rushed to his own vehicle and grabbed a Taser from under the front seat. The stun gun seemed like the best way to put him on the ground.

He jogged past the row of cars, stun gun ready. "Put the gas can down! Hands in the air!"

Burns glanced over at him, hesitated for a second, then dropped the red plastic container. He reached in a chest pocket and flicked the lighter in one quick motion. "Stop right there, or I'll scorch this piece of shit."

Jackson kept advancing. "Put your hands in the air!"

Burns tossed the lighter onto the hood of the car, and flames shot across the trail of gas. The suspect turned and charged toward the fence, only ten feet away.

Jackson sprinted, closing the distance as Burns scrambled up the pickets. As Jackson reached the flaming car, he pressed the trigger and let the prongs fly. One hit Gene in the leg, and the other smacked into the wooden fence. The suspect dropped to the other side, and Jackson heard him hit the ground running. *Crap!* He sprinted back to his car to radio for help, hoping that a patrol unit was already on the way.

CHAPTER 15

Sunday, November 23, 11:11 a.m.

In his car, Jackson gulped two naproxen sodium to calm the pain in his gut, then checked his watch. Time for his meeting with the chief. As he drove back to the department, he reflexively kept an eye out for Gene Burns. The ex-con's torching of the car indicated he wasn't rational about Trisha Weber, which meant he could have killed her new boyfriend as well. When Thompson's phone records came through, Jackson expected to find threatening calls from Burns. For now, he had a statewide alert out to law enforcement to watch for the suspect.

He found Chief Warner and Sergeant Lammers in the big main conference room with Jackie Matthews, the department spokesperson. They all looked up as he came in. Jackson squared his shoulders, telling himself he'd made the right calls yesterday in dealing with the twins. Or had he? If he'd booked them into jail, even on trumped-up charges, Henry wouldn't be dead. Not necessarily, he corrected himself. Jail was a dangerous place for people with mental illnesses or compliance issues. The deputies used Tasers on inmates, and one had died a few years back. Jackson greeted everyone and took a seat.

"We have a serious shit-storm developing," Warner said. "That activist, Willow, is outraged about Henry Walsh's death, and she's stirring up everybody." He pointed at Jackson. "You released the other twin last night, and he must have gone straight to Willow."

He'd braced for this, yet it still upset him. "Jacob Walsh was hysterical and needed mental health assistance. I had no reason to arrest him."

"You could have come up with something."

This bullshit from the chief? "I don't operate that way, and jail could have been dangerous for him."

Lammers cut in. "What's important is how we move forward. Do we have a plan?" She focused on the chief.

"We need to shut this down before anyone else gets hurt." Warner locked eyes with Jackson. "You need to make a public statement that Henry Walsh's fingerprints were on the weapon that killed Officer Thompson. But that his death was a tragic accident."

The chief wanted him to implicate the homeless man. "I can't do that. Not yet."

Lammers started to say something, but Jackson cut in. "One, the autopsy hasn't been done, and we don't know for sure that the broken bottle is the weapon." He counted off his points with his fingers for emphasis. "Two, the matching print is on the base of the bottle, not the neck, where it would be held as a weapon. And three, I have another viable suspect."

Before he could explain, the chief cut in. "I know it's premature, but we have officers out there who are grieving, scared, and outraged. Some have already been taking out their anger on street people. Now we have a gathering of homeless people and bleeding-heart citizens who are equally upset. This is potentially explosive." Warner raised his voice to a near shout. "You have to shut it down!"

This wasn't his fault. Trembling with anger, Jackson blurted, "It was your call to let the twins go yesterday."

The room echoed with silence.

Jackson hoped he hadn't gone too far. He tried to clarify his position. "Thompson was dating a woman named Trisha Weber. Her ex-boyfriend was jealous of their relationship, and this morning he set her car on fire. I have a statewide alert to find him. Gene Burns has more motive than the homeless twins."

The chief fiddled with a pen, mulling it over. "We'll hold off on publicly labeling Henry Walsh as the killer. But you only have twenty-four hours to get something solid on Burns. If you don't, you'll make the statement, shut down the investigation, and build a case against Walsh." The chief turned to the department's spokeswoman. "Put out a release calling Walsh's death a tragic accident. Tell the press we plan to investigate it thoroughly as well as take measures to make sure something like this doesn't happen again." Warner stood. "Move quickly, please. We have officers assigned to keep an eye on the protestors, and we can't afford another PR disaster."

Jackson nodded and started for the door. He understood Warner's frustration. The department had recently suffered serious blows to its reputation. Sexual assault of female detainees and thousands of dollars in cash, drugs, and valuables missing from evidence lockers. Just to name the worst of it. Now, a homeless man had been killed by a police officer. A man who might not be guilty of anything but leaving an empty beer bottle in an area frequented by dozens of homeless people.

In the bright foyer, the desk clerk called to him. "An officer just picked up Gene Burns and is booking him into jail."

"No. Bring him here." Jackson hated doing interrogations at the jail, but at least Burns' act of arson gave them a reason to hold him. "We'll take him over later."

"I'll let the officer know."

"I'll be in my office. Let me know when Burns is in the hole." He wouldn't call Evans or Quince for this one. They were searching Thompson's house this morning, and continuing the investigation was more important. Gene Burns was a long shot as a suspect. But his prints were in the system, and the crime lab would compare them to the evidence in the morning.

Jackson trudged upstairs, trying not to grimace in pain. The anti-inflammatories typically took half an hour to kick in. At his desk, he opened the Word file with case notes and did an update. But he didn't have much to add, so he keyed Gene Burns into the database to check his record. The man's file went back twenty years. A local with a drug and alcohol problem who went for periods of time with no trouble, then relapsed and got out of control. Reckless driving, drug possession, and intimidating and assaulting girlfriends was the typical pattern. Burns had also been charged with sexual assault twice, but had never been convicted.

Jackson called Burns' parole officer as a courtesy and left a message: "I've got Gene Burns in custody for setting fire to his ex-girlfriend's car. I'm also questioning him about Officer Dan Thompson's death. Call me if you have anything to contribute." Being Sunday, he didn't expect a call back. But POs worked odd hours, checking up on their charges, so it could happen.

His desk phone rang, and he wondered when the old-school devices would become completely obsolete. The front desk officer notified him that Gene Burns was waiting in interrogation.

• • •

Even seated, Burns was tall enough to be intimidating. But his arms were skinny, and the skin on his cheeks sagged in an unhealthy way. The arresting officer had left him cuffed with his hands behind his back, and Jackson didn't plan to spring him. Burns' dark, angry eyes watched Jackson's every move as he took a seat, set out his recorder, and spread out three crime scene photos facedown.

"Did the arresting officer read you your rights?"

"Yes, but it don't matter. I burned the bitch's car, and you saw me. Let's talk deal."

"This isn't about the car." His gravest tone.

Burns tensed, then overcorrected with an exaggerated shrug. "So what's the problem?"

"Where were you Friday night between six and nine?"

"Ah, let's see. That was two days ago. I went to Cottage Grove to apply for a job."

It sounded like bullshit. "At night? What job?"

"A construction job. I talked to a guy named Mike. I can't remember his last name."

More bullshit. "What time did you get back?"

"I don't know. Maybe eight."

Jackson leaned back, giving the suspect an amused smile. "So this is your story. Friday evening, you drove to Cottage Grove in the dark, thirty minutes away, and talked to a guy named Mike about a construction job, then drove back. And that took at least two hours. Is that correct?" Step one was to catch him in a provable lie.

A hesitation. "Yeah. Why? What's this about?"

"If you lie to me, everything changes. A judge will give me a subpoena for your DNA, then the district attorney will file charges and convene a grand jury. If you're convicted, you'll get the death penalty."

Burns' eyes flashed with fear. "Whoa. Whatever it is, you've got the wrong guy."

"You're sticking to your story? Does Mike have a phone number? Can you prove where you were?"

The suspect swallowed hard. "Tell me what the fuck this is about."

"Your ex, Trisha Weber, says you threatened her new boyfriend."

"No." He shook his head. "It wasn't like that." A desperate smile in an attempt to be charming.

"Now he's dead. Gutted with a broken bottle."

Burns squeezed his eyes shut, then leaned forward, his tone panicked. "I'm not a killer. I never even saw the guy."

"Here, let me show you." Jackson turned over one of the crime scene photos. "Officer Dan Thompson. We have the murder weapon, and your prints are on file. It's just a matter of time before we connect you to the crime."

"Oh Jesus." Burns looked away, focusing on the door.

"Tell me what happened, and I can get the DA to keep you off death row."

"I didn't do this."

Time to empathize, pry open his defenses, and get him to admit something. "I know you didn't just stalk and kill him. Something happened. Did Thompson tell you to back off? Were you intimidated?" Jackson didn't believe it for a second and silently begged his fallen colleague for forgiveness.

"We had words, and it got a little ugly. But that was a week ago."

"So you lied about not seeing him."

No response.

"Where did the altercation happen?"

"At Trisha's. I stopped by, and the cop was there. And it got to me." Burns was looking for sympathy now. "I loved her, and she said she'd wait for me. Then I find her with another man. And he's a cop! No offense, but that was salt in the wound."

"So you threatened Officer Thompson?"

"I yelled at both of them. I don't remember what I said." Deadpan tone, eyes rigid.

Another lie. "I think you do remember. And I'm sure Trisha does. Did you threaten to kill Dan Thompson?" He needed to talk to the girlfriend again.

"Maybe. But he said he'd call in more cops and arrest me, so I left."

"When did you see Thompson again?"

"I didn't." Burns grimaced in pain. "Will you take these cuffs off? And get me some water? Or take me back to jail. I'm done talking."

Jackson turned over the other photos. "You have no alibi. Your ex-girlfriend will testify that you threatened to kill Thompson. All we need is one piece of physical evidence, and you're going down for killing a police officer. You need to confess in exchange for a life sentence with the possibility of parole in twenty years."

"It's not gonna happen."

Jackson's phone rang, and it was a number he didn't recognize at first. Then he realized it was Burns' parole officer. "Jackson here. Thanks for the callback." He stood and turned away from the suspect, ready to step out if necessary.

"Why do you think Burns killed Dan Thompson?" the PO asked.

"Thompson was dating his ex, and Burns threatened him."

"Shit. How did Thompson die? I haven't heard the details."

Parole and probation were handled by the county, and those officers were more overworked than the city's safety department. "He was stabbed in the neck and stomach with a broken bottle of Colt 45."

"Goddamn. I just heard that Gene Burns had a run-in last week with another felon. And Burns threatened him with a broken beer bottle. I think you've got your man."

CHAPTER 16

Sunday, November 23, 11:55 a.m.

Schak stopped at Subway and bought a foot-long pastrami sandwich and oversize cookie. Hunger had burned a hole in his gut
since Danny's death. It didn't seem normal, but he had so much
on his mind, he didn't bother to resist. He took the food out to his
car, where he seemed to spend most of his waking hours during
the first week of an investigation. Even when he wasn't working,
he didn't spend much time at home, preferring instead to take his
boat out on the river. He and Tracy each had their own careers,
hobbies, and friends, but they connected every day in some small
way, and he couldn't imagine his life without her. He picked up
his phone to call her, but it rang in his hand.

"Rob, it's Kurt. I can't stop thinking about Danny. Do you
know anything yet?" His cousin's voice reflected the same grief
Schak felt.

Schak was glad to be busy. "The word is that a homeless guy named Henry Walsh killed him. Maybe aided by his twin brother. And we have Henry's fingerprints on the murder weapon." Schak had heard that from Joe at the lab, but he realized he needed to call Jackson for a current update.

"Thank god," Kurt said. "I'm glad they got the guy. It doesn't bring Danny back, but it helps."

"I know what you mean. How are you and Aunt Donna holding up?"

"We're okay. Mostly quiet and sad. Mom wants to plan a service but doesn't know when they'll release him."

"I'm sure they'll do the autopsy first thing Monday morning. After that, she can call and have a mortuary pick up his body." Schak felt queasy talking about his cousin that way. "But the department will plan a funeral procession too. Donna should call Jackie Matthews to coordinate."

"I'll tell her." A pause. "You and Tracy should come by Mom's tonight for dinner. It would be good to have you around right now."

"That sounds good." He meant it, but not with Tracy. Donna and Kurt would expect him to drink with them—and he wouldn't be able to say no—and that wouldn't go over well with his wife. "I don't think Tracy can make it. Plus, I'm working today, so I might not be there in time for dinner, but I'll stop by on my way home."

"See you then."

They hung up, and Schak worried about how his family would react to his quitting drinking. His dad wouldn't care, but his mother wouldn't understand, and neither would Aunt Donna or the rest of the Thompson clan. They didn't trust people who didn't drink. Thinking about it made him want a beer to wash down the last of his sandwich. He settled for the cold coffee in his thermos instead.

. . .

At the department, he searched the patrol logs for the dates of the incidents. No record of parties being broken up or sexual assaults on either day. Disturbing. Why wouldn't a police officer log a stop at a party house? Unless he was covering his tracks. Schak checked the criminal databases again, this time looking for a match to the perp's MO. Sexual predators galore, especially those who preyed on young women, but none that recorded their attempts to extort money from their victim's parents. He called Agent River at the local FBI office but got her voice mail. Of course, it was Sunday. He left a message, then called the main bureau in Langley and asked to talk to a profiler.

After a long wait, a gruff voice came on. "Special Agent Ward. How can I help you?"

Schak introduced himself and laid out his case. "Can you give me any kind of profile? His age? His background? Anything to help steer me in the right direction." He tried to push aside his worry that the perp was a patrol officer. A cop's presence at both parties could be expected. The department had cracked down recently on underage drinking events, especially around campus.

"It's a new one," Ward said. "I know of one predator who videotaped other people having sex, then blackmailed them, threatening to send the file to all their friends. He was Asian, forty-two, single, and an engineer. And lived in Chicago."

"Do you think this perp is a similar age? All the people at the parties the victims attended were young."

"Your predator is likely between thirty and fifty, and if he's smart enough to use a proxy server to upload the files online, then he's tech savvy too. He probably works in the STEM group—science, technology, engineering, or math."

Schak scribbled notes and wondered what else to ask. Blackmail and tech-based crimes were out of his comfort zone. He kept coming back to the unthinkable. "Both parties were broken up by the police, and one victim has a vague recollection of an officer talking to her. Do you think a cop could be the perp?" Schak knew the answer—he just didn't want to be the only one saying it.

"Interesting. Most law enforcement officers who abuse their power are more direct. They use intimidation rather than intoxicants to subdue their victims. But sure, it's unfortunately possible."

"Anything else?"

"How far apart were the crimes?"

"Six months."

"I'll bet there's more victims. He probably started out drugging and raping the victims just for jollies, then graduated to videotaping, then blackmail."

"If there are more victims, their cases aren't in our files. Why wouldn't the young women come forward?"

"Shame. And if they're drunk or drugged, some might not even know it happened."

How would he find them? "Anything else?"

"Not off the top of my head, but I'll take a look through our databases and see if anything pops up."

"Thanks for your time."

The thought of more young girls being drugged and abused revolted him. Why had he agreed to take this case? He ached to be with Aunt Donna and Kurt, drinking and reminiscing about Danny. Kindhearted Danny. His cousin had always stood up for the weak ones, protecting kids who were bullied in school and doing chores for the old disabled lady down the street. Danny's accidental shooting of Kurt had been devastating at the time, but it had forged him into the kind of person who put others first.

A true hero. For a moment, Schak was paralyzed with grief and despair at the evil that lurked in so many people. The violent murders happening every month in his town, the mass shootings of innocents. The world seemed to have gone mad, and he felt powerless to stop it. His job as the cleanup crew seemed almost pointless.

Get your shit together, he chided himself. *And get help on this investigation.* On impulse, he called Sophie Speranza at the newspaper, hoping she checked her voice mails on weekends, and left her a message: "It's Detective Schakowski. I need public help with a case I'm working. Intoxicated young girls are being sexually assaulted. Possibly after attending a party. And sometimes, they're blackmailed with a video of the event. I need more victims to come forward. Please get back to me."

His next call—to Ben Stricklyn, a detective in Internal Affairs—would be more difficult. Stricklyn wasn't in the building right now, but Schak wanted to talk to him first thing in the morning. He needed another investigator, and if the perp turned out to be an officer with the department, IA would take over the case anyway. He kind of hoped they would. He was in over his head.

Before he could dial, he heard shouting down the hall where the top brass had their offices. Training brought him to his feet, and he bolted out of his cubicle. What the hell was going on?

CHAPTER 17

Sunday, November 23, 1:47 p.m.

Sophie pulled off her jacket, made a cup of hot mint tea, and sat down at her computer. The view of the river caught her eye, as always, and she dreaded the thought of leaving this apartment. She'd never find an affordable place this nice in a bigger city. But she had to be a journalist, and if she lost her position in Eugene, she would move wherever she could to find work. Job hunting online was tedious and depressing, and she'd gone out for a walk to get away from it for a moment. She hoped like hell that she would find something in a warmer climate. Winters in Eugene had been wet and gray when she first moved here to attend college, but now they were drier and colder with occasional snowstorms. She couldn't handle the snow. Not after growing up in Tucson.

Her search produced a news-writing job at a TV station in Sacramento, so she emailed a cover letter and resume. She started to open her Facebook page, and her phone rang. Sidney Willow again. Sophie popped in her Bluetooth. "Hello."

"It's Willow. A cop killed Henry Walsh, and I need your help in exposing the police brutality of homeless people." The activist's voice had a catch at the end.

"What happened?" Sophie reached for a yellow paper tablet and pen.

"A police officer tried to arrest Henry last night in the bathroom at Albertsons. Jacob says Henry insisted on washing his hands first—because they're compulsive about certain things—and the cop tasered him. Henry fell and hit his head on the sink and died."

"Oh no. How is Jacob taking it?" The other twin had to be traumatized. Their bond had been intense and obvious in the time she'd spent with them.

"He's doing better than I expected. A detective came to the scene at the store and called CAHOOTS, so Jacob was given medication and counseling. But I'm still outraged, and we're staging a protest right now at the free speech plaza. Can you cover it?"

"Of course." Sophie couldn't believe what she was about to say. "I think you should call a TV station too."

"I already did. But I want you to write the full story. You know what I mean? A lot of homeless people have been beaten for no reason by cops, and it has to be exposed. I can connect you with people to talk to."

The logistics of interviewing street people would be challenging, which was probably why the incidents were not reported or covered. Assuming they were true. "Have the police made a statement about Henry's death?"

"They won't return my calls."

"Which detective was at the scene?" She hoped it was Jackson. He was handling the police officer's murder, so it seemed likely.

She had called him and asked for a statement, but calling once was never enough.

"I'm not sure. Jacob couldn't remember his name."

"I'll get down there now."

"I need you to do me another favor if you can."

"What's that?"

"Find the mayor's personal cell phone number and get her to the protest. The city council needs to know what's going on."

"Have you called the police auditor or the civilian review board?"

"I called my contact on the board, but it's Sunday and she didn't answer."

"I'll do what I can."

"Thank you."

They hung up, and Sophie searched her contact list. She didn't have the mayor's personal cell phone number, but she knew someone who did. Her real motivation in trying to reach the mayor was to get a quote for the story.

If the paper let her write it. Who else would? She was going out to cover it, and she doubted any other reporters knew the protest was happening. Sophie called her friend on the city council and left a message, then called Jackson. He didn't answer, and she left him a message too: "It's Sophie. I need to know about Officer Thompson and Henry Walsh. Maybe we can help each other again. Please call me."

After a vigorous internal debate, she called Jasmine Parker, the crime scene technician she'd dated for a year. Jasmine had broken up with her a few months ago, claiming she was tired of Sophie pushing her to come out about their relationship. Sophie thought it was more about Jasmine's fear of her parents' disapproval. To her surprise, her ex-lover answered. "Hey, Sophie."

"Hey. How are you?"

"Busy as hell. We had two bodies yesterday, so I'm working straight through the weekend. And Joe just got called in to process more fingerprints, so something else is going down."

"For Officer Thompson's case?"

"Is that why you called? You're looking for information?"

The truth of it embarrassed her, but only for a second. She'd already left Jaz a message asking for her help. "As you mentioned, we have two dead bodies this weekend, and I'm trying to save my job. They're getting ready to replace me with an intern."

"I thought they were just doing that to the old-timers."

"Around here, five years makes me the old guard. It's mostly about benefits. The new hires don't get health insurance, and it saves the paper a fortune."

"Bastards."

Sophie had tried not to think of her bosses that way. "I know the family is just trying to save the newspaper. But they're making it too personal and too painful for employees they can't afford."

"What do you want to know? I have to get back to work."

"Can you share anything about Thompson's murder? I know the suspect, Henry Walsh, is dead too. Did he do it?"

A long pause. "We have physical evidence that connects him to the crime scene, but it's not conclusive." Jasmine lowered her voice. "You can't use this, but the new fingerprints Joe is working on belong to a different suspect. So the investigation is still open."

"Any idea how the suspect is connected to Thompson?"

"He's in the criminal system. That's all I can tell you. We'll talk later." Jasmine hung up.

A second suspect was enough to lend credibility to Willow's claim that Henry was innocent.

Sophie grabbed her camera and her coat and headed out. The morning's snow had stopped, but everything except the middle of the street was still covered with a white powder. River Road, in the distance, was oddly quiet. She wondered how many people would actually come out for a protest in bad weather, then laughed at herself. The homeless were already *out*, and moving around when it was cold was in their best interest.

. . .

The plaza in front of the county courthouse was packed, and everyone was bundled in coats, scarves, gloves, and boots. You didn't see that attire often in Eugene, where most longtime residents didn't even use umbrellas. She stood back on the sidewalk and took photos, estimating the number of protestors at about a hundred. Yet more were coming, trudging up Eighth Avenue carrying backpacks, pushing carts, or riding bikes and pulling little trailers.

A dozen or so people in the plaza held signs, and they didn't have bundles of worldly possessions with them. Within the homeless community was a population of people who didn't sleep on the streets or at the Mission. They slept on couches and in friends' garages. Many had part-time jobs; some had a vehicle. They were the ones Sidney Willow had formed into a coalition, and the core group must have spread the word about the protest.

Sophie noticed families in the crowd as well. Many lived in their cars or in small mobile campers that they parked on side streets. She pulled out her recorder and made a verbal note for her story. "The homeless population in Eugene is as diverse as the rest of its citizens. They all have unique circumstances and stories."

When she'd interviewed the twins the day before, she'd learned of their parents' death and their determination to live their lives on their own terms. She'd been surprised to hear how ritualistic they were about collecting empty bottles and cans to turn in for cash. They had established routes they treated like jobs and paid their own way as much as they could. They also had attention deficit disorder, among other issues, so the interview had been challenging.

She walked the perimeter of the crowd and noticed four police officers, each at different spots along the sidewalk. Their faces were grim as they watched the gathering, but they didn't interact. Sophie made her way through the protesters, noticing two women passing out sandwiches. That was probably how they motivated so many to gather—by offering them free food. She took photos and asked for names. One young woman with a "Sleep Is a Right" sign looked like a college student. Sophie introduced herself, asked why she was there, and held out her recorder.

The young woman's response was passionate. "I'm tired of being arrested for trying to live. I'm tired of seeing my friends hit with a baton because they don't gather up their stuff fast enough. And I'm heartbroken that one of the twins was killed by a cop with a stun gun. This has to stop."

"How did you end up homeless?" Sophie asked.

"I lost my job, then my boyfriend kicked me out. But I've got a Pell Grant now, and I'm going to school at Lane. And I'm on a waiting list for an apartment with St. Vinnie's, so it's temporary."

Sophie couldn't imagine trying to attend college without a steady place to live. Out of the corner of her eye, she saw that Sidney Willow had climbed on a makeshift podium. She thanked the woman, excused herself, and moved toward the front. Willow held a megaphone to her mouth and called out, "Thank you for coming! I know it's cold, but we have to get justice for Henry! We can't let the police get away with this!"

The crowd began to chant: "Justice for Henry! Justice for Henry!" Sophie took more photos, then eased her way to the back to get out of the noise. Group chanting drove her crazy.

"How long do we have to stay?" someone shouted.

"Many of us will stay until Officer Bremmer is held accountable," Willow responded. "We'll camp right here."

"It's going to be freezing tonight," a woman shouted. "We can't be outside."

"The Egan Warming Centers will be open," Willow announced.

A roar of approval from the crowd. Named after a homeless veteran who'd frozen to death, the centers were a group of churches that opened their doors for the homeless to sleep when the temperature dropped below freezing. It had never happened this early in the season before, and the organization had been caught off guard trying to find volunteers for staffing.

A white van with bright red lettering rolled up nearby, and Trina Waterman climbed out. A spunky blonde reporter from KRSL. Sophie both loved her and hated her. As a cameraman joined the newscaster on the sidewalk, the crowd started chanting again.

"Fire Officer Bremmer! Fire Officer Bremmer! Fire Officer Bremmer!"

Sophie glanced over at the nearest man in uniform. His stoic face now had a twitch around the eyes.

Spotting the TV people, Sidney Willow made her way through the protesters, chanting and encouraging others to chant. As Willow neared him, the officer's face flushed with anger. She stopped in front of him. "We want justice for Henry Walsh *and* Officer Thompson."

"You're not fit to say his name," the man in uniform shouted.

"Justice for Officer Thompson!" Willow shouted, followed by "Justice for Henry! Fire Officer Bremmer!"

The crowd chanted louder. A scruffy man with a full beard staggered up to the officer and spat.

"No!" Willow grabbed the man to pull him away.

Panic shot through Sophie like an electric jolt. She rushed forward, yelling, "Trina! Camera!" Her hope was that having a TV crew in his face would keep the officer in check. She feared for his life if he got violent and the crowd went out of control.

But it happened anyway. She watched helplessly as the officer drew his baton, clubbed the spitter on the shoulder, then swung it at Willow. The activist ducked, but the baton caught her on the side of her head. She went down in a heap, blood dripping from her ear.

Onlookers screamed in rage and rushed the officer. Sophie grabbed her phone and hit 911 as another man in uniform charged into the melee, swinging his baton.

"What is your emergency?" the dispatcher asked.

"There's a riot at the free speech plaza, and people are hurt. Send ambulances."

CHAPTER 18

Sunday, November 23, 2:50 p.m.

Jackson climbed the stairs to his office space, weariness creeping in. He'd been in the interrogation room hammering at Gene Burns for the last hour, but the man had stuck to his stupid and unverifiable account of his Friday whereabouts. The suspect was still in the hole, so Jackson called the patrol sergeant on duty for assistance. Surprised that he didn't answer, Jackson left a message asking for a patrol officer to book Burns into jail on arson charges. He would call the sheriff later to ensure that Burns wasn't released. He texted Evans and Quince and relayed that the task force would meet at ten Monday morning. Right after Thompson's autopsy. It was time to go home and enjoy what was left of the weekend.

Jackson called Kera. "Hey, what do you have planned for dinner?"

"Nothing yet. Now that it's just me and Micah, I wing it more often."

"Let's go out. All of us. A big family dinner."

"Now you're talking. Where do you want to eat?"

That was tough, pleasing Katie and Kera and the kids. "What about Jung's?"

"Lovely idea. Are you feeling sentimental?"

They'd had their first meal together at the Mongolian grill. "Maybe so. Let's meet at five before it gets busy."

Lammers burst into his cubicle. "Don't make plans. We have another body."

Jackson bit his tongue to keep from cursing. To Kera he said, "Did you hear that?"

"I did." She sounded weary. "I'm sorry you have to work. Do you want me to take all the kids out to eat anyway? Benjie's with Katie, right? She probably needs a break."

"That would be wonderful. Thank you. I love you." He didn't care that Lammers was standing right there. Kera was a saint. They hung up and he turned to his boss. "What the hell have we got now?"

"For starters, there's a riot downtown, and we're arresting dozens of homeless people. So we've got no patrol units available for anything else."

Oh crap. "They're rioting about Henry Walsh?"

"That's the word, but I don't know much yet. I'm heading down there now." Lammers spoke rapidly, more rattled than he'd ever seen her. "But Officer Drummond called. He had his dog out searching the wetlands near Thompson's crime scene, and they found a body in a hidden campsite. They were supposed to search this morning but got delayed because of the snow."

Dread washed over Jackson. This would be bad. "Who's dead?"

"A homeless man." Lammers handed him a slip of paper. "Here's the location. He was shot in the head, possibly self-inflicted.

The weapon is a Sig Sauer, and Dan Thompson's cell phone was in his pocket. So it could be Thompson's gun too."

The news left Jackson reeling. What the hell had happened out there Friday night?

． ． ．

Jackson met Officer Drummond at the end of Wallis Street and took possession of the gun and the phone, both in plastic evidence bags. Wearing gloves, he checked the weapon's mag: only one cartridge had been fired. He locked the evidence in his car and changed into the boots he'd thrown into the backseat that morning when he saw the snow coming down. It had stopped after an hour, and only a little had stuck, leaving a light powder everywhere. The early cold weather had caught everyone off guard, but after two days, people were more prepared, and the warming centers had opened.

Jackson followed Drummond about a quarter mile through the wetlands, a gentle uphill climb. Near the peak, Drummond gestured to a clump of shrubs in a ring around a tree. "The body is in there."

Great. Jackson dropped to his knees and crawled through an opening, soaking the bottom of his pants. No wonder the search team that had been looking for bloody clothing hadn't found the body.

The dead man was on his back in a sleeping bag, in the middle of a tight clearing surrounded by wild rose bushes, swamp grass, and a small ash tree. Jackson stood at the perimeter, taking in the scene. A cold campfire, a folded tarp, and an oversize rucksack. The man either was new to the area or hadn't planned on staying long. Local homeless campers tended to collect things, including discarded furniture, canned goods from the food bank, and shopping carts full of junk they found and used for bartering. Something bothered him, but it hadn't fully registered yet.

He turned to Drummond, whose black lab had been commanded to wait just outside the camp. "How did you access the weapon and cell phone? Did you touch the body?"

"No. They were both on the ground near his head." Drummond pointed to the left of the corpse. "I picked them up, but I wore gloves and I took pictures first."

"They were on the right side of his body?" Jackson would need to see the photos.

"Yes."

"Did you call in the serial number on the gun to the department?"

"Right after I called Sergeant Lammers."

"Does the victim have ID?"

"I don't know."

Interesting that Drummond hadn't searched for it. Usually, that was the first thing the responding officer did. Maybe because the victim was homeless, it hadn't seemed important.

Jackson took a quick panorama of photos, then kneeled next to the body. Only his head and arms were visible outside the sleeping bag, and the gunshot had eviscerated much of his head. Consistent with the weapon being on the right, the bullet had entered on that side. A light frost clung to his dark beard, which covered half of his now-distorted face. Without ID, they might never identify this John Doe. Maybe he had some paperwork in the backpack that would give them a clue.

With gloved hands, Jackson unzipped the sleeping bag to search the man's many pockets. A knife, a nearly empty packet of cigarettes, and a gold wedding band, but no wallet. Why the ring? Was it sentimental or had he stolen it? The victim's hands were clothed in wool gloves, frayed and stained from outdoor use. If he had committed suicide—and it seemed likely that he had—the fabric of his right glove would hold gunpowder residue. Jackson stared at the victim's clothing. He wore layers, like most homeless people, but he wasn't particularly dirty, and his jeans didn't look any more worn than Jackson's weekend pants. He also had on decent boots. All of which could have been picked up free from a Catholic charity, but together they indicated he wasn't a drunken derelict. Jackson leaned in for a closer look at the dark peacoat. Was that blood spatter? Against the black, it was hard to tell, but there was a dried spray of something near the top button.

What the hell had happened? Jackson wished Evans would show up so he would have someone to brainstorm with. It was unusual to be at a crime scene with only one other officer. But the patrol staff was downtown with the protesters, and his task force detectives had probably taken the morning off, thinking that the Walsh twins were guilty and would soon be charged. But he knew Lammers had called them, and Evans would show up.

"What do you think went down?" Drummond asked, breaking the eerie silence.

Jackson stood to give his knees a break. "The obvious scenario is that this transient stabbed Dan Thompson, took his phone and weapon, then came back to his camp and killed himself. The question is why."

"Maybe he sobered up and felt guilty," Drummond suggested. "He probably knew he would be caught and executed."

Jackson held back a sigh. "Why kill Thompson in the first place?"

"Thompson probably tried to arrest him."

The first crime scene hadn't shown signs of a struggle, only those odd drag marks. But Thompson may not have been expecting a fight. Or maybe this John Doe had been angry and out-of-his-mind drunk. Or maybe he was a veteran who suffered from PTSD flashbacks and acted impulsively.

The chill seeped into Jackson's bones, making him eager to wrap this up and get back inside his car. His phone rang, and he retrieved it from his pocket: *Lara Evans.*

"Where the hell are you? I parked at the end of Wallis like Lammers said and walked two hundred yards south."

"Keep going. We're inside a clump of wild rose bushes around a little ash tree. Drummond's dog should be visible outside the camp."

"Stay on the phone with me until I see the spot."

"Thanks for coming out."

"What else am I going to do on a Sunday morning? Brunch with the girls?"

Jackson laughed. Evans was a bit of a loner, and he couldn't imagine her with a group of female friends. "This death looks like a suicide," he said, getting her up to speed. "But no ID so far." He heard footsteps making a squishing sound in the wet earth. "I hear you coming. Do you see the dog?"

"Yes."

"You have to crawl through an opening there."

"Lucky me."

She came through a minute later, moving more quickly than he had. "Where's Lammers?" Evans asked with a smile. "I thought she was working this case with us."

Jackson let out an amused scoff. He couldn't picture his over-size fifty-something boss crawling through the bushes. Schak would have done it, if he were on the task force, but he would have had choice things to say while coming through. The medical examiner would make the technicians clear an opening in the brush. Jackson didn't know if he would still be at the scene then.

He updated Evans on the placement of the gun and the phone, then showed her the contents of the man's pocket.

"I'll search his backpack and look for something with a name on it. We have to ID him." She started toward the pack, then stopped. "It's odd that he's lying down. Most people who shoot themselves are sitting up."

That was it, the thing that had bothered him. "It seems unusual to me too. But we've never processed a homeless suicide."

"Quince did. Remember that skeleton they found hanging from the tree when they cleared that area near Bertelsen and Roosevelt? That guy was homeless, but we eventually got a match on his dental records."

"That was a weird one." Jackson tried to imagine himself in this victim's situation. "I would have leaned against the tree and put the gun in my mouth."

Evans nodded. "Me too. But maybe he was too drunk. Or too cold."

Drummond cut in. "He's a bum who killed a police officer, who was a great guy with two kids. You shouldn't waste time on this human garbage."

Surprised by the outburst, Jackson turned to him. "Dan Thompson deserves a full investigation, and we're going to give him one. Maybe you and the dog should search the area outside this campsite."

"What are we looking for?"

Was that a real question or another objection? Jackson struggled to keep his voice calm. "Anything that might be connected to this dead body or Thompson's crime scene. Dropped personal items, bloodstained clothing, a sharp tool."

"I thought you guys found Thompson's murder weapon."

"The pathologist hasn't confirmed it yet. And until he does, we're still gathering evidence." Annoyed by the patrol cop's attitude, Jackson changed his mind. "Instead, why don't you get a hedge trimmer and cut a path into this area, so the ME and technicians can bring their equipment in." He didn't pose it as a question.

Drummond nodded and crawled back out. Now it was just he and Evans. Where the hell was Quince?

Evans reached for the backpack again. "We're going to get pressured to close this case out, aren't we?"

"The chief has already started, so let's do what we can before it gets dark." Jackson dropped to the ground and began to search. Something about this whole scenario seemed off.

CHAPTER 19

Sunday, November 23, 6:35 p.m.

Schak walked in the front door and smelled pork roast. Damn, he loved Sundays. His wife always made a nice spread for dinner because their son often joined them. But Brad's car wasn't here, and it was probably just as well. Tracy was upset, and he had work to do on the sexual assault case.

His wife called to him from her craft room. "I'll be right there. Dinner is basically ready."

Schak pulled off his coat and weapon and dropped them on a chair. He had a feeling he'd be going back out. If for no other reason than to grab a beer somewhere. He was trying not to drink around Tracy, so he'd stopped for one on the way home. Which reminded him to head for the bathroom to brush his teeth.

They met in the kitchen a few minutes later, and Schak pulled his wife in for a hug, drawing strength from knowing she was here for him at the end of every day, no matter how bleak his work was.

She squeezed back, but only for a second. They sat down to eat, and Tracy talked about her troubled nephew, her current quilt project, and Brad's new girlfriend. Schak nodded and made brief, appropriate comments.

"How was your day?" she finally said.

She always asked. "Sad. Stressful. Cold as hell out there." His body fat was supposed to keep him warm, but his ticker didn't function at full capacity anymore.

"You're not working Danny's murder, are you?" Tracy's brown eyes were still sympathetic. She hadn't changed much in the decades they'd been together. Still pretty in a farm-girl way, with strong features and lovely freckles.

"No, I've got another case. I think Lammers gave it to me to distract me."

"Can you talk about it?"

"You don't want to know."

She patted his hand. "I wish I was a better listener for your job."

"I'm glad you don't want the details. There's no reason for you to think about this ugliness."

Schak thought he meant that. He wasn't a big talker anyway. But sometimes Tracy's squeamishness annoyed him. Closing your eyes to crime and other people's pain didn't make them go away.

"How's Brad doing at the department?" she asked.

Schak updated her with what little he knew, then excused himself. "I have some files to look at. This case I'm working is critical, and there could be more victims." *Both past and future,* he thought, walking away.

• • •

In his man cave, a small bedroom at the back of the house where he also kept his camping and fishing gear, he inserted a thumb drive into his computer. In the device, he found the video of Ashley Devonshire being sexually assaulted. The thought of watching it revolted him, and he'd put it off until now, but he had no choice. What if the perp revealed something of himself? A tattoo? A birthmark or piece of jewelry? There might even be something in the room that could identify him or convict him later. This was his job. He clicked open the file and a naked young girl on a bed filled his monitor. Shame washed over him, and he froze the image.

Schak pushed out of his chair, the weight of his own body a burden after a long day. He located a shoe box in the back of his closet and opened it. A half bottle of Jim Beam—a Christmas present to himself from last year—and he still had most of it. More proof that he didn't have a drinking problem. He took a long pull and put it back. The bottle was meant for days like this, for tasks like this one. The bourbon warmed his belly and softened the tension in his chest. He sat back down and clicked on the video, notepad ready beside his keyboard. Just one important clue. Please.

The perp's manual penetration seemed to go on forever, but Schak focused on the details. A leather glove covered his hand and part of his forearm. Where would he buy something like that? Schak made a note. And who would own such a glove? Someone who trained birds of prey? Occasionally, there were glimpses of a gray sleeve. The material looked like a long-sleeved T-shirt. One of a million.

The perp abruptly switched and started probing the girl with a dildo. Schak reached for his mouse to fast forward through it.

The door opened behind him. "Are you watching porn?" His wife's tone was horrified.

He stopped the video, clicked off his monitor, then turned to face her. "I'm working a sexual assault case. I had to see if this video had any leads."

Her eyes and mouth tightened with skepticism. The doubt passed and her mouth turned down with disgust. "Why did you bring it home to watch it here?"

Schak deeply regretted it. "I'm sorry. I wanted to come home for dinner. I'll go back to the department and finish there."

Tracy brought her hands to her hips. "Why are you working a sex crime? That's not your unit's responsibility."

"Because the girl died. She committed suicide."

"Oh. That's sad."

"And there's another victim."

His wife was silent for a moment, her eyes undecided. "You've been drinking," she finally said, with a harsher tone.

"I had one shot of bourbon. To help me get through this. I'm as disgusted by"—he gestured at the monitor—"this filth as you are."

"I doubt that." She hugged her own arms, as if she were cold. "Have you been to an AA meeting?"

"Not yet. I'm working this case. It's critical."

"What will your excuse be next week?"

He didn't know what to say.

"I think you should pack a bag and go stay in a motel for a while."

No! A sharp pain pinched his heart. "You don't mean that." He racked his brain for the right thing. "We can get counseling and work through this."

"*We* don't need counseling. *You* need AA."

"I'll start going to meetings."

"I'll believe it when I see it. And until that happens, you need to live somewhere else."

Anger seeped into his bones, giving him new energy. "This is my house too. In fact, I've got more invested in the equity than you do. I'm not moving out." He took a breath to calm himself. "I will go to meetings. Because I love you. And I'm willing to compromise."

Tracy shook her head and walked out.

Confused, Schak put the thumb drive in his pocket. Tracy was taking this too far. He wasn't an alcoholic. And she'd been fine with his level of consumption for twenty-six years, so what was her problem now? Okay, so he'd been drinking a little more than usual lately. The workload at the department had been stressful ever since McCray retired and they hadn't replaced him. But he'd already cut back. There was no need to quit entirely. He strode to the living room and pulled on his weapon and coat. Where was Tracy? He heard the TV in the family room but didn't stop in to tell her he was leaving.

Out in his car, he wondered if he was legally okay to drive. He felt perfectly capable. The beer had been hours ago, so he only had one shot of bourbon on a full stomach. He started his sedan and drove to the department, hoping like hell it didn't snow again.

. . .

The video left him feeling ill, but he was no closer to knowing who the sick perp was. The man had been careful not to reveal any of his skin, and the bed was shoved up against a wall with no discernible marks. The next step would be to take a single slice of the video and enhance the image for closer inspection. Frustrated that he didn't know how, Schak emailed the file to Detective Dragoo in the tech department and asked for help. The tech guy wouldn't see the message until morning, and the enhancement wasn't a top priority. First, Schak had to drop off Ashley's laptop so Dragoo could hack into her Facebook page. Schak wanted to see all her exchanges, in case the perp had connected with her directly. He wished he had the skills to do it himself, but whenever he tried to learn new stuff on the computer, his brain froze like an overworked engine.

He remembered Ashley's phone in his carryall. He'd been so busy trying to track down witnesses, he'd forgotten to look at her recent calls. This wasn't a typical homicide investigation, so he let himself slide on the oversight. Schak fiddled with the phone and finally got her messages open. He scrolled back to Wednesday, the day of the assault. Ashley had texted with only two people about the party: Anna and Daren Sorenson. Schak had talked with Anna but hadn't located her brother yet. Nor had Daren contacted him, as requested. What did he have to hide?

There were no calls from men. He scrolled through Thursday and Friday and saw only more girl conversations. About the time he decided to call it a night, his phone rang, and he checked the ID. Why was his mother calling? "Hey, Mom. What's going on?"

"I'm at Donna's, and we're all reminiscing about Danny. You should be here."

His mother was a little tipsy, but she was right. He needed a dose of family. He wanted to honor Danny. "I'm on my way."

· · ·

His mother came to the door at his aunt's house and pulled his head close to hers. "Don't ever get yourself killed. I couldn't handle it." She kissed his forehead and pulled back. "Your unit will get the bastard, though, right?"

"I think we already did." The knowledge gave him less comfort than he'd thought it would.

His mother started across the foyer. "We're in the family room looking at photo albums. There's beer in the fridge."

Schak helped himself to a cold one, then joined his childhood family. It still hurt that he couldn't get these people together with his new family. Sure, once a year they all had Christmas dinner together, but his wife had never warmed to his mother or his cousins. He realized now it was because of the drinking. Before, he'd thought that Tracy was resentful of his bond with his mother and jealous of Donna's successes as a physician and a community leader.

His aunt greeted him, and he asked how she was holding up. "I don't know. Some moments, I think I'm fine. Then Danny's death comes crashing down on me. Plus, I have that damn malpractice suit, so it's been rough."

"I know what you mean. Thanksgiving will be painful and strange without him." Schak sat on the couch next to Kurt. "I'm glad to see you out of your wheelchair."

"I'm taking gene therapy now, and it's helping." His cousin held a photo album in his lap. Kurt pointed at a picture of the three of them around a big fire. "Remember the camp of a thousand frogs?"

Schak laughed. "Who could forget?" Aunt Donna had taken them camping twice every summer, always to remote campgrounds where they'd had to rough it. Kurt had been challenged by the adventures, but he'd never wanted to be left behind. Those trips were some of Schak's best memories.

Aunt Donna stepped up to the bar and poured everyone a shot of whiskey. "Now that Rob's here, we can toast Danny."

Schak held up his glass. "Danny was a great guy and a fine police officer. A humanitarian to the end."

Kurt went next. "Danny was a terrific brother. He always included me, waited for me, and made me feel like a whole person."

There was an awkward moment of silence while they all remembered that Danny had been the one who'd accidentally shot Kurt when they were little kids.

Choking back a sob, Donna said, "Danny changed my life. He made me realize that I had more love to give than I ever knew."

Schak's mother finished with, "I loved that kid. He made me laugh every time."

They clinked their shot glasses together and drank a toast to their lost loved one.

CHAPTER 20

Monday, November 24, 8:25 a.m.

Sophie strode through the parking lot, eager to be back at work in the *Willamette News* building. A sense of excitement she hadn't felt in a long time pulsed through her body. She'd witnessed a violent clash between police officers and protestors and had worked on the story all evening, wanting to get the emotions, images, and textures onto the page before they faded. It was some of the best writing she'd done in months, and she couldn't wait to show her boss.

She flashed her badge and trotted upstairs to her tiny cubicle. The red light on her phone was flashing. Excellent. People had returned her calls. She pulled off her jacket, dumped her big red bag on the desk, and clicked on her computer. While the system loaded, she listened to her voice mails. The first was from Detective Schakowski, asking for her help with a sexual assault case. What the heck? She'd never heard from him before.

The blackmail aspect of the case was particularly heinous—and intriguing. She called him back, excited when he answered.

"It's Sophie Speranza. I'd love to help. Tell me more about your case."

"I can't tell you the victims' names without their permission, but I'll ask the parents of the girl who committed suicide. They may be willing to go public to help stop the predator."

"A suicide?" That hit home, giving her a jolt. "How old was she?"

"Sixteen. She killed herself after the perp posted her assault video online."

How cruel! "You mentioned blackmail. Did he ask for money?" Sophie typed shorthand notes into a file as she talked.

"He wanted fifteen thousand in exchange for not uploading the video. Her parents couldn't meet his deadline, so it went live Friday evening. The girl took a bunch of sleeping pills and pain medication, and her parents found her dead Saturday morning."

"The poor family." Cyberbullying at its worst. Sophie pushed out of her chair and took deep breaths, too angry to focus. A good friend had killed herself in high school after being humiliated by a group of male athletes. She'd written about it to work through her rage, and from that experience, her love of journalism had blossomed.

"There was an earlier victim in May," the detective said.

"Give me a second, please, Detective. I need to catch up on my notes." Sophie eased back into her chair and started typing. This wasn't about her high school friend, and she had to keep her emotions in check.

"Call me Schak, and tell me when you're ready."

"I'm set. What else?"

"The first victim's parents paid the blackmail and never heard from him again. I want to know if there were more. And if so, I need those girls to come forward. The more we know, the faster we'll catch him."

"I'll get the story online today and in tomorrow's paper. How should they contact you?"

"Give my desk phone number and my email." He relayed the information, then said he had to go.

"Wait. How does the predator find his victims?" She needed to warn women as well as ask for their help.

"At parties. We think he picks the youngest, drunkest girl, then drugs her and takes her somewhere for the assault."

"Is he violent? Does he hurt them too?" It made her queasy to ask.

"No. In fact, he takes them home and drops them in front of their house when it's over."

"A predator with a conscience."

"I think he's just trying to make the parents feel grateful enough to pay him."

"I'll get on this feature right away. Keep me updated, please."

After she got off the phone, Sophie cleaned up her notes and sent the riot article to her supervisor, Karl Hoogstad. She uploaded the photos she'd taken to the server, and minutes later, the crime beat photographer stepped into her cube.

"Nice pics. Why didn't you call me? I would have come down." Brian was her age, and they'd started at the paper around the same time.

"I'm sorry. I got the call about the protest at the last minute. And you told me you were going to Bend this weekend."

"I did go, but you still should have contacted me."

"You're right. I'm sorry. I'm in a weird space here at the paper, and it's messing with my head. You've seen what's going on." Or maybe he hadn't. His job was safe because he was related to one of the owners.

"I'll process the photos and pick one to use," Brian said. "I hope to run it across the front page of the City section."

"Thanks."

Sophie couldn't decide what to do next. She still wanted to hear from Jackson about the police officer's homicide, but she was eager to write the story about the sexual assaults. That warning had to come first. As she crafted her lead sentence, her desk phone rang. An internal call. Nervous, she picked up.

"This is Chet Harris. Will you come into my office?"

An explosion of fear in her stomach. "Sure. I'll be right there."

She headed downstairs to the corner of the building the owners and managers still occupied. The rest of the floor was rented out to a real estate company. The managing editor occupied a corner office with tall windows and a view of the field across the street.

His door was open, so she stepped in. "Good morning."

From behind his desk, he gave her a bright, phony smile. Chet was an attractive middle-aged man who looked like he'd stepped out of an insurance commercial. This morning he wore a suit, and she wondered who he was meeting with next. Probably the banker who was calling in the loans that kept the paper afloat.

"Have a seat, please."

Sophie smiled and complied.

"We've been reviewing your work, and we have some concerns."

Oh no. This was it. She decided to go down swinging. "What concerns? I haven't had any negative feedback from Karl Hoogstad, and I hear great things from readers every day."

"Karl has been protecting you, but it has to stop. The quality of your writing has been slipping, and we don't think you're the right person to handle the crime beat."

It was all she could do to keep from shouting *Bullshit!* Sophie squirmed in her chair and chose her words carefully. "I respectfully disagree. I've covered three murder trials in the last six months, and I've heard nothing but praise for my work. I've even been on the scene for several breaking stories. I'm good at the crime beat."

A long pause. "A reporter shouldn't be part of the story. That's one of the issues we have."

Oh shit. She'd just given him a bullet to shoot her with. "Are you talking about the eco-terrorist situation?"

"That's one example."

"I was covering a story and was taken hostage!" Her defense burst out louder than she'd intended. But she wasn't done. "I reported the news from under a desk, while a man with a bomb threatened to blow up the building. I risked my life to do my job and help the police. How can you hold that against me?"

"I admire your passion, but you're a liability." The boss cleared his throat. "Also, the intern who's been covering a few crime stories is a better writer than you are."

A punch in the gut. For a moment, she was speechless. "I don't think a single other person in this building would support that contention."

"It's the opinion of the management, and we make the decisions. We're pulling you off crime and courts, and assigning you to cover Springfield."

Where reporters went to die. She made one last effort. "But I have relationships within the police department. Access to information that a new person won't have."

"You need to help Zee build those connections."

Not a chance in hell. Rage and dread fought for control. Rage won out. "I know what's happening here, and I'd respect you more if you just fired me." Sophie stood. "But if I still have a job, I'll get back to work."

"Turn over everything you're working on to Zee and go find out what's happening with the remodel of the Gateway mall."

She nodded, unable to respond.

Trembling, she climbed the stairs and returned to her desk. Her office neighbor stuck her head over the half wall. "Everything okay?"

"No, but I can't talk about it yet." Sophie feared she would cry. For a few minutes, she was paralyzed with indecision. She'd already sent in her piece about the homeless protest and riot, which included an update about Officer Thompson's murder. She trusted Hoogstad to run it with her byline. If Jackson ever called her back with real information, she would pass it along to the intern. She owed her readers that.

But she couldn't let go of the sexual assault story. It was too important to hand over to someone fresh out of college and too personal to turn her back on. Sophie decided to keep working on it in her free time. She would post the updates to her personal blog, *Safety Snapshot*, where she listed crimes in Lane County and posted articles about how to stay safe. If one of the victims who came forward happened to be from Springfield, she could legitimately cover the issue as part of her new assignment.

Impulsively, she called Detective Jackson again, and he startled her by answering. "I've got two minutes, Sophie, so make it fast."

"With Henry Walsh dead, will you close out the case? Are you satisfied that he killed Officer Thompson?"

"The investigation is ongoing. New evidence came to light yesterday that widened our focus."

"What evidence? Do you have another suspect?"

"We do, but he's dead too, so this will be a long, challenging investigation. I have to go." Jackson hung up.

Another body? A hum of energy pulsed in her veins. Sophie called the department spokesperson and waited through ten rings. She hated the thought of turning over a three-body story to an intern. Maybe she would write it anyway and see what happened. They would fire her for insubordination, but it was only a matter of time before they fired her for something. They'd laid the groundwork already by claiming the quality of her writing was in decline. Wouldn't it be amusing if she earned a Northwest Excellence in Journalism award for her eco-terrorist story? The winners would be announced next week. That was the kind of proof she could take into court for a wrongful termination lawsuit. But not if they fired her for insubordination.

The department spokesperson finally came on the line. "Jackie Matthews, EPD."

"Sophie Speranza, *Willamette News*. I'm calling about the body found yesterday. What's the connection to Officer Thompson?"

"I'm not authorized to share that, but we believe the two deaths are linked."

"What's the victim's name?"

"I don't have that yet."

That was odd. "Is the victim a transient?"

"Most likely."

"How did he or she die?" Sophie felt certain it was a man, but for the sake of objectivity, she had to pretend it could go either way.

"A gunshot wound is all I can say. I have to get back to work now."

"Whose gun?"

But the woman had already hung up. Sophie decided to go ahead and write the update, then quit before they could fire her.

The paper was dying anyway. Subscribers were not renewing, and advertising was shrinking everywhere but the Sports section. Besides, Jasmine had ended their relationship—leaving her lonely and confused about what she wanted. She wasn't serious about her current boyfriend and never would be. He was fun, and she enjoyed hooking up with a man for a change, but he wasn't intellectually curious enough or passionate enough about anything for her to stay in town because of him. She had to step up her job search and get out of Eugene.

Sophie made another cup of hot tea, then sat back down at her desk in cube world to write her last two stories for the paper. *Go cover the remodel of the Gateway mall.* As if she would waste her time. They expected her to quit. That was the point. Maybe there was another way to handle this. What if she just kept doing the job, covering crime, and hired a lawyer? They could fire her, but she wasn't going down without a fight. But would that hurt her chances of getting hired at another media company?

She pushed her employment issue to the back burner and wrote the sexual-assault-and-blackmail story, working through her morning break to get it done. She wanted the piece up on the website before this job blew up in her face. After closing the file, she uploaded it to the server for editing and wondered how her supervisor would handle it.

At noon, she made a quick trip to a nearby deli for a cup of soup, still shivering even after she came back inside. The temperature had dropped so quickly from the warm late summer that her body hadn't acclimated. Nobody's had.

Hoogstad came in while she was eating. Bald and round, he filled her narrow doorway. "You had a busy weekend." He gestured for her to follow. "Come into the conference room, please."

Sophie grabbed her recorder, slipped it into her sweater pocket, and followed him to the small interior room. Her supervisor had lost his private office when the newspaper moved everyone upstairs. Once inside the windowless meeting room, she reached into her pocket and clicked on her recorder as the door closed.

"I was still on the crime beat when I wrote that piece last night," she explained. "Sidney Willow called me yesterday about the protest, and I felt compelled to cover it. I'm glad I did."

"Yes, indeed. It's an excellent piece of writing."

"Can I quote you on that?" They were both still standing. This wouldn't be a long conversation.

"It wouldn't matter if you did." They were alone, but he still lowered his voice. "I'm sorry about what's happening to you, but I can't help. If I lose my job and my health insurance, I'm SOL."

Overweight, pasty, and coated in sweat, he was diabetic and took daily insulin. Even knowing he was going to screw her on the way down, she felt sorry for him. "I'll be fine. Just please run my last two stories. The second one I sent is even more important and needs to go up on the website today."

"I've already edited it." He shifted and crossed his arms. "I can't put your name on it though. It came in after I was notified of your transfer."

Not fair! "It doesn't matter. Run it anyway. Young women need to know about the predator."

"You're the best crime reporter I've ever worked with. I want you to know that, no matter what my official evaluation says."

"Thanks." It pleased her to have a digital record of that statement, even if she wouldn't use it to keep her job. It might prove important in landing a new position, in case no one at the paper would give her a decent reference. "Don't expect me to train Zee. I just can't."

"Go through the motions, please." He shrugged. "Or not. I'm technically not your supervisor anymore."

"Thanks again for giving me a chance to work this beat. I've loved it."

"You're welcome." He moved toward the door. "If you don't burn too many bridges on your way out, I'll give you a great reference."

She gave him a grim smile and held her tongue. She wasn't promising anything.

CHAPTER 21

Monday, November 24, 7:05 a.m.

Schak woke to an empty bed and the sound of someone slamming things in the kitchen, both of which were unusual. During the week, he was always the first one up, then Tracy would hear him peddling the exercise bike and get up shortly after. Head pounding, he headed for the bathroom. First, a long pee, then three aspirin and a long drink of water. Why did he feel so crappy? He hadn't had that much to drink. Or maybe he had. He had paced himself while he was with his family, declining a round of shots so he could drive home, but then he'd dipped into his bourbon again. What time was it? He stepped back into the bedroom and checked the clock. Whoops. He had to skip his twenty minutes of cardio and get to work. He showered, dressed, and rinsed with mouthwash, worried that he was still sweating alcohol. Some sharp-nosed busybody at the department could get him into serious trouble.

In the kitchen, Tracy grabbed stainless-steel bowls out of a cupboard.

"Good morning. What are you baking so early?" He walked over and poured a cup of coffee.

His wife ignored him.

"I know you're mad about the drinking, but you have to give me time. I'm dealing with a lot of shit right now." He noticed a cardboard container on the floor with a bunch of her kitchen stuff in it. "What's with the box?"

"I'm packing to stay with a friend for a while."

Oh shit. "Don't leave. We'll get through this." Why was she taking her baking stuff?

"I'm not coming back until you've been sober for at least a month." She glanced at him. "Aren't you late for work?"

He had to assume she wasn't making breakfast as usual. "This isn't fair. Danny was murdered. You can't leave me right now."

Tracy flinched. "I'm sorry, but it will always be something. You'd better go."

No time clock was waiting for him at the department, but he had a case to investigate. And he sensed that Tracy needed some space. She would change her mind. "I love you. Please don't leave." Schak left the house with his head, his gut, and his heart all aching.

He bought a cinnamon roll and a second cup of coffee at the Safeway on the way to work. The cold dark sky pushed him deeper into a foul mood. Why did everything have to turn to shit just as he felt like he was hitting his stride again? But he wouldn't wallow. He had a case to solve, a funeral to attend, and a supposed drinking problem to deal with. He would handle all of it as best he could. And if it wasn't good enough, too fucking bad.

Inside the department, he stopped in the tech unit, but no one was in yet. He left Ashley's laptop on Detective Dragoo's desk with a note to call him. Back at his own desk, he sent Dragoo an email explaining what he needed. Schak read though his notes and made a list of follow-up tasks. The first was to call Riverside High School and ask to talk to the principal. The receptionist transferred him through.

"This is Leslie Miller."

"Detective Schakowski. I'm investigating two sexual assaults, both female students at your school, and I'd like a list of all your male employees."

She was quiet for a moment. "You think it's a staff member?"

"I have to check out everyone. And since both girls are Riverside students, the staff seems like a good place to start."

"I understand, and I want to help in any way I can. Give me your contact info, and I'll send a list this afternoon."

"Thanks." Schak read off his ridiculously long EPD email address, then repeated it for good measure. "Can you suggest anyone I should talk to first?"

"No. I don't believe it's a staff member. A student seems more likely. Or maybe someone older, an ex-student perhaps."

"Do you have someone in mind?"

Another hesitation. "We had a problem two years ago with a student named Daren Sorenson, and we expelled him."

A pulse of gratification. He'd been right about the older brother who'd disappeared out of the house before he could question him. "What was the problem?"

"Several girls accused Daren of groping them. We advocated for getting him counseling, but his mother didn't follow through, so we had no choice but to remove him from the school."

"Can you give me the girls' names?"

"I'm sorry, but no. There's no reason to invade their privacy."

Schak could tell by her tone that she was done. "I plan to stop by the school this afternoon to question some of Ashley Devonshire's friends. I'll pick up the staff list when I'm there."

"I'll have it ready."

He found Daren Sorenson on Facebook, downloaded his photo, then called the desk officer and put out an attempt-to-locate for the young man. He had to find the kid and bring him in. It seemed plausible that his groping tendencies had escalated to sexual assault once he was free of the constraints of high school. Once the perp had recorded the sessions, the blackmail scheme for cash could have naturally followed.

Schak called Mrs. Sorenson again, but she didn't pick up. Remembering that he had other Monday morning calls to make, he checked his notes: Mobile Source and the passenger used as a money drop.

A subdivision of the local bus service, the company provided low-cost transportation to people with disabilities. The manager came on the line and asked how he could help.

"I need to know who you picked up on May nineteenth on the corner of Lincoln and Twenty-Third."

"Our records only go back four months."

Schak went for the long shot that the customer was a regular. "Have you picked up anyone at that location recently?"

"Just a moment." A short wait. "We transported Gracie McCormick from that location to a physical therapist appointment at the downtown hospital."

"Was that a recurring service for her?"

"Yes, for the last three months we have on record."

And the blackmailer knew her routine and had picked up the cash from her pouch when she got off the van there.

"Do you have Gracie's contact information?"

He made a funny sound. "She died recently, but I have an emergency contact number."

Schak took it down, but he doubted it would do him any good. He had the information he needed. The perp lived or worked near Gracie's pick-up or drop-off location. Did Daren Sorenson have a job downtown? Or go to the university? He made a note to ask when Daren's mother called back.

He glanced at the clock. Danny's task force was meeting now, and he wanted to know what was going on. Jackson wouldn't care if he stopped in.

CHAPTER 22

Monday, November 24, 7:35 a.m.

The small, brightly lit room in the basement of the old hospital was more crowded than usual. Surgery 10, as it was called, was designed as a one-person space, not counting the giant stainless-steel drawers that held bodies. But the county had hired a pathologist, so now Rich Gunderson, the medical examiner, attended crime scenes and prepped the bodies that came in, while Rudolph Konrad, the pathologist, conducted the autopsy, with the ME assisting. Today, the district attorney was in attendance, impatiently bouncing on his feet in a charcoal pinstripe suit.

They all turned to Jackson when he came in. "You're late." Konrad, a baby-faced blond man in his early forties, had said that to him a few times over the years. The pathologist was on the right side of the table, gloved and ready to go. Gunderson was on the left, his eyes drooping. The ME had been through a crazy, busy weekend with multiple bodies to process.

"I'm sorry." Jackson started to explain that he'd had a hectic morning with the kids, then changed his mind. This was not that kind of crowd. Konrad had never cracked a smile or a joke in his presence. Jackson pulled on a mask and gown—which was as much for his own protection as to guard against cross-contamination—and stepped up next to the DA at the foot of the table.

"Victor Slonecker, it's good to see you." He was never sure what to call the man. In the department, they used last names, but the DA's office was more formal.

Slonecker nodded. "I can't believe we're dealing with one of our own this time."

"We're all stunned."

"When is your next task force meeting?" the DA asked.

"Right after this, at ten."

The pathologist cut in. "I'd like to get started."

Jackson tuned out for the lengthy inch-by-inch inspection of Thompson's skin. Seeing another officer naked on the gurney table was disturbing enough without focusing on his moles, scars, and body hair. All he needed for this one were the basics: weapon, angle of entry, size of perp. The DA vibrated beside him, and Jackson guessed he was working on something else in his head.

Konrad began to explore the wound in Thompson's abdomen. He grabbed a tool and measured its length, width, and depth in several places, announcing the centimeters out loud for his recording. "An incised wound, made with a left-to-right slashing motion."

The wound was also on the left side of Thompson's body. "What is the killer's dominant hand?" Jackson asked.

"Right," Gunderson responded, as the pathologist continued his examination. "You pull with a knife."

"This wasn't made by a knife," Konrad corrected.

"I knew that."

The pathologist turned and measured the broken bottle lying on the counter behind him, even though the ME had likely already done it. Konrad held it next to the gaping wound. "See that tip?" He gestured to a sharp point at the base of the break. "This bottle made those lacerations along the bottom edge of the opening."

Jackson wanted to feel relieved. They had the right weapon. But the wrong fingerprints were still a problem. Unless both Henry Walsh and the John Doe had been involved in the murder. A nagging thought hit him. Was Henry left- or right-handed? He had failed to find out. After the twins had become distressed during questioning, Willow had shown up and demanded their release. His oversight bothered him, but he could still get the information. Henry's body was over there in one of the drawers. Typically, a person had slightly larger muscles on their dominant side. He would ask Gunderson to check. There was no reason to attend Henry's autopsy. Jackson had been there when he died, and Konrad would send him a full report. He might skip John Doe's post too, depending on how much the team could get done between now and then.

"What about the second wound?" Jackson asked. "Was it also made by a right-handed person?"

Konrad glanced over at him with stern eyes but didn't respond.

The DA spoke up. "I'd like to know too. After that, I need to go."

Relieved not to be the only one, Jackson said, "We have a task force meeting soon and a lot of evidence to review."

The pathologist nodded and shifted his focus to the wound on Thompson's neck. He took a series of measurements, said something Jackson didn't hear, then turned to the end of the table. "The neck wound is also incised, and the broken bottle was used for both thrusts. A powerful, right-handed person of approximately the same height as the victim. It's likely the abdominal thrust came first, because the angle of the neck wound indicates the victim may have been leaning slightly forward."

All of it served to confirm that John Doe had committed the crime. Henry Walsh was a couple inches taller than Dan Thompson and gaunt with scrawny arms. Not someone who would be described as *powerful*.

"Can you narrow down the time of death?" Jackson asked.

"No," the ME interjected. "The freezing temperature slowed the blood flow and decomposition, so the three-hour window is as close as we can get."

Jackson glanced at the body, not seeing any livor mortis on the front side. "Did he die right where he was? We saw signs of dragging at the scene."

Konrad stepped back from the table, as if to emphasize the interruption to his process. "If he was dragged, it happened either immediately before or after his death. His body wasn't moved after he had been dead for any length of time. But the lack of blood flow could also indicate that the victim was intoxicated or losing consciousness when he was stabbed. I'll know more after I examine the organs and complete the autopsy."

Had Thompson consumed the contents of his flask, then confronted a drifter in a drunken stupor? They would all have to wait for the toxicology report. Jackson decided not to stay for the internal examination. He looked at Gunderson. "Call me immediately if anything unusual turns up." He hurried out, eager to get away from Thompson's pale lifeless body. The DA followed him.

On the ride up in the elevator, Slonecker tried to pin him down. "I heard this morning about the homeless guy's suicide with Thompson's gun. Is he the killer? Making Henry Walsh innocent?"

"Most likely."

"His death was unfortunate. We have to find a way to placate the homeless community."

It wasn't Jackson's responsibility. "I don't have time. But it's best if they don't find out about John Doe's guilt until things cool down."

"Our office certainly won't comment publicly." They exited the elevator, and the DA excused himself. "I'll see you at the meeting."

Jackson called Katie on the drive to the department. She hadn't been feeling well that morning, and he was worried. She was so young to be pregnant and hadn't yet accepted the limitations that came with her responsibility. He didn't allow any alcohol in the house, and she was too young to buy it, but still, she managed to drink a beer every once in a while when he worked late—and wouldn't tell him where she'd gotten it.

His daughter finally answered after six rings. "I can't talk right now." Her voice was strained.

A flutter of worry. "What's wrong?"

"I have cramps."

Full-blown panic. "Call your doctor. Right now."

"It's not a big deal. I just have to make a trip to the bathroom and I'll be fine." She hung up.

Should he be worried? Jackson pulled into the parking lot at the department and called Kera, leaving her a message: "Will you check on Katie in a while? She's having cramps, but I have a task force meeting. Call me if it's serious." Maybe it was nothing, but Kera was a nurse and would know the right thing to do.

• • •

Jackson was the first to arrive in the conference room, so he read through his notes while he waited. Evans and Quince came in together. Both so attractive—and single. The two of them had never hooked up. But he knew why. Jackson had been Evans' mentor when she first came into the unit, and she'd bonded to him. Only he hadn't known how deeply until recently, when they'd had a tender moment that exposed their feelings for each other. But they were both committed to other relationships, so they'd pushed those feelings aside and moved on.

"Did you see the protestors at the county building?" Evans asked, dropping her shoulder bag on the floor. "They're gathering again, and they have even more regular citizens with them today."

Lammers strode in. "The department, or the city, needs to make a conciliatory gesture and get this under control. An officer was bitten yesterday, and another one had to have stitches in his cheek."

Jackson was torn. "But an innocent man is dead, and Sidney Willow is in the hospital. I understand their anger."

Lammers shot him a look. "Henry Walsh isn't innocent. His prints are on the murder weapon. He was at the scene." She plopped down in a chair. "Let's wrap this up. Orders from the chief."

Jackson's hands clenched, and he had to exhale before he could speak. "We have a new death. New evidence. New scenarios to explore."

Lammers took a seat. "Let's put it all out there and see if it adds up to anything other than a homeless altercation that ended up in an officer's murder."

The boss had made up her mind. Or the chief had, and she was the messenger.

As Evans went to the whiteboard, the DA walked in. "Have I missed anything?"

"We're just getting started." Jackson intended to run this like any other investigation. Every possibility was on the table. He turned to Evans. "Did you find the drifter's ID in his belongings?"

"Pete Scully. He had military discharge papers from twenty years ago." She wrote the name on the board. "I also found a prescription bottle of penicillin, but the label is faded and old, and I couldn't read the patient's name."

An antibiotic, probably irrelevant. "No mental health drugs?"

"Nope."

"Anything else of interest in his rucksack?"

"Just clothes and some personal items." Evans paused for effect. "And a thousand in cash."

What? "That seems odd."

"Unless he'd just cashed a VA retirement or disability check," Lammers countered. "Let's move this along. If it doesn't connect Scully to Thompson, it's not important."

Jackson struggled to control his anger. "We have a lot of unanswered questions about what happened that night. Such as, how did this drifter get close enough to Thompson to stab him?" But he probably knew that now. Thompson was intoxicated. He hesitated to share the information in front of Lammers.

Evans spoke up. "And why are Henry Walsh's prints on the bottle if Scully is the killer?"

The boss shook her head. "Don't make this complicated. The two homeless men got into a fight—maybe over the damn bottle of beer—and Thompson tried to break it up. Scully stabbed him, took his gun, then later shot himself."

It sounded reasonable. Yet, it bothered him. "But the suicide is still odd. He was lying down in his sleeping bag."

The DA turned to face Jackson. "What are you saying?"

"I'm not sure yet. What if someone killed Scully while he slept and tried to make it look like suicide?"

"Oh come on." Lammers' frustration was evident. "Both men involved in Thompson's death are transients, and they're both dead." She locked eyes with the DA. "There's no one to prosecute."

"I'm inclined to agree." Slonecker stood. "If anything changes, let me know." The DA walked out.

Jackson disagreed with Lammers' assessment of the two men as transients. Scully seemed like a drifter, but Henry Walsh had lived in Eugene his whole life. But Jackson kept it to himself.

He looked at Quince, who hadn't spoken yet. "Do you have anything to add to the board?"

"A business owner saw a light-gray sedan parked on Fourth Street the night of Thompson's murder. She said it seemed out of place." Quince shrugged. "But that was a block over from the crime scene, so it's probably not connected."

"See if you can find security camera footage of that area."

Evans wrote the car on the board. When she turned back, Jackson asked, "Did you find anything interesting in Thompson's house?"

"Nothing related to his death." Her eyes held a glint of mirth.

Jackson turned to Lammers. "What about Thompson's case log? Did you look at it?"

She nodded. "Routine traffic stops and a burglary at a warehouse. All of it irrelevant. What about you?" Lammers added, "Is there anything from Thompson's autopsy we need to know about?"

Rattled by her intractability, Jackson had to look at his notes. "The weapon is the broken bottle we found near the body. The killer is right-handed and about the same height as Thompson."

"How tall is Scully?"

"I'm guessing five-ten. But I don't have a measurement yet or even a time of death. The ME had three deaths to process this weekend."

"Four," Schak said, coming through the door. "A young girl committed suicide." He took the seat the DA had just vacated.

Schak met Lammers' stare. "I just want an update on Danny's death, then I'm out of here."

"He was stabbed by a transient named Pete Scully, who later killed himself." Lammers glanced at Jackson, as if challenging him to disagree.

"It seems likely Scully is the killer," Jackson conceded. "He had Thompson's gun and cell phone. He's the right size, he was in the area, and he had blood on his jacket."

"Who is Scully?" Schak's expression was a mix of anger and confusion.

"A drifter," Jackson said. "He's a veteran, but other than that, we don't know anything about him. But I'll find out what I can."

"Where did the drifter die?"

"Less than a mile from the original crime scene. A search dog found him in a hidden campsite."

Schak fought to control his emotions. "At least we got him."

"Yeah." Jackson wanted to share his concerns about how Scully died but not in front of Lammers. Or maybe not at all. Schak needed closure.

Lammers took charge of the meeting. "Update us on your case, Schak."

Jackson started to protest, but Schak looked so relieved, he kept quiet.

"We have a sexual predator targeting intoxicated girls, and I could use some help." Schak sat up straighter and looked at his notes. "Two victims, so far. Plus their parents, when you count the blackmail."

"Let's bring in a second whiteboard." Lammers stood. "I'll get a mobile one from the tech unit."

As soon as the boss left, Jackson said, "We're still going to find out what we can about Pete Scully. I want to understand his motive."

"Some people don't need a motive for killing a police officer," Evans reminded them. "Just the possibility of arrest is enough."

"But would a person like that kill himself?" Jackson posed.

For a moment, the only sound in the room was the heat system. Finally, Schak said, "I'm always surprised by the people who kill themselves. The department lost an officer to suicide recently, and we were all shocked. My wife's brother killed himself two years ago and didn't even leave a note. He had a family of teenagers at home."

Jackson pushed his concerns aside for the moment. He would continue to investigate on his own time.

Lammers pushed a mobile dry-erase board into the room and handed the marker to Schak.

"This will be interesting," Evans said. "Schak writes like a second-grader."

He cracked a small smile, then flipped her off. "Don't worry, I don't have much yet." He printed names, dates, and dollar amounts on the board as he summarized his case. "The first victim, Mara Andrade, seventeen, was assaulted last spring. The perp sent a partial video to her parents' cell phone and demanded ten grand or he would post the whole thing online. They paid him and never heard from him again." Schak paused, looking back at the group, then continued. "Last week, he assaulted Ashley Devonshire, age sixteen, with a similar MO. He wanted fifteen grand this time, and the parents didn't have it. They asked for more time. He posted the video, and Ashley took a bunch of sleeping pills Friday night. Her parents found her dead the next morning."

Schak turned to face the group, a troubled look on his face. "Both assaults occurred after the girls attended a party and got drunk. Both parties were broken up by a police officer."

Not again, Jackson thought. The stress made his guts roil in protest.

Quince broke the silence. "That doesn't mean it's one of us. Someone could be impersonating an officer."

Lammers asked, "Do you have a description?"

"Not yet. That's where I need help. I have to track down the people who attended those parties and find out who the victims were seen with and what the cop looked like."

"Give everyone a list of names," Lammers said. "I can be available if you need me, but I'm dealing with the fallout of yesterday's riot. We have five officers either injured or suspended and overtime issues to deal with because of the search for Thompson's killer." She closed her notepad. "The protestors are gathering again, and the chief has called a management meeting to decide how to handle it."

Jackson was relieved she planned to go back to her administrative role.

"The four of us can handle this," Schak said.

Lammers turned to his partner. "You may have to get IA involved eventually, but not yet." She glanced around at everyone. "No one outside this room is to know that we might be looking for a cop."

She stood, started toward the door, and locked eyes with Jackson. "It's time to move on."

"Yes, ma'am."

CHAPTER 23

Relieved to finally have help, Schak gave everyone a short list of witness names. He was glad he hadn't called Ben Stricklyn the day before. Lammers didn't want IA involved yet, and he'd rather work with his regular crew.

"Is the perp communicating strictly by phone?" Jackson asked.

"Yes, but no luck in tracking the number." Schak checked his list of things to do. Still overwhelming. "I'm heading to the tech department next. Maybe they can track the computer that uploaded the video of Ashley."

"Did you watch it?" Evans wanted to know.

Schak's cheeks flushed. "I had to. I needed to see if the perp showed anything that would help identify him." Tracy's disgust flashed in his mind. No wonder Quince had wanted out of the Vice Unit.

"Did you learn anything?" Evans wasn't judging him. He could tell by her tone. She just wanted to know who they were looking for.

"No. He only films the—" Schak searched for an inoffensive phrase. "The manual part of the assault. So he's careful not to reveal himself. And I don't think he ejaculates inside them."

"They don't remember anything?" Jackson squinted at him.

"I think he drugs them. And these assaults may be as much about the money as the sex," Schak said.

"That would be unusual," Evans countered. "Rape is more about power and violence than anything else."

Schak didn't know if he believed that. "I called an FBI profiler, and he says the perp is probably between thirty and fifty." Schak turned and scribbled the profile on the board. "Tech savvy too. Most likely someone who works in science, technology, or engineering."

Evans let out a snort. "I could have told you that."

Schak ignored her. "Both girls attended Riverside, so he could have some connection to the school. But the parties were in the campus area, hosted by young men in their twenties."

"Are the victims friends?" Jackson asked.

"They knew each other through a male classmate, Daren Sorenson, who graduated last year and slipped out of his mother's house before I could question him." Schak wrote his name on the board. "He also has some groping incidents in his past, so he's my prime suspect."

"So the connection might not be the school," Jackson commented. "But the social circle."

"Right. He's targeting families with money."

Evans jumped in. "Then watching to see when those girls go out drinking? Maybe by monitoring their social media pages?"

"Dragoo is breaking into her Facebook account for me." Schak updated the board with *Riverside* and *Facebook*. "The profiler also thinks there's likely more victims. I called Sophie Speranza at the paper and asked her to run a piece calling for victims to come forward. If we get flooded, I'll need your help talking to them too."

A weary tension filled the room.

"I know," he said. "You all worked straight through the weekend, and so did I."

"I got called out with the SWAT unit yesterday to handle the riot," Evans added. "And it could happen again. So I might not be much help."

Jackson spoke up. "The perp is smart to ask for small amounts of money and to give parents only a few hours to comply. That's why no one has contacted us until now . . . when a girl died."

Could he find the guy? Fear of failure gripped Schak. What if the perp gave up his blackmail business to avoid being caught or moved to another town to continue? "Any ideas how to catch him?" He wasn't too proud to ask.

"What about a sting?" Evans suggested. "We set up a party inside his territory, then send in an undercover cop to play a drunk young woman." She grinned. "I would do it, but I'm not sure I can pass for under twenty-five."

Schak liked the idea and said, "I'll talk to some of the Vice detectives and see what we can come up with."

"It's a long shot," Jackson said. "So it can't be our only plan of action." Jackson made a face. "Lammers might not approve the resources."

Schak decided not to tell the boss. "Let's all meet again tomorrow morning." He stood, ready to dig into the investigation again. "Call me if you get anything useful."

Back at his desk, he downed two more aspirin with his lukewarm coffee. Not exactly a hangover, but feeling deprived, he'd drank too much too quickly the night before. He had to find a compromise, a way to keep his drinking in check so that Tracy would get off his back about it. He wanted to feel better physically every morning too.

Time to get on Facebook and see if he could find a connection between the victims or between the parties. A rush of anxiety made him push away from his desk. He hated social media. Sometimes it made his job easier, but combing through all that personal information felt like sniffing everyone's underwear. Why did people share so much detail? So much pain and humiliation? To find anything useful, he had to sift through so much garbage—cat pictures, religious mumbo jumbo, feminist poetry—it overwhelmed him.

He walked across the building to the tech unit, and Dragoo looked up from his desk. His receding hairline and green Ducks jacket made him look like a used-car salesman. But the tech guy was sharp and aggressive in a good way.

"Hey, Schak. I just finished tracking the video. The perp uploaded it at the Eugene library."

"Damn. So he's too smart to use his own computer."

"Yeah, but if he was really tech savvy, he could have used a series of proxies and made it impossible to track. So he's not a pro, and that's good news."

"How do we find him?"

"Maybe set a trap. Have the parents contact him and offer to pay to take down the video. I could watch the file and target the location it's pulled from."

Another good idea, but unworkable. "The phone number he was using is out of service. He's moved on."

"He was smart to communicate by text only."

Schak was tired of hearing how smart the predator was. "Have you hacked into Ashley Devonshire's Facebook page? I need to see her connections."

"You're all set." Dragoo handed him the silver laptop. "I changed her log-in and password to *Schak*."

"Thanks."

He stopped in the break room for coffee, then braced himself and logged into Ashley's account. Her last post had been Friday evening at 7:47: *This world is not suited to people like me. Or maybe I'm just not tough enough. But I feel like I'm screaming in my head all the time and it's exhausting. Thanks for listening.*

Two friends had responded with concern, asking if she was okay. Neither was on his list of witnesses, but he made a note of their names. He scrolled back to Ashley's posts for Wednesday, the night of the assault. She'd been chatting with Anna Sorenson about the party, but neither mentioned meeting anyone specific. He read all her page posts between the party and her final note. Half were links to funny videos and photos of cute pets. The rest were random observations and teenage girl chatter about movies and clothes. And a few jokes about how cold global warming was. A waste of his time. Twenty minutes of teeth-grinding hell for nothing. But he'd had to check. His gut told him the predator was someone who had access to these girls.

Schak scrolled through Ashley's friends, looking for someone older, a male face that seemed inconsistent with everyone else. He didn't find anyone like that except a teacher who seemed to be friends with all his students. But the predator could be hiding behind another persona, pretending to be a young female friend. Schak checked his notes. Taylor Crenshaw and Daren Sorenson. The two people who'd been at both parties. He'd stopped at the Sorenson home on Sunday, but the mother had claimed Daren hadn't been home and that it was typical for him. She'd given him the name of a friend he might be staying with, but he'd had no luck tracking the boy down.

Taylor Crenshaw was likely in school today. Unless she was home, grieving for Ashley. Schak made a note to check with the Devonshires about when the memorial service would be held. The predator might show up to target his next victim. Schak called Riverside High School, identified himself, and asked if Taylor Crenshaw was in attendance. She was, indeed, so he pulled on his overcoat and headed out.

• • •

An elite school on the bank of the Willamette, Riverside had more masonry and glass than most high schools, which tended to look like prisons. Not this one. Lush landscaping, fresh paint, and red-brick at the base. Schak hurried across the parking lot, head down against the cold wind. Inside the school, he smelled pizza and realized it was lunchtime. His stomach growled in response. Pizza and beer. Damn, that sounded good. He headed for the main office, feeling self-conscious as the young people gave him curious glances.

He recognized the older receptionist's voice as the woman he'd spoken to earlier and moved to her side of the counter. Ahead of him stood a young girl in a short skirt who had to be freezing. The teenager finally moved along, and he spoke to the receptionist. After a little back-and-forth about where the interview with Taylor would take place, the woman sent an office helper to her classroom to bring the witness to him.

"And would you check with the principal? Mrs. Miller said she'd have a list for me."

"She brought it to me earlier, and I've got it for you here." The receptionist handed him a manila envelope.

Five minutes later, he was seated in a small yellow conference room with a pretty young woman who was taller than he was. Schak held back a basketball joke and introduced himself.

"Is this about Ashley?" she asked, her lips trembling.

"Yes. I need to know about the party you both attended Wednesday night."

"Are you going to tell my parents?" Worried eyes blinked at him.

"About your underage drinking? No."

A slump of relief. "We're all upset about Ash. I can't believe she's dead."

He had to keep her focused. "Who did Ashley talk to at the party?"

"Everyone. That's the point of a party."

He inhaled and nodded. "Who did she leave with?"

Taylor's blonde eyebrows scrunched in concentration. "I'm not sure. A lot of people split when the cop came and told the minors to go home. I didn't see Ash after that."

"Did you see the cop?"

"Yeah. I was in the kitchen, ready to bolt out the back door." She blushed, then laughed. "But I look older than my age, so he didn't run me out."

"What did he look like?"

She shrugged. "He was cute."

"Please be as specific as you can."

"That's all I remember." Her eyes went wide, thick lashes blinking rapidly. Then she quickly whispered, "Was it the cop?"

Oh hell. He didn't want to start that rumor. "No. I'm just trying to find the officer so I can get information from him."

Taylor fidgeted, unzipping her orange leather jacket. "He seemed a little taller than me, so about six-foot. Short brownish hair and good cheekbones."

"Age?"

She shrugged. "In his thirties, I think."

"Would you be able to recognize him again from a photo or a lineup?"

"No. Sorry."

Schak recalled the task force meeting that morning. The witness had just described Michael Quince. A heavy rock landed in his empty stomach. *No.* It had to be coincidence. "Was the cop in uniform?"

"Yes, dark blue."

Quince had once been a patrol cop and could still have his uniform. He'd also worked Vice for a few years, so he was an expert on sex crimes. If anyone in the department could pull it off . . . *No.* He had to search the school's employee database and find another match. "Did you see the police officer talking to Ashley?"

Taylor shook her head. "But I was pretty drunk. A lot of that night is a blur."

"Yet you remember the police officer in detail?"

"Of course. Even when you're drunk, the thought of getting arrested makes your head clear for a moment. Besides, he was hot." She shifted again. "I hope you find the creep who assaulted Ashley. I'm afraid to go to parties now."

Schak wanted to shake his head. Or maybe shake her. "You should be afraid to get drunk at parties. It's stupid and dangerous, and he's not the only predator out there."

The girl pressed her lips together as if she were about to cry, then abruptly zipped up her jacket. "Can I go?"

Schak didn't regret his comment. "Not yet. Did you attend a party at a house on Eighteenth and Patterson last May?"

"I'm sure I did. That's where my brother lives."

Right. He knew that. "Do you remember anything about the party?"

"Not really."

"Can you think of anything else that might help me? Anyone suspicious Ashley may have come into contact with recently?"

"Sorry. We hadn't been hanging out that much lately. She was kind of depressed."

Schak gave her his card, watched her hustle out, then headed for his car. He had to grab some lunch, then search the EPD files for someone who looked just like Quince. And, to be professional, he had to find a way to ask Quince what he'd done last Wednesday night.

CHAPTER 24

Monday, November 24, 12:25 p.m.

Jackson sat at his desk, eating a BLT sandwich he'd bought from a vendor truck that came to their parking lot every Monday around noon. He missed being downtown, close to restaurants and, most important, Full City coffee. He scowled at the cup of crappy stuff he'd picked up in the break room. Evans had come into the task force meeting with a cup from Dutch Bros., but for the first time, she hadn't brought him one. That was good, he decided. They both needed to take a step back and keep their relationship more professional.

He had already called the three names on the list Schak had given him, but no one had answered. He would try again later, then make the rounds to their houses around dinnertime, when they were more likely to be home. Relieved to have the afternoon somewhat free, Jackson leaned back in his chair, closed his eyes, and mulled over Thompson's case—his own version of meditation, which often led to a breakthrough. Despite Lammers' orders to close the case, he wasn't finished. So much left undone, too many questions unanswered.

But his mind refused to relax. He kept coming up with investigative steps he hadn't yet taken, such as perusing the phone and bank records that hadn't come through yet. This case had been intense and unusual from the beginning. They'd rounded up suspects almost immediately and gone into interrogation mode before they'd had a chance to dig into the victim's life. Then the first suspect had died just as a second suspect came to light. Now they had a third—and in theory, final—suspect with physical connections to the murder. But since the man was dead, there was no real need to build a case against him.

Yet the motive remained elusive. Lammers seemed to think that homeless men didn't need a motive for murder, that all they needed was to feel threatened. And that might be true for some. But Pete Scully's suicide bothered him. Why the prone position and a thousand in cash in his rucksack? But the drifter had Thompson's gun and cell phone. Could they have been planted by someone trying to frame the drifter for the murder? It seemed unlikely. The twins weren't capable of that kind of planning, and it didn't explain the cash.

A headache built up in his forehead, and Jackson sat up and rubbed his eyes. *Oh dear.* He'd forgotten to check on Katie. Guilt and worry made his pulse race as he called his daughter's cell phone. She didn't answer, so he called Kera, who picked up. "Hey, Jackson."

"Did you check in with Katie? I haven't heard from her since this morning."

"She's with her obstetrician now, and I'm in the waiting room with the boys. So I don't know anything yet."

"Thanks for taking her. Thanks for being so good to Benjie."

"My pleasure."

He heard the toddlers chatting with each other in the background.

"Speaking of the boy," Kera said. "Don't you have a custody hearing this week?"

"I do. But did I tell you about the letter from the court?"

"No." She gave a soft laugh. "You've been preoccupied since this case started, as always. But that's why you're good at what you do."

And why he was such a crappy dad at times. "One of Benjie's supposed relatives has filed for custody, and both cases will be heard this Wednesday."

"Do you want me to call and remind you, if you're still obsessed?"

That stung. He might miss a dentist appointment during a homicide investigation but not a court date. "Don't worry. I'll be there. And so will Mariah Martin. She's going to support me." The social worker had seen Benjie bond to him, and hopefully she would convince the judge that separating them would be devastating to the boy. "Update me when you know what Katie's doctor says. Even if it's just a text."

"Okay. I'll let you get back to it." She hung up.

Jackson shifted gears and tried to remember what came next in the investigation. He needed to back up, do the basics, and look more closely at Dan Thompson's life, starting with his work as a police officer. Lammers had supposedly checked his case log, but only for the last two days of his life. Jackson opened the database of recent arrests and searched for Thompson's name. It came up twice. In his last week on the job, Thompson had arrested a young woman for driving under the influence and a middle-aged man for public nudity at Alton Baker Park. Jackson expanded the search to include the previous month, but the arrests were more of the same—all benign, except one case of domestic dispute.

Jackson opened the domestic file and skimmed through the details. Two weeks earlier, Thompson had gone to a home in the Cal Young area after a neighbor called about a noisy altercation. He'd arrested Eric Marston for slapping his daughter and shoving his wife. The man had gone with him cooperatively, and the family had said little about their dispute. Sadie Marston had later bailed her husband out of jail, called Thompson, and told him she wouldn't testify against her husband. The charges were still pending, but the district attorney wasn't pursuing the case. A typical response. Charges could be filed and left on the books for a year without taking the person to court, and the DA's office used the tactic to keep people in line without the expense of prosecuting them.

Was it worth checking out? Probably not. How could a mild domestic dispute in a nice neighborhood be connected to Thompson's murder near a homeless camp? Jackson moved on. Now that he had Thompson's cell phone, he could check out who the victim had talked to prior to his death. Jackson pulled gloves out of his carryall, noting it was his last pair. He would have to restock before he left the building again.

The phone was a personal item, smaller and older than those the department issued to detectives. He tapped open the call history. Thompson's last call had been to his girlfriend, Trisha Weber. He'd contacted her at noon, and they'd talked for a couple of minutes. His only call that day. Jackson clicked over to the text list. No messages on Friday either. His last text had come from someone labeled only as Josh. Reading the exchange made Jackson's heart ache for Thompson. Josh was obviously his son, and Thompson had pleaded with the boy to spend time with him that weekend. Jackson felt sorry for the teenager too. He would have to live with the knowledge that his last words to his father had been *I want to see my friends instead.*

Jackson tapped back into the call history, checking out Thursday. That evening, the victim had called Donna Thompson, his mother, and talked for eight minutes, like the good man that he was. Scrolling back to Wednesday, Jackson saw that Thompson had received a call from Sadie Marston. *Interesting.* If Thompson had called Marston, that would seem like a standard follow-up to a case. But she had called him. Jackson checked to see if she was returning a call from Thompson. No outgoing calls to Marston showed up.

Lammers stepped into his cube, blocking the sunlight that beamed over the partial wall. "Is that Thompson's phone?" An unhappy tone.

"Yes." Jackson offered no explanation or apology.

"It should be at the lab, getting dusted for prints." She held out her hand. "I'll take it over. His weapon too."

He started to protest, then remembered he could get complete phone records from the provider. Slipping the cell back into its evidence bag, he said, "Joe's pretty swamped, so it could take a few days." He turned over the weapon too.

"The chief wants this case closed, Jackson. We don't have the time or resources to satisfy personal curiosity." The edge dropped out of her voice. "I'm not asking you to stop thinking about Thompson. None of us ever will. But the department needs closure. The homeless community needs closure. Stop picking at the wound."

"Yes, ma'am." He said it so softly, she cocked her head and stared at him.

Finally, she said, "The reason I came in here was to ask about the other twin. Do you know where he is?"

"No. Why?"

"With his brother dead and Willow in the hospital, I'm a little worried about him."

It took a moment to process what she was really saying. "You mean you're worried he'll go nuts and cause a scene or end up frozen under a bridge or something. And the department will look bad."

The sergeant's shoulders tensed. "We're trying to get him connected with resources that can help him, but no one has seen him since he left White Bird clinic yesterday morning."

Irritated and confused, Jackson said, "Jacob isn't my responsibility. And you can't ask me to drop Thompson's case, then expect me to follow up on it at the same time."

"I just wondered what you knew. I'm not asking you to find Jacob Walsh." She shook her head, as if he were being unreasonable. "If you hear anything about him, let me know."

"I will."

She left his space, and Jackson popped an aspirin, along with a mix of other anti-inflammatories—a pain-relief cocktail. He grabbed his carryall and coat and headed downstairs. He would call Sadie Marston on his way to see Tristan Channing, a potential witness in Schak's case. It couldn't hurt to see if Sadie or her husband held any animosity toward Thompson.

Outside, the frigid gray sky threatened more snow. Unusual for Eugene. They'd had more snow in the last two winters than in the decade before. He hoped it was a fluke and not the new normal. Jackson put in his earpiece and called the number he'd written down. A woman answered, sounding rattled. "If you're calling to ask for money, take me off your list."

"This is Detective Jackson, Eugene Police. I'm calling about your encounter with Officer Dan Thompson."

"Hang on a second." The sound of footsteps and voices could be heard in the background. She came back on. "Sorry, I'm on a break at work and had to get some privacy."

"Where do you work?"

"At Southern Valley Title. Why? What is this about?"

"Officer Thompson was killed Friday night, and I'm looking at his recent case files. I'd like to discuss this in person." Jackson drove out of the parking lot. The title company was only a few minutes away.

"There's nothing to discuss. My husband and I argued. That's it. But our busybody neighbor called the police when she heard shouting, and an officer came out."

"The report says your husband slapped your daughter and pushed you."

A harsh breathing sound. "Yes, Eric slapped our daughter *on the shoulder*. She was being verbally abusive. I stepped in between them, and Eric moved me out of the way. Nobody got hurt. It was just a bad moment for our family. The charges are ridiculous, and our attorney says the DA isn't going to pursue them. Please let this go." Weary and begging now.

"This isn't really about the incident at your house. It's about Officer Thompson." He turned toward Coburg Road.

"I was stunned to see on the news that he was dead. But didn't a homeless person kill him?"

"It looks that way." He needed to gauge her feelings about Thompson, but it needed to be done in person. "I'll be at your workplace in a minute. Meet me outside if you'd like to keep this private." He hung up before she could argue.

The title company was inside a building at the edge of the Oakway mall. Jackson had signed closing documents there when he and his ex had sold their house. He climbed from his car and went inside to wait in the lobby. It seemed unlikely that she would try to give him the slip, but he'd learned to be cautious.

A woman in a long beige coat stepped off the elevator. She noticed him immediately and came his way. Mid-forties, well dressed, and anxious. A pixie face that looked as if it had been compressed from forehead to chin. "Detective Jackson, I assume?" She kept her hands on her purse strap.

"Yes. Where would you like to talk?"

"It's too cold to stand outside. We'll sit in my car." She hurried out the glass doors and across the lot to a Pathfinder parked near the street. She climbed into the driver's side and unlocked the doors. Jackson took the passenger's seat. It wasn't the strangest questioning setup he'd ever experienced, but it came close.

She started the car, cranked up the heat, and turned to face him. "What do you want to know?"

"Why did you call Thompson last Thursday?"

"It doesn't matter now, and I don't want to talk about it." Marston clamped her mouth shut and crossed her arms, signaling she was closed off to that line of questioning.

Jackson decided to circle back to it later. "Do you blame Officer Thompson for your husband's arrest?"

"What do you mean?"

"Were you angry with Thompson for taking Eric in?"

"At first, yes. But he said he had to. He said the department would rather make unnecessary arrests than to walk away and let a woman be killed."

"What about your husband? Did he harbor a grudge against Thompson?"

"A grudge?" She blinked a few times, as if trying to process the real question. "What are you implying? That Eric might have killed a cop out of revenge for a stupid arrest?"

"Police officers have been killed for less." *Such as a blanket,* he thought.

"That's insane." She made another harsh sound. "My husband is a lawyer. He's probably going to sue the department for false arrest, but he's never hurt anyone, including me."

Had his instincts on this one been completely wrong? He still had to ask about the phone call. "You contacted Officer Thompson on his personal cell the day before he was murdered. I want to know why."

She started to speak, then stopped and rubbed her arms, as if suddenly cold. A moment later, she burst into tears. "I called Officer Thompson to tell him the whole truth. Our daughter had been sexually assaulted, and we were being blackmailed. That's what Eric and I were fighting about."

CHAPTER 25

Monday, November 24, 3:05 p.m.

Schak spotted Sophie Speranza in a corner booth, and a wave of apprehension rolled over him. He'd never met with a reporter before. It went against his grain, like inviting the IRS to look at his finances. But she'd called him and said a victim had come forward already and was eager to talk. He didn't see anyone with her and thought she might have manipulated him. Oh well, at least he could have a decent burger for lunch. He'd missed the burger-and-brew specials at the Sixth Street Grill since the department had moved out to Country Club Road. He hated the sound of their address. A police department should seem more accessible than that.

Schak slid into the booth across from her. "Hello, Ms. Speranza."

"Call me Sophie." She smiled and reached out a hand.

He shook it, thinking she was pretty and tiny and had the reddest hair he'd ever seen. Her photo on the paper's website didn't do her justice. "You said the victim was meeting us."

"She said she would be here." Sophie's expression held a hint of worry.

"Give me her name and contact information in case I need to follow up."

"Eden Soboda. Here's her phone number." Sophie jotted it down and slipped him a sticky note.

A waitress came by and they ordered. He wanted a beer, but wouldn't drink in front of the reporter. If the new victim didn't show up, Schak wondered what he and Sophie would talk about for the next thirty minutes. He didn't plan to answer questions, and he'd never been good at small talk. "Did Soboda tell you what happened to her?"

"She's not really sure. She'd been drinking with friends at a bar one evening, and they were pulled over on the way home. That's all she remembers. Except, when she woke up the next day, she knew she'd been assaulted."

"Pulled over by a police officer?"

Sophie's brow flinched. "Of course. Why the clarification?" She made a quick note on her yellow tablet.

"Just getting the facts."

A young girl hurried up to their booth. "Sophie?"

"Yes." The reporter scooted over, and the girl sat down. Her hair was a mess of braids that looked like dreadlocks, but she wore typical college student clothes: jeans and a green Ducks sweatshirt.

"Thanks for coming." Sophie gestured at him. "This is Detective Schakowski."

The girl stuck out her hand. "Eden Soboda. I'm sorry I'm late. I had to stay after class to ask the professor a question, and it took longer than I thought it would."

"You're a student at the UO?"

"A sophomore."

"Do you live here in Eugene?"

She giggled, a nervous little burst. "For the moment. But this isn't my hometown. I'm from Boise, Idaho."

"So your parents don't live here?"

"No. Why?"

She didn't fit the pattern, except for the possible involvement of a police officer. Schak tried not to look disappointed. "Tell me the details of your assault."

"It was June fifteenth, and I got really drunk. My boyfriend had just dumped me, so I changed my plans and decided to go home for the summer. I went out with friends to say good-bye, and I pounded down a boatload of margaritas." Soboda looked around, as if to find the waitress. "I don't remember much after my third drink, but I know we got stopped on our way home because they told me we did."

"How did you get home after you were stopped?" A real patrol officer wouldn't let them drive away drunk.

"We were only a few blocks from the complex where we live, so we walked."

"Did the officer escort you?"

A blank expression. "Nobody mentioned it."

"Did he issue a DUI ticket?"

"No. He let us off easy."

That was unusual. "So you and your friends walked two blocks home. Then you passed out?"

Another nervous giggle. "No. They said we ran into some guys who lived in the complex and partied with them for a while."

This one could go either way, Schak thought. The cop could have followed her home and sexually assaulted her. Or, more likely, she was raped by one of her friends. A guy who thought he was having consensual sex because she was too drunk to say no.

"Why didn't you report the assault?"

"There was no point. The guys we partied with were athletes. No one would have believed me anyway." She twisted one of her braids and didn't meet Schak's eyes. "I didn't want to send anyone to jail. What if it was my fault?" Soboda glanced at Sophie. "I only came forward because the article online made it sound like a predator was out there and more women were vulnerable. I wanted to help stop him."

"You're doing the right thing." Schak did his best to sound reassuring, but he couldn't fake a smile. "I'd like the names of the guys you partied with."

Soboda looked distressed. "I'd rather not tell you. Everyone turns against you if you accuse an athlete of anything."

Hells bells. How could he do his job if she wouldn't name anyone? "I need to talk to everyone who was with you that night. Did you wake up in your own bed?"

She nodded.

"I need to know how you got there."

"I told you. I don't remember anything." Soboda suddenly shut down. "I have to go back to class." She climbed out of the booth. "I'm sorry I couldn't be more help."

"Wait!" Schak wanted to get up and stop her, but he couldn't slide out of the booth fast enough.

She turned back, clearly impatient.

"Tell me the names of your girlfriends."

"It doesn't matter. Neither of them returned to the university this year, and I've lost contact." She spun and headed out.

Schak sipped his coffee while Sophie wrote out a long note, and the waitress brought their food. He dug into his burger like a starving man. His wife hadn't made him breakfast, so he'd grabbed a banana on his way out. What if Tracy left him? He would learn to get by, but it would be painful.

"What do you think?" Sophie asked. "Is she one of the predator's victims?"

"I don't think so. There's no blackmail involved, so it's probably just another college date rape."

"I hate that term." She stared at him until he put down his burger.

"What else do you call it? She doesn't even know if she consented or not."

Sophie leaned forward, eyes blazing. "If a woman is too intoxicated to make a rational decision, it's rape. Regardless of anyone's age or social connections." The reporter's voice was intense, and the people in the booth behind them had likely heard her.

He didn't disagree, but he resented her all-or-nothing attitude on the subject. "Let's keep this quiet, okay? This is sensitive investigative information."

"I'm sorry. I appreciate your trust, and I won't share anything you don't want me to."

Schak took another bite, focusing on his food. He just wanted to eat and get out of there.

"The best way to catch him would be during the money exchange," Sophie finally said.

He'd thought about that. "*If* we get that opportunity. We can't intercept him if the parents don't involve us until it's too late. Or not all."

"That *opportunity*—" she gave the word a special twist— "would mean that another girl would have to be assaulted. And filmed. And harassed." Sophie shook her head, repulsed. "What about a sting to catch him in the act?"

"We're considering it, but it's a long shot."

"Does he have a territory?" A little excitement in her voice now. "I mean, is there a pattern to where and how he picks his victims?"

Schak had to be careful about what he shared with her. Yet, if the paper printed information about the parties, maybe young girls would be more careful. "Both of the victims had been drinking at a party. So we think he targets gatherings where young girls will be."

"The campus area?"

"So far. But singling out the right party in the campus area is like trying to find the right hippie at the Oregon Country Fair."

Sophie laughed, snorting a little salad. "But it's not impossible, right? What else do the victims have in common?"

Should he tell her? Why not? "They both attended Riverside High School." The information about the cop had to stay discreet. If she printed it, their perp would shut down and disappear, and the public trust would be shattered again. Whatever was left of it. The activist was in the hospital, and the local TV station had showed clips of Officer Garcia striking her. Citizens were already calling for new policies and training.

"He must have some connection to the school," Sophie said, taking more notes.

"Don't publish that. I'm still looking into school employees, and I don't want to alert anyone."

"You said 'attended,' past tense. I know one committed suicide, but what about the other one?"

"She graduated."

"Will you tell me their names?"

"I can't."

"Give me the names and addresses where the parties were held. I have a lot of connections, and I'm good with social media. I think I can help you."

Could she? His own Facebook effort that morning had produced nothing except a desperate need to drink. With this case, he needed all the help he could get. His biggest concern was that the predator was a cop and the reporter would find him first. But the perp was probably using a fake online profile, so she wouldn't find his real identity. With mixed feelings, he flipped back through his notes and gave her the information about the party houses.

His phone rang: *Jackson.* "I have to take this." He pushed his plate aside and scooted to the edge of the booth before he answered the call. "Hey, partner. What have you got?"

"Another sexual assault victim. Guess who knew about it?"

Schak was on his feet. Jackson had to be talking about a police officer. "Who?"

"Dan Thompson."

CHAPTER 26

Sophie wanted desperately to hear the other end of Schak's conversation. It had to be Jackson. And he could be updating Schak on a lead involving Officer Thompson's murder. But the detective had stepped into the lounge, where she couldn't hear. She paid the check, rushed out the back door, and caught up to him as he climbed into his car. "Hey, we didn't finish our conversation."

"Sorry, I have to go."

"Was that Jackson? Is something breaking on Officer Thompson's case?"

"It's another sexual assault victim."

"What's her name? I want to interview her."

"You know I can't tell you. What do I owe you for lunch?"

"Don't worry, I got it."

"Thanks."

"Tell the victim to call me if she wants her story to help other women."

He rolled up his window and started backing up. Sophie got out of his way. A blunt man with rough edges, but he'd made her laugh, so she liked him. More important, he'd met with her and discussed strategy for catching the sexual predator. It was more time than Jackson had ever given her. Except for the interview his boss had forced him to sit through with her years ago.

What now? Officially, her job was to cover Springfield. But she could do that by phone in an hour this afternoon. She needed to know the assault victims' names. With that info, she could get on Facebook, Twitter, and Instagram, then map their connections in half an hour. She might even be able to pinpoint a party circuit. They were probably on Snapchat too, but those messages automatically deleted too quickly to be helpful.

On the drive back to the newspaper, she called Riverside High School and took a gamble. "Hello, this is Sophie Speranza with the *Willamette News*. I'm writing a profile about the suicide victim. Will you spell her name for me, so I get it right?"

"Ashley is just like it sounds, but with an *e*." The receptionist also spelled out Devonshire.

Yes! "Thanks. Does the school have anything planned?"

"We're holding a commemoration for her this afternoon in the gym at two."

"I'll see if I can make that. Do you have a photo file you can send?"

"The yearbook team probably does. I'll ask."

"I appreciate that." Sophie rattled off her email. "Who else should I interview to get a full picture of Ashley's personality and what her final days were like?"

"You should ask her parents that. I have to go."

It snowed for the last few minutes of her drive, and she cursed it but kept driving. The first time it had snowed in Eugene, it had been a novelty, a new experience to savor. Now she hated it like most rational adults.

. . .

Back at her desk with a cup of hot tea, she noticed a new message in her personal Gmail account. It was from her union rep, who was sitting twenty feet away: *Let's have lunch and talk about your situation.* The older woman clearly didn't want the newspaper's management to have access to the message. Sophie replied and suggested Wednesday. After she hit Send, she laughed and thought, *If I'm still here.*

Keeping her voice low, she called Detective Jackson, and he surprised her by answering. "Sophie?"

Was he sitting somewhere killing time, waiting for Schak to show up? "Hey, Jackson. Do you have an update on Officer Thompson's murder?"

"A lot has happened, but it's too early to make any announcements."

"I think I know something you might not. Let's trade. You first." It was the only way to get him to share real information.

A long pause. "We have a new person of interest with physical links to Thompson's crime scene."

Huge news! "Does that mean Henry Walsh has been cleared?"

"Not exactly. He may not have committed the actual murder, but it's still likely he was at the scene."

"Who's the new suspect?"

"A drifter. I can't give you his name until we confirm his identity."

That was odd. "Is he in custody?"

"He's dead."

Whoa! "How? What happened?"

"I'm still investigating. Now tell me what you have."

"Jacob Walsh thinks he saw someone sitting in the truck with Officer Thompson."

"Who?"

"He didn't say. It was a brief mention. Then the twins started talking about something else, and Willow asked them how they'd been treated in custody, and we didn't get back to it." The time Sophie had spent with them had been bizarre. "It's hard to keep them focused, if you know what I mean."

"Do you have any sense of the time frame? Such as before or after Thompson gave away blankets?"

"No. As I said, it was just a brief mention that was buried in an avalanche of words."

"I wish you had told me this earlier."

"I'm sorry. I meant to. But Henry was arrested and killed, making the case look solved. Then the riot happened, and I was there, so I had to write the story. It was a crazy weekend news-wise." All true, but it probably seemed lame to him. "I did call you, but I kind of thought you might already know. You questioned the twins for hours."

"I need to talk to Jacob. Do you know where he is?"

"No, but I can call SIRA and ask Willow's partner if anyone knows."

"Thanks." Jackson's tone shifted, and she knew he was done talking about the case. Yet there was so much more she wanted to report. "What's happening with Officer Bremmer? And Officer Garcia?"

"You'll have to call our department spokesperson."

"Will the department offer Jacob Walsh any compensation for the loss of his brother?"

"I'm not privy to such decisions. Text me if you find out where he is."

She almost laughed. Jackson didn't want to talk in person again. And texting was a new skill for him. "Then you can text me the killer's name when you've confirmed it."

"Bye, Sophie."

She hung up and realized Zee, the intern, was standing at the entry of her cube.

"I need your help."

Oh boy. Nothing like training the person who took your job. "With what?"

"Getting information from the police. I've been assigned to take on the Thompson murder, but no one at the department will talk to me, and I can't locate the family."

Sophie couldn't bring herself to share what she'd just learned. Not only was it the only leverage she had, but as a reporter, Zee needed to hear it directly from sources. "Detective Jackson is handling the case; have you tried him?"

"Of course. He won't return my calls."

"What about Detective Evans? She's more helpful sometimes, and she tends to work his cases."

"Evans." Zee wrote it down. "We need to talk about the sexual assault story too."

The big woman towered over her, but Sophie didn't have a chair in her small cube to offer. "Let's go to the conference room." She hated the windowless space, but there was nowhere else to talk privately.

She headed for the little room, and Zee followed. The intern took a seat near the door, looking uncomfortable. Sophie reminded herself that Zee was fresh out of college and trying to jump-start her journalism career, the same position Sophie had been in five years ago. Only now, it was much harder, thanks first to the internet and Craigslist, then to the digital revolution that gave everyone a platform from which to publish their thoughts.

Zee launched in. "Hoogstad says I have to follow up with the sexual assault story too. So I need you to update me on what you have."

Sophie had a wild thought. But she had to present it at the right time in the conversation.

Zee took her hesitation to heart. "Hey, I'm sorry to take your beat. I didn't expect this internship to displace anyone. It's nothing personal."

"I understand. Just remember the newspaper could do the same thing to you. After your internship is over, they might say you just didn't cut it and bring in another intern. That may be the only way the paper will survive—by keeping their employee costs to almost nothing."

The young woman slumped in her chair. "What am I supposed to do? I went thirty thousand into debt to get a journalism degree, and no one will hire you without an internship on your résumé."

"If I were you, I'd keep looking for a job. Which is exactly what I'm doing." Sophie tapped her yellow pad. "Let's get to work. The sexual assault story is intriguing, but the police are stumped." She summarized the details as Zee took notes.

"Have you called the school?" the intern asked.

"Only to confirm the latest victim's identity. But she's a minor, so the paper isn't likely to run it. But we can use it to find the connections between the victims."

Zee stared at her. "You said 'we.' I thought you were assigned to cover Springfield."

"I am. But without my help, you'll never get anywhere with either of these stories. Do you want to write fluff pieces with no real information, or do you want to dig for the truth? I'm offering to show you how it's done."

Zee's eyes narrowed. "Whose byline goes on the story?"

"I'll push for a double byline, but it will probably be yours. Because I'll likely get fired for insubordination."

"Shouldn't you just cover the beat you've been assigned and keep your job?"

"After we've broken open this story and you see what it's like to really investigate, you'll understand why I can't just write about shopping malls in Springfield."

"Thanks for working with me. I want to be good at this."

Sophie leaned forward and lowered her voice. "Are you willing to take risks?"

The intern blinked a few times. "Like what?"

"I'd like to do a sting." She got a rush of adrenaline just thinking about it. "We find the perp's pattern and watch for the next party. Then one of us pretends to be the most intoxicated girl at the party, hoping to lure the perp. The other one keeps watch, takes photos, and calls the police at the right moment."

Zee's mouth fell open. "That's crazy."

"It's real journalism."

"Shouldn't the police be doing this instead?"

"They don't have anyone who can pass for seventeen." Sophie grinned. "Except for your height, you look twelve."

Zee gave her a shitty smile.

Sophie continued. "Plus, the police department is busy keeping officers at the free speech plaza, where the homeless are still protesting."

"If the predator is targeting girls with wealthy parents, he's not going to pick me."

Well, hell. "Good point." Sophie could still attend the party, keep an eye on the young drunks, and watch for the predator.

"By the way, that protest story was a great piece of writing. I hope Hoogstad submits it for next year's Northwest Journalism awards."

"Thanks." Sophie hoped so too. "I still plan to dig through all the social media connections between the victims and see if I can find the next party."

Zee looked at her with admiration and a little fear. "I can't believe the newspaper is pushing you out of the crime beat. You're the best."

Sophie jumped up, deciding to mentor Zee after all. "Let's get to it. Bring your laptop to my cube and we'll work together."

Fifteen minutes into the project, they had a list of twenty names that were all connected to Ashley Devonshire. But the teenagers didn't discuss the parties on Facebook. Probably because some of their parents and teachers had profiles. Sophie switched over to Twitter and searched for the names. She finally found a series of tweets about a party the previous Wednesday. That had to be the one Ashley had attended the night she was assaulted. Sophie turned to Zee. "We need to interview some of these kids. Someone might have suspicions about who the predator is."

Heavy footsteps made her glance out the opening of her cube. Hoogstad.

He stopped in the doorway, sounding a little breathless. "There's been a school shooting in Corvallis. Zee, I want you to go with the photographer and cover the story. He's leaving now."

Zee slammed her laptop closed and bolted out.

Jealousy was her first reaction, but Sophie shrugged it off. School shootings were hardly news anymore and not much of a challenge to write about. But depressing as hell. She would keep working the homicide and the assaults and dare the paper not to run her breaking stories. Even if they didn't, she'd still have them for her portfolio, and she could always publish them on her blog.

CHAPTER 27

Monday, November 24, 3:55 p.m.

Schak drove to the Marston home, pushing the speed limit, his mind racing. Danny had taken a report about a sexual assault two days before he was killed. It had to be coincidence. But why wasn't the report in his log? Had the parents tried to keep the incident to themselves like in the other cases? Tension pulsed in his temples. A breakthrough was playing around the edge of his thoughts, teasing him to find it. Maybe Sophie would come through and track down the next party in the perp's trolling field.

At the house, Jackson's sedan was parked on the street, but no vehicle was in the driveway. Jackson said he'd spoken with Sadie Marston at her employer's, then arranged to meet her at home so they could both talk to her daughter. But it didn't look like they'd showed up yet. He hoped the family didn't blow them off. People did that sometimes, rather than talk to the police. Especially teenagers who'd been drinking or smoking pot and didn't want to admit to it.

Schak climbed out of his car and into Jackson's, which smelled like wet boots. "What do you think? Are these cases connected?"

"I don't know how they could be." Jackson shifted to face him. "I don't even know if this incident is connected to the other assaults."

"I just met with a college girl who was sexually assaulted near campus. No blackmail in that case. They were pulled over by an officer, then met up with a group of athletes and partied some more."

Jackson scowled. "If not for the mention of the police officer, I'd say your college victim isn't connected. It sounds more like a case of date rape."

"When I said that, Sophie bit my head off." Schak was still mulling it over. "She says rape is rape. But the last girl I talked to didn't know if she had given consent or not."

"But if she was unconscious . . ."

"She may have just been really drunk. What if she said yes, then later couldn't remember?" Schak recalled the last time he'd been blackout drunk and how fuzzy his memory had been the next morning. "But that's part of why she didn't report it."

"One thing is clear," Jackson said. "There's a lot more sexual assault going on than we ever realized."

A car pulled into the driveway, so they both climbed out and stood on the sidewalk. A cold wind made Schak wish he'd put on his overcoat, but he wasn't going back to his car for it. They'd be in the house in a moment. "It's supposed to drop down to twenty-five tonight," he said, remembering what little he'd seen of the morning's paper.

"Rough weather for people on the streets," Jackson commented. "Thompson's murder has got me thinking about the homeless."

Schak didn't let himself think about them. The issue was too complicated and distracting. "We need to meet with the team."

"I'll set it up for the morning. It's late and we all need a break."

The woman and her daughter hurried into the house without looking back at them. *What the hell?*

Jackson started up the walkway and Schak followed. Sadie Marston opened the door as they stepped onto the patio, waved them in, then slammed it closed.

"Christ, it's cold," she said. "I just turned up the heat, but it will take a minute. Coffee?"

Jackson declined, much to Schak's disappointment, so he said no thanks as well. "Where's your daughter?"

"She'll be right back. Let's sit at the dining room table."

Sadie Marston generated a nervous energy that made Schak eager to get it done and get out. Maybe it was best she didn't make coffee. They all sat down, and he and Jackson both took out notepads. A moment later, a teenage girl stomped into the room, glared at her mother, and didn't look at them. *Oh joy.* This would be a pain.

"This is Grace." Mrs. Marston gestured as the girl sat down, then introduced the two detectives. Grace nodded but didn't speak.

Long brown hair, dark eyes, slender, and an eyebrow piercing. She seemed familiar. Had he met her recently? Then it clicked. Grace looked a lot like Mara, the first victim, the one who'd gotten pregnant. He tried to visualize Ashley, the dead girl, wishing he'd focused more on her face. She also had long brown hair. *The perp had a type.* Schak scribbled it down, then asked, "What day did the assault happen?"

"Friday, November seventh." The girl's voice was pleasant, despite the look on her face, which indicated she would rather be having a root canal.

"Tell us what happened."

"Mom went to the Hult Center, so I invited a few friends over. Janelle brought some vodka, which we drank, but it wasn't much. We smoked some pot too. Mom has a prescription."

Mrs. Marston's mouth tightened. "It helps my fibromyalgia, so I can sleep. I thought I had it hidden. So I didn't know Grace had been stealing small amounts."

Teenagers taking their parents' pills and drinking their booze now had a new twist. "We're not going to report it," Schak said. He stared at Grace until she met his eyes. "What happened next?"

"My friends went home, then I got a message from an online friend who said she wanted to join the party. So I headed out to meet her at Joe's Pizza."

Jackson cut in before Schak could. "How did she know you were partying?"

Grace rolled her eyes. "We'd been posting updates on Twitter."

"What's the friend's name?" Schak asked.

"Kelsey."

"Last name?"

"I can't remember. I hadn't met her in person yet."

A bad feeling landed in Schak's chest. "Did you meet her?"

"No. I was pretty wasted by then. Some guy stopped by and offered me a ride. That's all I clearly remember. After that, I have a couple of flashes, one of a small room and the other of me coming in the front door, but they both seem more like a dream than something real."

Schak hated to ask, but he had to. "What makes you think you were sexually assaulted?"

Grace glared. "My vagina hurt, and I felt violated."

Schak shifted his gaze to Mrs. Marston. "But you didn't call the police?"

Mrs. Marston bit her lip. "I wanted to, but the asshole sent a text saying he had a video of Grace smoking my pot and would send it to my boss if I didn't pay him fifteen thousand."

"What did you do?"

"I demanded to see the video, but he wouldn't send it. He said he had a file of her naked too, but when he couldn't produce any proof, I told him to fuck off."

The perp had somehow failed to record the assault and consequently failed to collect a payment. That must have infuriated him. "I'd like to see his texts."

"Grace took my phone and deleted them all."

This girl was a pain. "Where was your husband during all this?"

"Traveling for his job. When he came home, I told him about it and he freaked out. That's when Officer Thompson came to the house."

"But you didn't report the assault at that time?" Schak tried to sound factual, rather than disbelieving, but he failed.

"No." Mrs. Marston struggled to control her emotions. "I was afraid I'd lose my job if the blackmailer followed through on his threat. Maybe even be arrested."

"It's not Mom's fault," Grace blurted out, showing her first sign of distress. "I didn't want to report it. I can't even tell you what the guy looked like, so what's the point of going through all this?"

Should he ask about a police officer? Schak didn't want to put ideas into her head. "Can you tell me anything about the guy who gave you a ride? His age? Size? Voice?"

"He seemed kind of in the middle, like not forty yet. Even though I can't picture him, I remember thinking he was cute. For an older guy."

"Did he offer you a drug? Or something to drink?"

"I don't remember."

"Can you think of anything else?"

"No. Just that he seemed safe. Which is why I wasn't scared to ride with him." The girl made a strange choking sound. "I was so wrong. You can't trust anybody."

A cop? Jackson glanced at him, and Schak gave a small nod. "The friend who contacted you and invited you out, Kelsey. Tell me everything you know about her." Schak stood. "Or better yet, show me her profile online."

They learned little about Kelsey Walker from her profile. She listed her age as eighteen and her school as Riverside. Schak left the small bedroom to call the school. As he identified himself and talked to the receptionist, he smelled coffee and walked to the kitchen. "I need to know if Kelsey Walker is a student."

"I don't recognize the name, but I'll check."

After a long wait with annoyingly upbeat music, the receptionist came back on. "I checked last year too, but we don't have anyone by that name."

"Thanks."

Schak hung up and took the coffee Mrs. Marston handed him. "Where does Grace go to school?"

"Sheldon."

Now he had a victim that wasn't from Riverside. They would have to widen the perp search. "Your daughter was lured out of the house by someone posing as a student. But we'll catch him."

"But if Grace can't identify him . . ."

"There are other victims. He's left a cyber trail somewhere."

A tear rolled down Mrs. Marston's face. "I warned Grace about online predators. I warned her about underage drinking. Is this my fault? Because of the medical marijuana?"

He didn't think so. "A lot of teenagers experiment with drugs and alcohol, no matter what their parents say or do." His own mother had let him drink at home, so he didn't go out "and get himself killed," as she always said.

Jackson joined them in the kitchen. "I have a meeting with my custody lawyer soon, so I'm going to take off."

Schak handed Mrs. Marston a card. "Please call me if your daughter remembers anything else."

Outside, Jackson strode toward his car, a man in a hurry.

"Wait," Schak called. His partner turned, and Schak said, "There's something we have to talk about."

"What's that?" A snowflake drifted down between them.

He didn't know how to say it diplomatically. "The descriptions of the police officer match Quince."

Jackson stared, wide-eyed. "I don't believe it. There has to be someone else in the department who fits."

"I've looked. There's Officer Barton, but he doesn't work patrol."

"Quince doesn't work patrol either."

More snow fell, and Schak thought about his coat in the car. "The perp could be a poser. In fact, I'm betting that he is." Stress constricted his chest, and he had to pull in a deep breath. "But what if it's Quince? We've had other sexual predators in the department, so we can't be blind to this. Quince is on our team. If we plan a sting or a raid, he'll know."

"Oh crap." Jackson, who rarely swore, added, "We'll hold back until we can rule him out." His expression grew even more distressed.

"What is it?"

"Quince mentioned having money problems, *and* he worked sex crimes."

"I know."

The snow fell harder, and Jackson bounced on his feet. "One of the twins said he saw someone in the truck with Thompson."

Who would Danny let into his vehicle? "You think it was Quince?"

"I don't want to believe it." But Jackson looked like he might.

"If he's posing as Kelsey, we have to find out. I'll go write some subpoenas." They headed for their cars, and Schak worried that he didn't have enough suspicious activity to convince a judge or the social media site to reveal the user's information. Even more challenging, how could they effectively investigate if they couldn't trust a member of their own team?

CHAPTER 28

Tuesday, November 25, 7:45 a.m.

Katie's cramps had subsided the evening before, and her obstetrician had diagnosed a UTI and recommended cranberry juice and rest. Feeling guilty, Jackson dropped off Benjie at Kera's, vowing to find the boy a regular day care soon. Before he'd left the house, he'd told Katie to call him if she needed medical attention again, but they both knew she'd contact Kera instead—so he could work. They had to go car shopping this weekend. His daughter would need her own transportation, especially once the baby was born. On the way to the department, he picked up doughnuts for their meeting. Schak loved them, and after what his partner had been through in the last couple of days, he needed a little comfort food. As cold as it was, they all did.

At his desk, he updated his Word file and added a question in bold: *Is Thompson's murder connected to the sexual assaults / blackmail?* Investigative instinct told him there were no coincidences.

Yet, Thompson had been killed near a homeless camp with a broken bottle that had a homeless man's fingerprints. Another homeless man had been found with Thompson's gun and cell phone. So his death seemed more obviously connected to street people. But both suspects were dead, and that was suspicious too. An odd thought hit him. Was Officer Bremmer involved? Had he killed Henry Walsh and Pete Scully to cover other crimes?

Jackson printed copies of the case file, then glanced at the time. The meeting was starting soon. He sent Kera a quick text: *I'll make it up to you, and take both boys for a whole day.* He'd done it before. The first half was great fun, but by mid-afternoon, he'd have them in front of the TV.

Jackson headed for the conference room, hoping that brainstorming with the team could help break through the logjam of contradictions in these cases. He hadn't told Quince about the meeting so they could talk freely and be selective about what information they gave him. Evans was in the room, typing on her tablet. She took her case notes electronically, and as much as he wished he could be that efficient, he just couldn't make it work for him.

"Hey, Jackson." She looked up and smiled. "I'm glad you're here early. I wanted to tell you something."

He stepped toward her, sensing it was personal and that she'd keep it soft. "What is it?" Apprehension strummed his spine.

"I'm trying to transfer into Special Investigations. It might take a while, but I wanted you to know."

He knew why, but the socially appropriate response was to inquire. "What's going on? I thought you liked working Violent Crimes."

"You know I do." She gave him a sad smile. "But I have to move on. It's best for both of us."

He knew she was right. "I'll miss working with you. But you'll be great in SI."

"If they'll take me. I've also applied for a patrol supervisory position."

The only way to be promoted to sergeant. "You'll hate that."

"I know. But it will be temporary. I need to make sergeant if I want to advance in the SWAT unit."

"Best wishes in whatever you do." Should he brief her on the concern that Quince was a potential suspect? He heard footsteps outside the door. "Stay after the meeting, so we can talk again." He turned to the door, greeted Schak, and took a seat. His partner seemed more disheveled than usual—a stain on his white shirt that looked like he'd spilled mustard and wiped it up, dark circles under his eyes, and a pinched expression that indicated pain.

"You okay?" he asked, looking his friend in the eye.

"Yep." Schak gave a half grin, then glanced away. He took a seat next to Jackson then elbowed him. "So who's running this meeting?"

Good question. Their cases seemed to have merged. "You are. According to Lammers, the Thompson and Scully deaths are resolved. So this is now the sexual predator task force."

Schak turned to face him. "You don't think the drifter killed Danny? What don't I know?"

Jackson got up and closed the door. Lammers' office was ten feet away. "It's a bunch of little stuff. Like drag marks near Thompson, and Scully shooting himself while lying down. Plus the fact that the twins saw someone in Thompson's truck." He knew they weren't reliable, so he added, "But it would help to have another witness."

"If it's true, it changes things." Evans stood and went to the murder board. "We questioned everyone at the camp and everyone we could find in the area. Should we ask the public for help?"

"I can't. This case is closed, remember?" But Schak deserved to know all his concerns. "Pete Scully also had a thousand dollars in cash in his rucksack."

"What are you saying?" Schak looked troubled.

"I'm not sure, but now that we know Thompson was aware of the sexual predator, we have to rethink the motive."

"What?" Evans spun toward him. "When and how did you learn that?"

"Late yesterday," Jackson said. "I dug into Thompson's shift logs and noticed a domestic dispute from a few weeks earlier. Then I saw in his cell phone that the wife had called Thompson two days before his death. Men involved in domestic violence can be vindictive, so I checked it out." He stood to add the names to the other case board. "Sadie Marston said she'd called Thompson and told him her daughter had been assaulted—the reason for their fight. Schak and I went out to interview the family, and they're the third victims of our predator."

"That's weird," Evans said. "I see why you think Thompson's murder might still be open."

"Did the perp blackmail them?" Evans asked.

"He tried." Jackson summed up the scenario. "We think he failed to record the assault, then, without a video, couldn't collect an extortion payment."

"He failed again with the Devonshires," Evans added. "And the assaults were close together. Maybe he's desperate for money."

"That could work for us," Schak said. "I'm still thinking about a sting."

"Where's Quince, by the way?" Evans asked.

"I forgot to tell him about the meeting." Jackson started to mention their suspicion when his phone rang. The medical examiner's office. "It's Gunderson." He put his phone on the table and set it to speaker. "Jackson here. We're in a task force meeting, and you're on speaker. What have you got?"

"A couple of updates on Dan Thompson's autopsy. Since you left early." A little jab.

"And?"

"This may be irrelevant, but he had heart disease. A serious condition called hypertrophic cardiomyopathy. He was probably taking medication for it."

Schak touched his own chest. "It must run in the family." He had experienced a heart attack a few years back.

A moment of silence. They all knew Gunderson had called about something else.

The ME finally added, "I sent Thompson's blood to the state lab Saturday morning and asked them to rush it. I just got preliminary toxicology results. Thompson had a point-one-eight blood alcohol level and lorazepam in his system. It's a benzo, a mild tranquilizer."

That was also unexpected. "Just how intoxicating is that combination?" Jackson asked.

"It's hard to say. For some people, that pharmacology would have put them under. But if Thompson was a drinker, and his liver indicates he was, then he was buzzed but probably functional."

Jackson looked at Evans. "Did you find any prescriptions at Thompson's?"

"Just an antidepressant."

Where did he get the tranquilizer? Jackson got back to Gunderson. "Thanks for the update. Anything else?"

A pause. "Konrad and I have some disagreement on the angle of the stab wounds, but he's the pathologist, so his opinion is in the report, which I'll send over soon."

"What do you think?" Jackson glanced at Schak, concerned about how he was taking the discussion of his cousin's stabbing. Stoic, as usual.

"I think the perp was taller than the victim—that the thrust had a slight downward projection."

Jackson thought about the alcohol/benzo stupor. "Or maybe Thompson was hunched over."

"Maybe. But Konrad disagrees, so forget I said it. Besides, you've got the guilty guy, correct? He's in the drawer over there, chilling, waiting for us to unlock his secrets."

Jackson cringed. Another autopsy to attend. "When's the post scheduled?"

"Tomorrow morning at ten. Konrad has an early meeting with the DA."

Schak cut in. "What about Ashley Devonshire? Have you completed her autopsy?"

"Yes. But there's nothing to report. No body trauma, no real signs of sexual abuse, nothing in her stomach. We'll see what her blood analysis reveals when it comes in."

"No signs of sexual abuse?" He and Schak said it in unison.

Gunderson cleared his throat. "I'm not saying she wasn't assaulted. But there's no tearing, swelling, or bruising."

Schak's brow furrowed. "I'm confused."

Evans explained, "She was unconscious, remember? Rape isn't always violent. It's about non-consent."

"I'm hanging up now." Gunderson clicked off.

Jackson pocketed his phone. "These assaults may be more about the blackmail money than the sexual gratification." He glanced at Evans. "Or domination, or whatever."

"You think he'll try again soon?" Evans bounced on her toes. "We have to figure out how he targets his victims."

"We think he's using a fake online profile named Kelsey Walker." Jackson realized he'd taken the lead again, out of habit. "Maybe we need to monitor that profile round the clock."

"I called the Facebook office this morning and asked about the profile's source, but they said I needed a subpoena." Schak shrugged. "It was worth a try. And I'll take the paperwork to a judge today."

"I'll take the first Kelsey shift," Evans said. "I don't have dinner plans."

Jackson grabbed the next one, not wanting to be up late. "I'll watch from eight until midnight."

"Can't we set up our own fake profile and lure the perp out?" Evans said, pacing now.

"He may be suspicious if a new person pops up and starts interacting with him," Jackson said. He thought about his teenage daughter and her online profile, but he would never risk drawing attention to her.

"I'll talk to Dragoo," Schak said with a pinched brow. "Maybe he can hack into Kelsey's account. He got into Ashley's for me."

Jackson shook his head. "That was different. The victim was dead, and you had her parents' permission. You and Dragoo will need a court order to violate Kelsey Walker's privacy." Sometimes he hated being the stickler.

"I know that." Schak rubbed his buzzed head. "I asked Sophie Speranza to help me find more victims. So far, only one has come forward, and I don't think she fits the profile."

"What exactly is the profile?" Evans picked up the marker, ready to add to their case board.

"Ashley, Mara, and Grace all are high school students with long brown hair and petite bodies," Schak said. "The college student I talked to yesterday didn't fit that physical type."

"Can you get pictures?" Evans asked.

"Sure." Schak nodded. "I should have done that already." He glanced at Jackson. "Sophie is looking at the victims' connections online to see if she can spot a pattern. Or a new party developing." He cleared his throat. "I want to share the third victim with her."

"It's your case." Jackson was relieved it wasn't his call. He never wanted to give information to Sophie, but he rarely regretted it.

Evans paced impatiently. "Do we know anything about the perp? Have any of the victims given a description?"

Time to tell her. "Quince matches the description of the cop who broke up the parties."

Evans' mouth fell open. "You don't really suspect him, do you?"

"We have to be open to all possibilities."

"In theory, yes, but I don't believe it's him." Evans crossed her arms.

"I don't want to believe it either." Jackson realized how challenging it would be to have him on the team. "We don't want Quince to know he's a suspect, so I'll call him later and update him with nonessential information."

"What exactly is the description?" Evans asked.

Schak said, "Six-foot, late thirties, and attractive, but that's all we know."

"That's so broad, it's almost meaningless," she muttered.

Another connection popped into Jackson's head. "It also describes Gene Burns, the ex-con who threatened Thompson. Burns was charged with sexual assault years ago but not convicted."

"Is he still in custody?" Evans asked.

"I hope so." Jackson made a note to call the jail.

"But if Burns is the perp, maybe we should have him released," Schak argued. "So we can monitor him, maybe catch him in the act."

"The Burns idea helps explain Thompson's involvement in the sexual assault cases," Evans said. "The men knew each other through Trisha Weber. If Thompson connected Burns to the assaults and confronted him, the ex-con may have killed him, then framed a homeless person because it was convenient."

Relief settled into Jackson's bones. He'd been thinking something similar, and the theory made sense all the way around. It also meant they weren't looking for a cop. *Thank god.* He stood. "I'll call the jail now and put a hold on Burns."

The door burst open and Lammers shouted, "We need you downstairs. Homeless people are protesting in the lobby, and this could get ugly."

CHAPTER 29

Jackson pounded down the stairs as the chanting sounds grew stronger. He stepped into the crowded lobby and resisted the urge to touch his weapon. The other detectives fanned out around him. Jackie Matthews, the department spokesperson, stood on a chair near the front counter and tried to get everyone to quiet down. Two uniformed officers flanked her, and Ben Stricklyn, an Internal Affairs detective, had just come in the front door. A few feet from him, Sophie Speranza took pictures.

About fifty people crammed into the narrow space. Some held signs, but the rest were simply shouting, "Justice for Henry! Justice for Willow!" Mostly men, layered in heavy winter clothes, but a few women as well, ranging from late teens to one who looked seventy. Jackson scanned the group, looking for Jacob Walsh, but didn't see him. *Damn.* He really needed to question him again. Internal Affairs needed to talk with him as well. Jacob was a witness to the Taser incident that had led to his brother's death. "Search the crowd for Jacob Walsh," he said to Evans. "I'm going to grab Stricklyn and see if we can get control here."

Jackson pushed through the mob to reach the IA detective. Through the glass front doors, he saw dozens more people spilling down the wide stairs and into the front parking lot. Many didn't look homeless. This was the same crowd that came to the citizens' advisory board meetings. "I need your help," Jackson said. "Come with me to the front."

"We need a SWAT unit," Stricklyn countered.

Bad idea. "No, we need to give these people some hope. Come on."

Jackson resisted the urge to grab his arm, then turned and headed for where Matthews was still trying to get the crowd's attention. He motioned for her to get down from the chair. "You haven't called for the SWAT unit, have you?"

"Sergeant Lammers did."

"Tell them to stand down. No one else needs to get hurt!" She started to argue but then charged toward Lammers, who had seniority. His supervisor was near the stairs, probably waiting for the chief to come down. Stricklyn had followed him and was standing by. The two patrol officers had their batons at their sides but stayed back, watching the crowd. Jackson stepped up onto the chair. He held his arms in the air and waited. It took a couple minutes, but the tactic gained people's attention, and the chanting slowly died out. When it was quiet, a young man yelled, "Who are you?"

"Detective Jackson. I'm investigating Officer Thompson's death. He was a friend to the homeless community, and he needs your help. I need your help."

The young man stepped forward. Dark shoulder-length hair, short beard, and a long leather coat. "Why should we help you?

We want justice for Henry Walsh. And for Willow. Too many of us have been assaulted and treated like garbage."

"That has to change. I agree." Jackson touched the IA officer's shoulder and raised his voice. "This is Detective Stricklyn. He's with Internal Affairs, and he's investigating Henry's death and Willow's assault. The officers involved in those incidents are on leave and will be held accountable." Jackson knew it wasn't true, but he needed the crowd to feel placated. Officers were almost never disciplined for excessive force. The underlying belief was that it was bad for morale. That it would intimidate and hamstring patrol cops, putting them at risk in dangerous situations.

"No officers are ever charged with wrongdoing!" the man yelled.

"But they are reprimanded and taken out of fieldwork. And policies do change. In response to the recent incidents, the department is starting a new training program." Also not true—at the moment—but he would push for it. "Instead of gathering here, where you're at risk, take your concerns to the city council. Send representatives."

"You mean like Willow? Who's now in the hospital?"

Jackson had no comeback for that. "Things will change, I promise! Does anyone know where Jacob Walsh is?" A wild impulse jumped into his head and out of his mouth. "I want to help him. I want to buy him a home in Opportunity Village. If you see him, please let him know. Please send him to me."

About half the crowd cheered. The young man who'd spoken glared, skeptical. Jackson tried to calculate what one of the little mobile huts would cost him.

Lammers cruised toward him, and people parted to get out of her way. She signaled for Jackson to get down. When he did, she hauled herself up onto the chair.

Lammers called out, "I talked to her doctor this morning, and Willow is improving. She'll make a full recovery."

A loud cheer for that news. When they'd quieted down, Lammers added, "We support Willow's efforts to get people off the streets and into regulated camps. So the police department will make a generous donation to SIRA."

Another cheer.

"But you have to get out of here and let us do our jobs. You're putting others at risk by taking our time. Please! A SWAT unit is on the way, and I don't want anyone to get hurt!"

She shouldn't have said that. Some people jeered, but others headed for the door. The young spokesman stepped toward Jackson. "I know where Jacob might be."

"Tell me."

"He sleeps in a shed somewhere around Third and Monroe. But no one has seen him since Henry died. We're all worried."

Nothing he didn't already know. He just had to find time to get over there. "Thanks. I'll make sure he gets help." Jackson meant that. He would call Willow's organization and arrange to pay for a camper and get Jacob set up at the village—where people would keep him company and help him with his grief.

More of the crowd moved toward the door, and relief flooded his body. Now if they would just leave the parking lot before the SWAT unit arrived, primed with adrenaline and carrying surplus military gear. Sergeant Bruckner, who ran the unit, was a good man, but he loved using the door knocker and stun grenades. Jackson couldn't bear for another person to get hurt, all because he'd brought the twins in for questioning. He was starting to think Henry's fingerprint on the broken bottle didn't mean anything except that he'd drunk it or picked it up at one point, then left it lying along the road.

He turned to Lammers. "Did you okay the donation with the chief? Is it real?"

"Not yet, but he'll be on board. We need to repair public trust."

"We need Willow to come out of this all right."

Lammers flinched. "I made that up too. But I'll call her doctor now."

"You did good. We had to get them out of here before anyone got hurt." He heard Kera's voice in his head calling *bullshit*. But she'd never worked in law enforcement. Their job was to protect people, not make their lives better. And to protect the public, they had to protect themselves first. "I have to get going."

"What's happening with the sexual-assault-and-blackmail case?"

He wasn't about to bring up Thompson. Schak could tell her about the connection. "We've found more victims. And we think we found the perp's fake online profile, so we're closing in."

"Good to hear."

Schak and Evans walked up as they talked. "What's the plan?" Evans asked.

Schak nudged her. "Will you go see if Dragoo can track the source of the Kelsey Walker profile?"

"I'm on it." Evans headed upstairs and Lammers followed her.

Jackson decided not to question what Schak and Evans were up to. "We need to locate Gene Burns," he said. "I'll call the jail." As he pressed a speed dial key, he added, "And I need to find Jacob Walsh and see if he can tell us more about the person in the truck."

A female deputy answered. "Lane County Jail."

"Detective Jackson here. Is Gene Burns still in custody?"

"I'll check." A minute later, she said, "He was released this afternoon on bail."

Damn. "Who posted the money?"

"I don't have that information, but I can transfer you to the records department." The connection broke after a few minutes on hold. Jackson pocketed his cell. No one in records ever picked up the phone.

"Someone bailed him out?" Schak asked.

"Probably his mother or a girlfriend."

"Or his ex-girlfriend." Schak looked like he wanted to spit.

"You think Trisha Weber bailed him out after he set fire to her car?"

"I've seen abused women do dumber things." Schak turned toward the stairs. "I'm going to find out."

"I'll drive over to the shed where the Walsh twins sleep and see if Jacob is around."

They both headed back to the conference room where they'd left their casebooks and carryalls. Jackson grabbed his overcoat too. He might have to question Jacob where he found him—outside in the cold.

· · ·

Fifteen minutes later, he was knocking on the door to Ella's house. The shed was locked, a sign that Jacob wasn't inside. He had called out anyway, with no response. The kindness Ella had shown in giving the twins a place to sleep had not been extended to him the last time he'd been there. He hoped to do better today.

The door opened, but a screen door remained locked. The older woman in a red tracksuit said, "You again."

"I need to talk to Jacob. Do you know where he is?"

"No."

"This is important. He may have witnessed something."

She made a scolding sound. "He witnessed a cop taser his brother, his only companion. He watched Henry die. Jacob is crushed!"

More guilt. "I'm sorry it happened. I tried to prevent it." Jackson reached for a business card. "I want to help Jacob with a more permanent housing solution. Please give him this and have him call me." He held out the card, and she reluctantly opened the screen door and took it.

He started down the walkway.

Ella called after him, "When it's cold, Jacob hangs out at the deli inside the Albertsons on Eighteenth and Chambers. They have tables and free newspapers."

Jackson turned back. "That's where Henry died. Would he go there?"

"They are creatures of habit. So yes, he would."

"Thank you."

. . .

It started snowing on the drive over, and Jackson thought about all the people out there without housing. A recent survey had counted nearly 1,800 in the county, a number that had stuck in his mind. As much as he hated the snow, it meant something entirely different to people without a home. Most didn't have cars either, so even if they could go to the Mission or one of the warming centers, they'd be cold and wet before they got there. He felt powerless to change their circumstances, except maybe the way EPD officers treated them. He made a mental note to take his concerns directly to the chief—as soon as he had time.

Jackson pulled into the crowded parking lot and had to cross over to the area near the bike path to find an empty space. Everyone was making a quick grocery stop in case the snow kept falling. He spotted the gangly man on the side of the building, shoving empty cans into a recycling machine under a protected overhang. Jackson approached cautiously. "Jacob, it's Detective Jackson."

The man wouldn't look up or acknowledge him. He just kept feeding the machine in a rhythmic motion.

"I know you're upset and grieving, but I'm one of the good guys, remember? I called the crisis team instead of taking you to jail. And I know Henry didn't kill Officer Thompson."

Jacob stopped. For a few seconds, he was still. Finally, he turned. "Where is Henry?"

Oh no. Starting from scratch. "He's in the morgue. They're cleaning and examining his body, and they'll release it soon." What happened to homeless people who died? Did a local mortuary cremate their bodies? Who paid? The city? He'd never considered it before. Poor Jacob needed closure, and it seemed unlikely he could afford a service. "Would you like to see him?"

"Yes."

"I'll take you now."

"I have to finish these cans."

Jackson glanced at the man's shopping cart. It was nearly empty, so he would wait. "You can turn in the money slip later," he said, hoping to head off a trip into the store. "I'll bring you back here."

"I'm hungry now."

"What do you want? I'll go get it."

"A turkey sandwich. With mustard and a pickle."

Jackson worried about letting the man out of his sight, but he knew how obsessive the twins could be about food—or whatever was on their minds. His mind, he corrected. They were no longer plural. He hurried into the store, bought the sandwich, and came back. Jacob had finished and was talking to another man with cans. The snow had stopped for now. Maybe they'd get lucky and it wouldn't stick again. Jackson led Jacob to his sedan, hanging on to the sandwich until they were in the car and rolling. He eased into the conversation. "Do you know about Opportunity Village?"

"Of course."

"Would you like to live there?"

"I don't have a little house or a sponsor."

"I can help you with that."

His voice perked up. "Really?" Then grew skeptical. "Why?"

"I want you to be safe and to have company."

A quick glance his way. "I'm okay. I don't need meds."

"This isn't about medication. I'm trying to be nice." But it was time to do his job and get information. Jackson turned down Thirteenth and headed east. "Jacob, I need to ask you about Friday night, when Officer Thompson was handing out blankets."

"That was last week. Before Henry died. I don't remember much."

Was this a complete waste of time? He had to know. Jackson set his recorder on the seat and clicked it on. "Did you see Officer Thompson in his truck?"

"He was behind the truck, handing out free stuff. But not to us."

"What about before?"

"Not that day. We saw him at the Mission once."

"What about after the blankets were gone? Did you see him get into the truck?"

"No." Jacob faced forward, never once glancing at him.

"Did you go back to the truck after he sent you away? Did you see someone sitting with Officer Thompson?"

"Henry said not to talk about it."

A flash of dread. Were the twins guilty after all? "Why not? What happened?"

"Nothing! We didn't do anything."

"What did you see?"

"I don't want to be blamed."

"You're a witness, Jacob, not a suspect. What did you see?"

"Just someone in the truck." His voice got quiet. "I think they were drinking. Cops shouldn't drink in uniform."

"Who was drinking with Officer Thompson?"

"I don't know. It was dark, and they wore a coat with a hood."

Still, the confirmation of a witness was enough to convince him that the investigation was still open. Unless it had been Pete Scully in the truck. But why would Thompson let a drifter into his vehicle? A dark and bizarre scenario eased into his head. Thompson had heart disease and depression. And maybe a drinking problem. Had he hired Scully to take his life? So he died looking like a hero instead of a suicide? It seemed unlike Thompson, but the combination of depression and alcohol could warp people's thinking. The scenario also explained the drag marks and the cash in Scully's backpack.

Jackson pulled into the parking lot at the old North McKenzie hospital, now functioning as an urgent care clinic. Jacob looked out his window at the building. "Henry's in the hospital? I thought he was dead."

Oh god. Jackson reached over and gently touched his shoulder. "Henry is dead. His body is here because this is where they cleaned him up and did the autopsy."

"Oh." The grieving man hung his head.

Jackson parked the car. "Let's go say good-bye to your brother."

CHAPTER 30

Tuesday, November 25, 9:25 a.m.

Sophie opened an email from a woman who'd been sexually assaulted, and braced for another outpouring of rage, frustration, and shame. Nine so far, plus five voice mails. None had mentioned blackmail, and only two victims had officially reported the crime. The others had refused to put themselves through what one described as a "pointless act of a self-inflicted annihilation." Were women becoming more afraid than ever to report a rape? She knew she should be working on the Gateway mall story, but this was too important. How many more victims were out there who hadn't contacted the paper?

Her work cell phone buzzed, and she glanced at the number, not recognizing it. "Sophie Speranza, *Willamette News*."

"This is Octavius Krause. I wanted you to know we're protesting at the police department in a few minutes."

It took a moment to shift gears. Had she met this man? "Are you connected to Willow?"

"We're partners. I'm the cofounder of SIRA. She would want you to be there today."

"How is Willow?"

"The same. Still unconscious, but stable."

Sophie vowed to get out to the hospital and see the activist as soon as she woke up. "What's the focus of your protest?"

"Same issue, police abuse of the homeless. We want the officers disciplined or fired. It's a nationwide problem, especially for people who are mentally ill."

"I'll meet you there, and we'll talk more."

Sophie hurried out to her Scion without telling her supervisor. The protest was just as important to cover as the sexual predator. But why was it all happening now, as she was being pushed off the crime beat? She hoped the newspaper would run her stories anyway . . . and not fire her.

On the drive to the police department, she called the photographer and told him about the protest.

"I thought you were off the crime beat," Brian said.

"I am. But I can't walk away from this one. Can you make it down here?"

"No, I have a zillion photos to process from the school shooting."

One student had died, and three more had been wounded. "Heartbreaking story. I hope I never have to cover one."

"I'm still shaking. Gotta go." He hung up.

• • •

The crowd in the parking lot of the police department surprised her. She was forced to park across the street at the golf club and walk over. A quick visual survey revealed that about half the crowd was probably not homeless, just good-hearted support for fellow citizens. She took photos, then went inside the packed lobby. The group inside looked more like street people, but they were younger and more coherent than most of the men she saw on street corners with signs. Her respect for Willow and Octavius jumped a notch. Organizing and motivating homeless people had to be challenging. Getting this many out here on such a cold day was a small miracle. Had SIRA brought them in buses or vans?

A young man spotted her taking notes and approached. He had shoulder-length hair, a beard, and a long overcoat, making her think of someone from *The Matrix*. "I'm Octavius Krause. Thanks for coming."

He answered a few questions, then spun toward the front when the crowd got quiet. Jackson, standing on a chair near the counter, addressed the crowd. Octavius rushed forward to respond to the detective, who promised there would be changes in the department. Sophie scribbled notes as fast as she could, doubtful that Jackson had any real authority on the issue. But he also promised to personally help Jacob Walsh, a gesture she found touching and believable.

A big woman in a dark jacket took the chair next and announced that Willow would make a full recovery. It was good to hear, but again, Sophie was skeptical. The woman also pleaded with the crowd to leave so law enforcement could do their jobs. The crowd responded and started breaking up. Relieved, Sophie tucked her yellow tablet back into her oversize bag. She really wanted to get back to her computer, continue connecting online, and find the profile the perp was hiding behind. She'd created a new profile on both Facebook and Twitter at home the night before, listing her name as Sophie Lynn and her background as a high school student. She sent out dozens of friend invitations on Facebook and started following local high school students on Twitter. She was making progress, but she needed support from someone inside the social circle. Maybe Ashley's mother would help her.

. . .

Ninety minutes later, Sophie parked in front of the Andrade house, cursing the snow. *Damn!* The weather wasn't supposed to get like this until January or February. But after a few days of it, she'd learned to dress in pants for work and kept extra clothes and boots in the car. She liked to be prepared. She grabbed her red leather bag, climbed out of her car, and carefully made her way up the stone walkway. She'd learned Mara's name after a series of phone calls. Mrs. Devonshire, the mother of the suicide victim, had been reluctant to talk at first, but her anger had finally driven her to complain about Ashley's friends and their bad influence on her daughter. Afterward, Sophie had texted Ashley's friend Anna Sorenson, who'd eventually connected with her online, told her about the parties, and given her a list of names. At the top was Mara Andrade, who was rumored to have been assaulted in the spring. Another call, and the young woman had agreed to tell her story if Sophie used a pseudonym.

She rang the doorbell and was surprised when an older man greeted her. "Sophie? I'm John Andrade, Mara's father. Come in."

He led her to a family room in the back of the house with a view of the river.

"Mara had second thoughts about talking to you, but she said I could speak for her."

Well, hell. She could have done this over the phone. "I'm disappointed, but thank you for standing in."

The father's eyes were sad. "Mara went over the whole incident with a detective recently, and it left her shaken. She agreed to speak with you, but then she regretted it."

"I understand." Sophie took out her notepad and recorder, determined to get a quote or some backstory she could use. "Tell me what happened."

Mr. Andrade took his time and gave a full account of the party, the sexual assault, and the follow-up blackmail, giving much more detail than Detective Schakowski had provided. When he mentioned a police officer breaking up the party, Sophie recalled Schak's reaction to the college student's account of being pulled over. A rush of adrenaline made her hand shake as she wrote: *Cop as predator?*

But Mr. Andrade was not the person to question about it. "How is Mara handling things?" she asked, forcing herself to focus on the victim. "Is she getting counseling?"

"She did, and it was helpful, especially after the abortion. But she's moved past it now. Mara's planning to attend community college next term and eventually become a counselor."

"I'm glad Mara is doing well. At least she's here in Oregon, where they don't force women to have their rapist's baby."

Mr. Andrade nodded sadly. "We probably should have called the police instead of paying the blackmail, but Mara wanted it to be over."

"Didn't you worry that he would come back for more money?"

"We considered it, then decided the criminal wouldn't want to take the risk again."

She understood the unspoken background thought. "Because there are so many potential victims? Because he enjoys the assaults and would likely move on to another young girl?"

He stiffened and scooted his chair back. "We didn't really consider that."

Sophie couldn't bring herself to apologize for the comment. That was why rapists often got away with their crimes. She now knew how much victims dreaded talking to authorities. But their parents should know better. "How do you feel about the police department? Is that part of why you didn't report the assault at the time?"

"We were mostly concerned that the predator would make good on his promise to release the video if we called the police."

"But how would he know?"

"We worried he was watching the house and would see."

"Why not report it after you paid him?"

"Because he still had the video. And we were never optimistic the police would catch the pervert." Andrade stood. "I need to get back to work. You should have plenty for your story."

Sophie stood too, wondering what he did at home to make enough money to afford the house. "Thank you. Can I call if I need clarification?"

"If you must."

• • •

Ten minutes after she returned to the newspaper, her boss stepped into her cube. "What are you working on? I'm supposed to keep an eye on you."

She hated to lie to him. There was no point if she planned to turn in the copy anyway. "The sexual predator story. There are more victims."

"It's not your beat." Hoogstad clenched his fists, but she knew his frustration wasn't directed at her.

"One of the victims is from Springfield." Not exactly the truth, but she needed to give him an out.

Her boss let out a sigh. "What have you got that's new?"

It was too soon to mention the possibility of a police officer's involvement, whether he was phony or not. "I found the victims' connections online, and I'm hoping to uncover the predator's profile."

"Be careful." After a pause, he grinned. "I just heard you're a finalist for the Northwest Journalism award for your story about the eco-terrorist."

Hot damn! "Will a win keep me on this beat?"

"It might." He lowered his voice to a whisper. "Other newspapers cover the awards. If you're interviewed by, say, the *Oregonian*, and it becomes news that you're being railroaded out of your crime beat . . ." His voice trailed off.

The glimmer of hope made her smile. But she knew better than to hang on to it. Other reporters who'd been with the newspaper for twenty-plus years had been forced out. Her salary wasn't in the same bracket though, so maybe management could afford to keep her for a while.

"For the record, as far as I know, you're working on a Springfield-based story and training the intern." Hoogstad nodded and left, without the least bit of shame for covering his own ass. She didn't blame him.

Sophie turned back to her computer and continued friending every young person connected to Anna Sorenson and commenting on her new friends' posts. Later, she took a break from writing to check back and discovered that two more students had accepted her on Facebook and Twitter. Taylor Crenshaw and Kelsey Walker. She sent a friendly message to both, knowing it could take time to earn their trust. She suspected Anna Sorenson had paved the way. The girl seemed eager to help find the predator, as well as excited to be involved.

Sophie kept friending people, posting comments, and working her way in. Her stomach growled, and she heated a cup of instant miso soup in the microwave. When she sat back down, her Facebook notification pinged and a dialogue box opened. Kelsey Walker had messaged her: *Hey, I like your hair. What brand and color do you use?*

The comment made her smile. She'd uploaded a photo of herself from college, but she still looked much the same. Or so she told herself. She keyed back: *Thanks. It's my natural color. Lucky me.*

Kelsey messaged again: *It must be nice not to have to pay a stylist for color every six weeks.*

Yeah, right. Like she could afford that. She keyed in: *Not on my allowance. My parents—*

Sophie stopped mid-thought. A rush of excitement filled her belly. Had Kelsey steered the conversation toward money on purpose? What if she/he was the perp and was trying to scope out whether her parents were loaded enough to pay the blackmail? She'd used Riverside High School in her profile, so it was easy to assume her parents were at least upper-middle class. She recast her message: *My parents can afford it, but they're saving up for me to attend an out-of-state college. If I get in.*

She sat back and ate some soup to keep busy while she waited for a response.

From Kelsey: *What's your fav?*

Sophie replied: *Stanford.* It was true. She'd settled on the UO because she'd goofed off too much in high school to get her GPA above 3.7. She added: *Too bad it's not really a party school. :(*

Kelsey took the bait: *I know it's only Tuesday, but I'm in the mood to suck down some blueberry vodka, maybe chill on some benzos. Let's get a party going.*

Great idea. Your place?

Ha! As if my parents didn't exist. If you can find a house, I'll round up the partiers.

I'll get on it.

Pulse humming, Sophie stepped out of her cube to pace the landing. Could she pull this off? She knew a couple people who might loan out their houses for a party. One being Gabe, the guy she was dating. But the young age of some of the attendees was a problem, both morally and legally. Maybe Zee or Anna Sorenson would have better luck finding someone who would throw a party and not care if teenage girls came. If she did manage to get it set up, she would have to contact Detective Schakowski.

What if Kelsey wasn't a scammer or a predator? She had no way of knowing or checking. Would the police be able to? Would a hacker? She knew a guy with hacking skills.

Sophie went back to her desk and called Zee, whom she hadn't talked to since she went to Corvallis to cover the shooting. The intern didn't answer, so she texted Anna. First, they needed a big house with a casual owner or landlord. Once they had the party rolling, Sophie would try to bait Kelsey into revealing more. Schak wouldn't take her seriously unless they had a solid reason to think Kelsey might be the predator.

CHAPTER 31

Tuesday, November 25, 1:05 p.m.

Schak watched the last of the protestors leave the department. Didn't any of these people have jobs? That was always his first thought when he saw groups gathering, regardless of their politics. It was too bad Sidney Willow had ended up in the hospital, but Officer Garcia had probably just been doing his job. Schak hoped he didn't get fired just to appease the Citizens' Review Board. He was glad not to be a patrol cop. They walked such a fine line between maintaining control and using excessive force. In the heat of the moment, it could be hard to tell the difference.

Time to find Gene Burns. Relieved to have another focus besides the social interactions of his teenage victims and witnesses, Schak headed to his desk to check email and update his case notes before shifting gears. A call to Parole and Probation connected him to Gene Burns' PO, who gave him the ex-con's phone number and address and asked to be notified if anyone found him. Schak called the number on the off chance that Burns would be stupid or cocky enough to meet with him voluntarily, but his service had been disconnected. He might as well drive over and grab some lunch on the way. Food always made him think about his wife, a great cook who spoiled him. Tracy was still at her friend's house, and he'd woken up alone that morning for the first time in twenty-six years. Schak called her for the third time since she'd left, and again she didn't answer. He left another message, this one more desperate: "I love you. I miss you. I can't do this without you. As soon as I arrest this perp, I'll start going to AA meetings. Please come home."

He pulled on his overcoat and grabbed his carryall, the weight causing a familiar twinge in his lower back. Was it time for his monthly chiropractor appointment? He'd been going since his patrol days, when he carried twenty pounds of equipment around his waist. Law enforcement was hard on the body and the soul. How was he supposed to *not* have a drink at the end of the day? The thought terrified him.

He pulled on a knit cap as he crossed the parking lot, not caring that it didn't look professional. His crew cut didn't keep his head warm, and the snow kept starting and stopping, keeping everyone on edge. The drive to Burns' apartment took less than ten minutes, even with slow-moving, snow-scared drivers. The ex-con lived in the new Sponsors complex, charity-based housing that helped people transition from jail or rehab into the real world. Burns had failed, despite the support system. Some people just weren't right in the head. Schak hoped to help put the ex-con back where he belonged.

Surprised by how well kept the property was—considering its location at Four Corners, a.k.a. meth central—Schak parked and climbed up to apartment sixteen. Pounding on the door didn't produce a response, so he tried the knob just to check. Locked.

He knocked again then went in search of the manager. An older man with permanent worry lines, the manager refused to open Burns' apartment for legal reasons but assured Schak that the tenant hadn't been around for days. Schak gave him a card and asked him to call if he saw the ex-con. Where else would he be? His thought earlier about who had posted the bail echoed in his head: Burns' mother or his girlfriend. He called the PO, who didn't have information for either. On impulse, Schak decided to stop by Trisha Weber's place.

In his car, he dug out Jackson's printout of case notes and found her address. Trisha might be at work at the clinic, but Burns could be holed up at her place, running his predator scam from her computer right now. With the ex-con facing arson charges, would he try to score another blackmail payment, then take the money and run?

. . .

Trisha Weber lived in a small cottage on a panhandle lot, about a half mile from the Sponsors complex. Schak pulled down the long driveway and parked between the fences bordering it. Neither of the two vehicles in front of the house was going anywhere until he moved his car. One was the red Toyota that had been burned, and the other, an old Ford Escort. He glanced in the Escort as he passed. No weapon on display and no packed bags.

Trisha opened the door as he approached. "Hey, Schak."

She seemed older and less pretty than he remembered from the one time they'd met at a family dinner. She'd lost Danny too, he reminded himself. But he didn't trust her. "I'm looking for Gene Burns. Is he here?"

She shook her head. "I'm done with him."

"Then who's driving the Escort?"

"I am. Gene trashed my car, so I bought something cheap to get me by." She stood in the half-open door, wearing leggings and a bulky sweater, and didn't invite him in.

What was she hiding? "Can I come in for a minute? I want to talk about Danny."

A flash of fear in her eyes. "Now is not a good time. I've got to get ready for work."

A door closed softly inside the house.

Liar! "I just need a minute of your time, and it's too cold to stand out here." He stepped toward her.

She didn't budge. "I've got to go." She started to close the door.

Schak grabbed the door, bracing to have his hand slammed. "Get back!"

Trisha froze and gave him the stink eye. "Just leave. It's not what you think."

"I think your ex killed Danny, and if you don't get the hell out of my way, I'll cuff you and charge you with obstruction."

Trisha finally stepped back and opened the door, shouting over her shoulder, "He's here, but you're wrong about Gene!"

The betrayal burned him, and Schak charged into the house. "You screwed your ex three days after Danny was killed? Two days after Burns torched your car? What the hell is wrong with you?"

"Don't judge me." Trisha burst into tears. "And don't judge Gene. He's changed."

Schak wanted to laugh, but it would have hurt his already tight chest. He shook his head. "You go from dating a criminal to dating a cop then back to the scumbag? Can't you make up your mind?"

She shrugged. "Cops are bad boys too. They just get away with it."

Burns waltzed through a door near the kitchen. Schak yelled, "Hands in the air!" Itching to pull his weapon, he reached for his cuffs instead.

"Why?" Burns pretended to be casual. "I'm out on bail, and Trisha isn't going to press charges."

Idiot. "Get 'em up! This isn't about arson. It's about murder, sexual assault, and blackmail."

"What the hell are you talking about?" Burns put on a good show of innocence as he raised his arms.

Schak moved toward him. "Turn around. Now!"

Trisha rushed up, looking worried for the first time. "What sexual assault and blackmail? I thought this was about Danny. Gene has an alibi for that night."

"Quiet!" Schak took another step toward the suspect, wishing he had his Taser handy.

"Are you arresting me?"

"I'm taking you in for questioning."

Burns' face registered relief, and he finally complied. "You're wasting your time."

Schak cuffed him, read him his rights, then turned to Trisha. "Don't come to Danny's funeral. You're not welcome." She started crying when he led the suspect out the door.

On the drive to the department, his phone rang on the dashboard. He usually used the speaker function, but he had Burns in the backseat, so he put his earpiece in. He hoped it was Jackson. "Schakowski."

"It's Sophie Speranza. I wanted to update you on my progress."

"Go ahead, but I might have the suspect in custody."

"Oh." She sounded disappointed. "I've got a party rolling for tonight with all the players."

Sophie was setting up for a sting. A surge of excitement jangled his nerves. He hadn't felt that in a long time.

She continued. "And I invited a profile that could be the predator."

"What profile?"

"Kelsey Walker."

Interesting that she'd come up with it too. "We're watching that profile already."

"Great minds and all." Sophie gave a nervous laugh. "What happens if the Kelsey profile stays active while your suspect is in custody?"

Good question. "As I said, we're monitoring the situation. But text me with the location of the party." Just in case they were wrong about Burns. The man almost seemed too stupid to run a blackmail scheme. But Schak would hold him for as long as they needed to. The prick had threatened Danny, then fucked his girlfriend. He could sweat about murder charges for a while.

"I interviewed Mara Andrade's father this morning," Sophie said. "He never thought the police could catch the guy."

"He's wrong. We'll get him." Schak started to hang up. "Hey, don't do anything stupid at the party. Stay sober and alert."

"I plan to. Will you be there? I mean, as a backup?"

"Of course." Before that, he had to see a judge about subpoenas and call Mara's father to get the name of the officer. Schak hoped like hell it wasn't Quince.

$$\cdot \quad \cdot \quad \cdot$$

At the department, he put Gene Burns in an interrogation room, leaving him cuffed, then went to round up some coffee. He stopped by his desk to call Mr. Andrade. Mara's father didn't answer, so he left a voice mail, then checked his email. A message from Agent Ward at the FBI: *I found another perp in Washington who loosely fits your profile. He wore a security officer's uniform and lured young girls from shopping mall parking lots, then drugged and raped them. He was never caught and could be operating in Oregon now.*

Oh hell. He didn't need another suspect. He needed search warrants and evidence. Or a confession would be nice. Schak responded and thanked Agent Ward, then checked Jackson's cube. His partner had his feet up and his eyes closed. Was he sleeping? Jackson's eyes popped open and he sat up, looking embarrassed. "I was processing information, hoping for a breakthrough on this case."

"Sure you were."

"I had a strange thought." Jackson stood to look him in the eye. "Your cousin had a heart condition."

"So do I. It runs in the family. I think that's why my aunt became a heart surgeon."

"He also had a drinking problem."

Schak stiffened. "So?" *Why was he drawing this out?*

"Trisha Weber told me he was depressed too, and he had the prescription for it. What if he was burnt out? And didn't want to live? What if he wanted to kill himself and not have it look like a suicide?"

"What the hell are you saying?" The idea was crazy. Yet, he remembered Danny talking about suicide when he was thirteen and still reeling from the guilt of putting Kurt in a wheelchair. But that was long ago, and his cousin had made peace with himself.

Jackson shrugged. "It's just a thought. The drifter who had Thompson's gun also had cash, and the twins both saw someone in the truck with Thompson after he finished handing out blankets."

"How could he trust someone like that to follow through? And why would the drifter kill himself afterward and not spend the money?"

"Good points." Jackson changed the subject. "Did you find Burns?"

"He's in the interrogation room. Want to join us?"

"Sure."

On the way downstairs, Jackson asked, "When was the first girl assaulted?"

"Mid-May."

"Burns went to jail in June, then was released three weeks ago, right before the second assault and blackmail. The timing fits for those two cases."

Schak stopped in front of the interrogation rooms. "Sophie already pinpointed the Kelsey Walker profile as a possibility too. We have to see if the profile stays active while we have Burns in custody. Who's monitoring it now?"

"Evans."

Schak called her, knowing she was probably right upstairs, and put her on speaker. "Hey, are you watching the Kelsey profile?"

"Yep. Earlier, Kelsey invited a bunch of people to a party this evening. Then the profile went quiet for a while. I'm working on a subpoena for Facebook to see if we can get the profile's location."

"Thanks. We're interrogating Burns, then I'll pick up the subpoena and go see the judge. Stay on the profile, please." Schak hung up.

"Is the perp trolling for his next victim?" Jackson's eyes sparked with intensity.

"Seems likely. If he's desperate for the money, he'll try again." Schak decided to give Jackson the whole story. "Sophie set up the party, and she plans to be there."

"Why am I not surprised?" Jackson looked worried. "It's a long shot, but we need to be outside that party, in our cars, ready for anything."

Doubt flooded Schak. Did he have the wrong man in the interrogation room? They would know soon enough. "If the Kelsey profile stays active while Burns is in the hole, we'll focus on our other suspects. But let's hold him as long as we can. I hate the prick."

CHAPTER 32

Tuesday, November 25, 3:45 p.m.

Gene Burns' second interrogation was over quickly. He denied everything, including owning a computer, then asked for a lawyer. They let him make the call, then put him back in the hole.

"What do you think?" Jackson asked, as he and Schak climbed the stairs.

"He may not be smart enough to pull off the blackmail and money drop. But I still want to search his apartment and see if he has a computer. Or a blue uniform."

Jackson stopped before they entered the Violent Crimes workspace and kept his voice low. "We need to monitor the Kelsey Walker profile even when Quince is supposed to be watching. If his report matches what we see, it could be the best way to clear him."

"Unless we're wrong about the profile." Schak rubbed his head. "I still need to find Daren Sorenson. He's the nineteen-year-old who used to attend Riverside and was expelled for groping girls."

The age seemed wrong. "Nineteen is young for blackmail, and it doesn't match the age the witnesses gave for the officer who broke up the parties."

"Maybe the cop isn't involved. You know the department has been cracking down on campus drinking."

"I hope you're right. How can I help?" Jackson offered.

"I've got an ATL out on Sorenson, but we may have to check all his friends' homes."

Jackson realized he hadn't followed up on his list of witnesses. The homeless protest and his search for Jacob had eaten up most of the day. He looked at his notes from that morning. "I'll drive over to the house shared by Tristan Channing and Alex Crenshaw. They hosted the first party, the one Mara attended."

"Call Sorenson's mother again. She probably knows exactly where he is." Schak started for his office.

"What about Burns?"

"We can leave him for a while." His partner gave a sheepish grin. "Unless you want to take him to jail."

Jackson didn't see the point. "I'll pass. I've got plenty to do." He went to his desk to check his notes. There were still a few things he'd planned to follow up on from Pete Scully's death scene. But the distractions and merging cases had sidelined it. *The prescription.* He wanted to know who'd written it. The faded and worn label would make tracking the information challenging, but he had to try. He pulled the small plastic container out of his carryall, used his cell phone to take a close-up of the label, and sent the photo to Jasmine Parker at the lab. The prescription had a retail number that was still visible and a blue-and-white background that might be associated with a particular pharmacy. Jasmine might even recognize it. If not, he would call pharmacies in the evening, on his own time.

The other unfinished item was Thompson's recorder. He hadn't had time to listen to all the personal files yet. But they would have to wait. A sexual predator was out there, potentially preparing to victimize another young girl and her family. That investigation had to come first. Jackson pulled up the ATL on Daren Sorenson to check his photo. An attractive young man with dirty-blond hair, wide-spaced hazel eyes, and perfect teeth. He printed the image, tucked the paper into his notebook, and headed out.

. . .

The house shared by the two young men was in the university area near the corner of Eighteenth and Patterson. A small ugly bungalow with a sagging front porch. It was only a matter of time before the owner sold the property to the development company that was tearing down all the rental houses in the area to build student apartment complexes. Two cars were in the driveway, and there was nowhere to park on the street. Jackson went around the corner and left his sedan in a nearby apartment complex, ignoring the tow-away sign. He walked back to the gray house and noticed a one-foot-tall snowman in the front yard. The occupants had spent a lot of time gathering up yesterday's light dusting of snow to create it. Young people with lots of free time. He'd forgotten what that felt like.

Music vibrated through the walls and annoyed him before he reached the door. Would they even hear his knock? He pounded hard and called out, "Answer the door!" No need to alert them to his law enforcement status.

A minute later, the door flew open, and a tall young man looked him over. "What do you want?"

Jackson showed his badge and gave his name, shouting over the music. "Are you Tristan or Alex?"

"Alex. Why?"

Jackson barely heard him. "Turn the music down, please."

Alex Crenshaw signaled to someone inside the house, and the volume went down a notch.

"May I come in? I want to talk about a party you held May seventeenth."

The young man laughed. "We've had a lot of parties, and May was an eternity ago."

"This one was significant. I'd like to question your roommate too." Jackson stepped forward. Crenshaw seemed to weigh his options, then finally let Jackson in. With all the blinds closed, the house was dark, and it reeked of dirty socks and stale beer. Two young men sat on the couch playing video games. One matched the picture he'd just printed and stuck in his notepad.

He stepped toward him. "Daren Sorenson?"

He looked up, then cursed, his face twisted in anger and fear. "Yeah, so?"

"We need to talk about Ashley Devonshire." Jackson pulled out his phone, speed-dialed Schak, and hit the speaker button, keeping his eyes on the suspect.

"I heard what happened," Sorenson said. "But it wasn't about me."

Schak answered. "What's going on?"

"I've got three witnesses, including Daren Sorenson. I could use some help."

"Will do."

They both hung up. Jackson focused on Sorenson. "Did you attend a party here on May seventeenth?"

Sorenson scoffed. "I don't know—that was months ago."

Jackson shifted his gaze to the other young man on the couch. "Tristan Channing?"

"Yes, sir." Half-respectful, half-mocking.

"Do you remember the party on that day?"

"Of course. It was my birthday. Thus, the party." He grinned, but his eyes were nervous.

"Was your friend Daren in attendance?" He nodded at the suspect.

"Sure. So was Alex and about fifty other people."

"Who did Daren leave with?"

Channing rolled his eyes. "Now you're asking too much. It was my twenty-first birthday, and I was blasted. I don't remember anyone leaving."

"What about Mara Andrade? Did you see her?"

The name drew a lascivious smile. "She is unforgettable."

"Who did she leave with?"

His face went blank. "Uh, I really don't know. She was here until the cop came, but I didn't see her after that."

"Didn't the party break up after the officer intervened?"

Another incredulous look. "Hell no. We sent the minors home, turned down the music, and kept right on partying."

Crenshaw, still standing next to him, asked, "What's going on? Why do you care about that party?"

Jackson focused on him. "Did you see Mara leave?"

"Yeah. She went out with another high school girl when the cop made them step outside."

Finally. A witness who saw a victim with an officer right before the assault. "What did he look like?"

Crenshaw shook his head. "I'm not sure. I just saw the uniform and the badge and got a little panicked. But he seemed average, you know. Not real tall. Not short and fat. Nothing I would remember."

"What color was the uniform?" Jackson still hoped he wasn't one of their own.

"Dark blue."

Loud pounding on the door. "It's my partner. Let him in."

Crenshaw complied, and Schak bustled in. "There you are, you little shit." He strode straight for Sorenson. "Get up. We're going to the department."

Jackson felt a little sorry for the young man. Schak's grief seemed to have moved to the anger stage already. "We just want to ask some questions. Cooperation will work in your favor."

"About what?"

"Ashley Devonshire," Schak said. "You heard me talking to your sister about her the other day. You know she was sexually assaulted."

Sorenson put up his hands. "Hey, I didn't do that. I'm good with girls, you know?"

Schak took Sorenson's elbow. "You were kicked out of Riverside for groping them. This is your chance to explain."

"That was high school," Sorenson whined. "I grabbed a couple girls' butts. I didn't know it was a big deal." He grudgingly walked out with Schak.

Jackson decided he'd learned all he could from the roommates. He would follow Schak to the department and sit in on Sorenson's interrogation. His partner had almost punched Gene Burns during his questioning—something he'd never seen from Schak before—and Jackson didn't want anything to happen to their young suspect. Now that Thompson's death seemed linked to the assaults, Schak was emotionally engaged with the investigation, and it was worrisome. Approaching his partner about the subject wouldn't be easy.

On the drive back, his daughter's ring tone buzzed in his pocket. Jackson touched his earpiece to answer. "Hey, Katie. What's up?"

"I'm bleeding. I think I need to go to the hospital."

CHAPTER 33

Tuesday, November 25, 5:30 p.m.

Schak wanted to leave Daren Sorenson in the hole while he grabbed a quick meal, but he decided this one had to be handled delicately. He didn't want the kid to feel like he was in custody, and he didn't want to stir up any parental indignation. At the last moment, he changed direction and took Sorenson to the soft interrogation room they usually reserved for minors and witnesses.

"Have a seat." He gestured at the overstuffed brown couch. "I'm going to get some coffee. Want some?"

"Bottled water would be good."

Right. As if they kept a stocked refrigerator of it. Schak hurried to the break room and rounded up a cup of burned coffee for himself and a plastic cup of tap water for his suspect. When he returned, Sorenson was stretched out on the couch. What the hell? Didn't this kid realize what kind of trouble he could be in? Was he a sociopath who didn't experience the same fears and social concerns as everyone else, or was he innocent? Schak remembered another kid, a fifteen-year-old boy who'd fallen asleep during questioning about vehicular manslaughter. Later he'd mentioned it to his wife, who worked as a counselor, and she'd claimed some people sleep to avoid stress.

He walked over to the couch. "Sit up and let's get started. I'm going to record." Schak clicked on his device.

The boy sprang up, looking wide-awake. Schak handed him the plastic cup. "It's all we have."

Sorenson set it on the floor. "How long am I gonna be here?"

"That depends on how much you cooperate. Where were you last Wednesday, November nineteenth, between eight p.m. and midnight?"

"Tristan Channing's party. But you knew that."

"Did you talk to Ashley Devonshire?"

"I don't know. It was crowded. I talked to a lot of people."

The kid was lying. So Schak would lie too. "Strike one. Witnesses say you hung out with Ashley. Why did you lie about it?"

"Because I didn't assault her, and I don't want to go to jail." Annoyed and defensive.

All at once, Schak realized why the kid might lie. Why he'd snuck out of his house before Schak could question him. "How well did you know Ashley?"

"We were good friends."

"People tell me you were friends with benefits. Did you have a sexual relationship with Ashley?"

For a long moment, Sorenson's eyes jumped around while he tried to make up his mind. Finally, the kid cried out, "Please don't charge me with rape. I know she's sixteen. But so what? I'm only nineteen. The sex was consensual."

Barely. Yet because the teenagers were only two and a half years apart, the DA wouldn't prosecute him. Oregon law had more compassion and common sense than other states. But Sorenson didn't know that. "It's called statutory rape. Tell me what happened that night." Schak still wanted to nail him for the blackmail. The greedy little shit.

"Nothing happened. We weren't a couple, and we hadn't hooked up in weeks. She was with some other guy at the party."

Schak wasn't sure if he believed him. "Which guy?"

"I don't know him, but his name might be Chris. Ask Tristan."

"What does this guy look like?"

"Shorter than me. Maybe five-eight. Dark straight hair. You know, like an Asian, but maybe mixed race."

Schak jotted it all down. "What time did you get home from the party?"

"I stayed over. I was too drunk to drive."

"Will your friends swear in court at risk of perjury that you never left the party house that evening?"

He swallowed hard. "I think so."

Schak's phone rang. He hated to be interrupted during an interrogation, but with the Kelsey profile and party sting pending, he felt he had to check. He pulled out his cell: *Evans.* He stood and stepped out. "What have you got?"

"The Kelsey profile is suddenly active again and chatting with people about the party. I know you're interrogating someone, and I thought you should know."

So they were either wrong about the profile or wrong about Burns and Sorenson. There was a third possibility. "Have you heard from Quince?"

"No, but I left him a message about our meeting so he wouldn't be worried."

"Do you have the subpoena ready?"

"Yes."

"Will you take it to Judge Cranston at his home? Tell him a teenager's life is at stake."

"I can't. The SWAT unit was just called to an armed stand-off. I missed the last rollout for the downtown protest because Lammers called me out to the second crime scene. I can't give Bruckner an excuse to cut me from the team."

She was the only female SWAT member, and he admired her ambition, courage, and energy. But Evans needed to make up her mind. Detectives couldn't be called off their duties the same way patrol officers could. But it wasn't his responsibility to tell her that. "I'll pick it up and run out there myself. The party won't get going until eight or so."

"I'm sorry, Schak."

"It's no problem." He hung up. But it was a problem. With Quince as their last viable suspect, someone else had to monitor the Kelsey profile. He couldn't do it. The subpoenas were critical to locating the predator, and he had to sit watch in the party house neighborhood. That left Jackson. He called, but his partner didn't answer, which was unusual. Schak left a message, updating him and asking for help. Quince didn't answer either. The uneasy feeling in his gut deepened.

• • •

Schak stopped for a burger at a fast food place on the way. The first bite triggered an intense longing for a beer to wash it down with. He told himself the beer craving was about the flavor and the need to settle his stomach, but the tension in his arms gripping the wheel told a different story. He carried a lot of stress, and his body liked the after-work wind down. During the first few days of a homicide investigation, when he worked long hours, the time usually flew by, and he didn't think about alcohol until he got home. Knowing he had to quit was making him crave it all the time now. *Life was a bitch, and then you died.*

He ate in the car and dripped ketchup on his white shirt. *Hell!* Right before seeing the judge too. Not that it should matter. He'd called before he left the building, and Cranston was expecting him. The judge hadn't promised he would sign, just that he would read the subpoenas. Schak felt optimistic. Cranston had daughters and little sympathy for men with histories of violence toward women.

The climb up Chambers—with traffic crawling slowly in the dark on a slick road—was excruciating. Tempted to use his siren, he made calls instead. First Tracy, then Jackson again. Neither answered. Once he crested the hill and made his way to Blanton Road, he was able to pick up speed but couldn't relax. He parked in Cranston's driveway and climbed out, trying to shake off his tension. But a sense of urgency gripped him, and tremors ran through his hands as he walked up the stone steps.

Cranston, an older man with a year-round tan, opened the door, shook his hand, and led him to a study.

"I'm not sure why this couldn't wait until tomorrow," the judge said, taking a seat at his desk. "Social media companies are notoriously slow to respond to user-information requests."

"I've already talked to the person who handles these things. She said she would release the information as soon as I sent her a subpoena."

"Let me read it then." Cranston reached for the stack of papers. "Sit down, please. You're making me tense."

Schak didn't want to sit. Or wait. But he had to settle himself. Staking out the party meant sitting in his car for hours. He regretted his last cup of coffee.

"Have a snifter of cognac." The judge gestured to a service table with a variety of liquor bottles.

Why not? It would calm him down for the long stakeout. "Thanks. Do you have bourbon?" He didn't care for liqueurs. Too sweet.

"In the big decanter." Cranston didn't look up.

Schak scooted to the bar, picked up a shot glass, and poured from the decanter in front. He downed the bourbon, feeling the heat almost instantly. The allover softening came moments later. God, that hit the spot. He took a seat on the leather couch, leaned back, and tried to relax. His phone rang a moment later: *Jackson.*

Schak took the call, getting to his feet. "Hey, partner, where are you?" He hurried out of Cranston's office and stood in the hall.

"I'm at the hospital. Katie's having a miscarriage."

"Oh damn. Is she okay?" He didn't know the right thing to say. Although, considering her young age, it was probably for the best that she didn't have a baby.

"I think so. She wanted me to wait out in the lobby, so I'll have to check with someone in a while."

Damn! He needed the whole task force on deck tonight, and they were all bailing on him. "Give her my best."

"I got your message, and I'm sorry about the timing. I called Katie's aunt Jan, and she's coming out here. I'll join you as soon as I can."

"You sure? Your daughter needs you." He really needed to shut up and stop being so damn nice. "Do you have your laptop with you?"

"No. Sorry. Katie was bleeding, and I didn't even think about it."

But he wouldn't be alone. Schak let out a chuckle, his first in days. "Not to worry, I've got Sophie on the case."

"Oh brother. She needs her own monitor." Shack heard voices in the background, then Jackson said, "I have to go."

The connection broke, and Schak put away his phone. For any other investigation, he would have called for patrol backup. But if a Eugene officer was their perp, alerting a night-shift patrol cop who worked the university area could be a huge mistake. He could do this by himself. He would borrow a laptop from the tech unit and monitor the Kelsey profile while he sat in his car, staking out the party. No, not without internet, he wouldn't. Their city-issued sedans weren't equipped with wifi access like the patrol cars. It had never been much of a problem until now. But still, he would be in the vicinity, watching the party house. If a man in uniform showed up, he would call the desk officer and try to determine if the guy was with EPD. Schak would wait, watch, and tail the perp if he left with a young girl.

All of which was unlikely. This was a long shot, he reminded himself. Kelsey was probably a high school girl, and the predator was probably someone he hadn't pinpointed yet. The Washington state rapist mentioned by Agent Ward was still on the table. Schak stepped back into the judge's office.

Cranston stared at the fireplace, where phony gas flames burned in a bluish light. The judge grabbed a pen. "I'll sign the Facebook subpoena and the one giving you access to Kelsey Walker's account—because she won't know and won't be harmed in any way if you're wrong. But I can't let you search Gene Burns' apartment. You have no physical evidence connecting him to the assaults or blackmail. As an ex-convict, he's already vulnerable to the overreach of law enforcement."

An ex-con, vulnerable? Cranston had gone soft. "I'm not look-ing to bust him for anything else. I don't care if he has drugs or weapons, and I'll ignore them if he does. I just want to know if he's impersonating an officer to rape young girls." *Who might later kill themselves*, he thought.

"Find a witness who can put him in the vicinity, at least. Sorry." The judge stood and handed him the paperwork. "Good luck. I mean that."

Schak forced himself to say thanks and hurried out. He would stop and fax the subpoena to the legal department at Facebook, then grab a laptop from the tech unit and head for the university area. His luck could change, and he still might catch the perp as he zeroed in on his next victim.

CHAPTER 34

Tuesday, November 25, 7:15 p.m.

Sophie pulled on faded jeans and a tight sweater in forest green, her best color. She reapplied makeup, but there wasn't much she could do with her hair to make herself look younger. Maybe a little glitter? It didn't matter. The sexual predator wasn't likely to target her. She didn't look sixteen, and she didn't plan to get drunk enough to seem vulnerable. Her role would be to watch the young girls who did get shit-faced and let Detective Schakowski know if they left the party with someone who—

She plopped on the bed, realizing she didn't have enough information to be effective. Did Schak have a description of the predator? If so, why hadn't he told her and let her print it? Because he thought the guy was a cop? Women still needed to be warned. Where was her phone?

She found it by her laptop and called the detective. He answered on the second ring, sounding tense. "What's up?"

"Do you have any idea what this guy looks like? I can't be effective if I don't know." She stepped out the door to check the weather. Cold as hell but not snowing. Thank god. She especially hated driving in the stuff at night.

"One description puts him with medium brown hair, late thirties, and good looking."

The age struck her as odd. "He should be easy to spot at the party, if he shows up. This social group seems pretty young." Sophie scrambled to grab her notepad.

Schak was silent.

"What? I need to know everything I can."

"This is off the record, and I'm only telling you for your own safety. But the description matches a police officer who broke up two of this crowd's parties."

He did think it was a cop. Juicy! And scary. "You think the predator is one of your peers?"

"Or maybe he's just wearing one of our uniforms. Or maybe it's a coincidence. We really don't know."

"Two parties, two victims, both had a cop show up. Same description?" She scoffed. "That doesn't sound like a coincidence."

"You have to keep this to yourself."

He was protecting the department. "If we"—she quickly corrected her mistake—"if you don't get the guy tonight, we have to go public with the information. Young girls trust cops, and not knowing that one is dangerous puts them at risk."

"He's probably not a real officer." Schak sounded defensive.

"And my article can say that, but if the predator is wearing a uniform and pretending to be a cop, people need to know." Sophie recalled the victim who'd met with her and Schak. "What about Eden, the college student? She and her friends were stopped by a police officer the night she was assaulted."

"She doesn't fit the profile," he argued. "And EPD has been cracking down on campus parties and underage drinking, so the pattern isn't as clear as it seems."

"You'll be nearby the party tonight, correct?"

"Of course. Is there any update on the Kelsey Walker profile?"

"Nothing recent. Earlier, he or she was inviting people to the party but didn't seem to focus on anyone in particular." Sophie had hoped to see who he/she would target.

"Stay in touch with me," Schak ordered, as if she were one of his minions. "I want to hear from you every fifteen minutes."

"Yes, sir." Another shiver of excitement rippled through her chest, mixed with a little fear. She tried to laugh it off. "If a high school girl named Kelsey walks up to me at the party, I'm going to feel silly."

"Me too. But we think the perp is going to try again soon, so even if Kelsey isn't his profile, he could still strike tonight."

Suddenly, the whole scenario seemed more real. A knot formed in her stomach. The creep could be anywhere in the city, targeting a teenager they'd never heard of. "I'll check the online crowd and see what's new, then head down to campus."

"Thanks, Sophie."

She sat down with her laptop and clicked back to Kelsey's page. The profile was engaged in dialogue with a young woman named Skylar Norton. Reading back through previous posts, Sophie realized they'd started out chatting about the party, then segued into favorite TV shows. She tried to see Skylar's personal information, but the page was private and didn't open. After a few more posts, Kelsey suggested to Skylar that they switch to chat, and the public conversation stopped. *Oh damn.* She would have given anything to know what Kelsey was saying to the young woman. Sophie scrolled back through Kelsey's posts but didn't see anything of interest. She texted Schak: *Kelsey chatting privately with Skylar Norton. Young, pretty, dark hair. No other information.* Time to go. She pulled on her coat and grabbed a red wool cap and gloves. At the last second, she grabbed a blanket in case it snowed while she was out and her car went off the road and she had to keep warm. The thought of walking home made her change into boots. Not exactly pretty party shoes, but she hated being cold.

Sophie's phone rang and she snatched it out of her pocket. *Jasmine Parker.* Again. Did Jaz miss her? Sophie took the call on her earpiece and went out to start her car. "Hey, Jasmine. Good to hear from you."

"The snow made me think about you, and I got worried. Are you okay?"

Her ex-girlfriend did miss her. Did they still have a chance? Sophie went back inside to wait for her car to warm up. "Honestly? I'm stressed. The managing editor called me in yesterday and said I wasn't good enough to work the crime beat. He assigned me to cover Springfield. I'll either quit or get fired very soon."

"That's so sleazy. Is he giving your job to Zee Schrock? I saw her byline this morning on an article about Officer Thompson's death."

Sophie pulled off her coat and sat back down. "She's an intern. She'll cost them half as much and no medical benefits." Sophie decided to give Jasmine—and their relationship—one last chance. "I'm looking for journalism work in other cities. Now that I don't have a reason to stay here."

A pause. "You could become a private detective and stay because it's a great place to live." Jasmine laughed. "Wouldn't Jackson be totally annoyed if you gave him competition?"

The private detective idea intrigued her, but Sophie didn't want to be distracted. "Or you could tell me to stay because we belong together."

A deathly pause. "I love you, but nothing has changed." Jasmine's voice shifted back into business mode. "The reason I called was to tell you about the second death. I noticed the intern's article didn't mention it."

Sophie's pulse quickened. Jackson had mentioned it, but he hadn't given her any details. "What do you know?"

"A homeless man supposedly shot himself with Officer Thompson's gun. He also had his cell phone. So the working theory is that Pete Scully killed Thompson, stole his possessions, then killed himself out of guilt."

Suicide? Weird. Sophie jotted down the name. "But you don't think that's what happened?"

"I'm not a detective, and I don't have the background information. You should call Jackson."

"I will. Thanks." Sophie checked the time and reached for her coat. "I've got to get going. I'm working on another story."

Jasmine laughed again. "You mean there's something happening in Springfield on a Tuesday night?"

"Ha!" Sophie was too tense to joke. "This is the sexual assault investigation. I'm still going to follow the story—even if the paper won't print it."

"This is why I love you. Be careful." Jasmine hung up before she could respond.

Hearing that made her heart sing. But only for a second. If they couldn't be together, it would be easier if Jasmine didn't love her. Now was not the time to think about her love life. Or the murder/suicide story she wasn't supposed to write. She had a sexual predator to help catch.

CHAPTER 35

Jackson paced the ER lobby, his mind jumping back and forth between loyalties. Katie was having a crisis. Her body was rejecting the baby, and she was bleeding badly. He kept seeing the red-stained towel on the seat of the car. Intellectually, he knew she would be okay. No one died from miscarriages, did they? But his heart ached for her. Another lost life, so soon after her mother died. How much could she take? Even though her aunt was coming to provide more support, he knew he should stay.

Yet Schak needed him on the job. Jackson had never failed his partner in thirteen years of working Violent Crimes together. The sexual predator's recent pattern indicated he might strike again soon, and the party tonight was an ideal trolling ground, with all the usual players in attendance. If something went down, he needed to be there. Why hadn't he brought his laptop? *Stupid!* If he had it, he could log into Ashley's Facebook account and monitor the group's activities, especially the Kelsey profile. Assuming the hospital had free wifi.

He stopped by the window and stared into the dark parking lot. At least it wasn't snowing. He called Quince but got no answer. Where the hell was he? Technically, he wasn't obligated to work after hours. None of them were. But that was the expectation of law enforcement. No one was ever really off duty. Investigative work required them to connect with witnesses and suspects whenever and wherever they could. He'd once questioned a man at his middle-of-the-night bakery job, because that was the only time he could pin him down. So Quince's behavior was unusual.

Jackson didn't want to believe his task force member was the predator. But what did he really know about him? They never saw each other outside of work, and Quince hadn't shared anything personal since he'd transferred from the Vice Unit. The thought gave him pause. Working sex crimes could mess with a man's head. Overexposure to unhealthy sexual activity could generate an unwanted sexual response. Had Quince become addicted to sex videos? Or some other predatory behavior?

A woman in blue scrubs approached him. "Mr. Jackson?"

He spun toward her, ready for good news. "Yes. How's Katie?"

"She's fine. The bleeding has stopped, and she's sedated."

He tried not to think about the baby she'd lost, but images kept popping into his head. What did they do with its body? Should they have a service? "I'd like to see her, if only for a moment."

"I'll take you back."

They walked through a maze of short hallways, passing several exam rooms, most of which were empty. Katie slept in a narrow mobile bed, covered by a white blanket. Without makeup or her usual expression of disdain, she looked about twelve. Relief, love, and guilt all washed over him. Relief that she was physically fine, followed by another, more subtle sense that this was for the best—that she wasn't meant to be a mother so young. And guilt for being glad she wasn't pregnant anymore. Katie opened her eyes for a brief moment, saw him standing there, then drifted off again.

Jackson stepped back out of the room. "I should let her rest." He turned to the woman in scrubs. "How long will she sleep?"

"Probably a few hours. We gave her a valium to calm her down."

His ex-wife's sister was in the lobby when he came back. "Jan. Thanks for coming." He hugged her, grateful for her presence in their life. "Katie's in room nineteen. They sedated her, so she may sleep for a few hours. You don't have to be here." It was the right thing to say, but he hoped she would disagree.

"I'll stay. You can take a break or go run an errand." Jan was blonde, soft, and sweet. Unlike her sister, who'd been dark, sharp, and sexy.

"I really should check in with my task force. We've got a sting going down right now."

"Then go. I'll be here when Katie wakes up and call you."

"Thank you."

He walked out the door, then started running. In the car, he called Kera, but she didn't answer. She was probably putting the boys to bed. He left her a message, updating her on Katie's health, while he drove out of the massive parking lot. His next call was to Schak. "What's happening?"

"I'm parked at Seventeenth and Pearl, watching a house that's about three blocks from the one we visited this afternoon. The young people just keep coming. They all look fourteen to me, but that's because I'm old and crotchety."

"Who's watching the Kelsey profile?"

"No one. Quince isn't returning calls. I brought a laptop from work in the hope I'd pick up a wifi connection, but no luck."

"I just left the hospital, and I'm heading to the department." Jackson crossed the empty intersection and drove onto the expressway. "I'll monitor the online activity and keep you posted. If anyone in uniform shows up, call me and I'll be there in a few minutes."

"Do me a favor and check out a girl named Skylar Norton. The Kelsey profile started interacting with her, then took the conversation private."

A pulse of panic. "That's what happened right before Grace Marston was assaulted."

"I know. And Skylar fits his type."

"Text me the name. I'm still driving." He took the Delta exit, only a few minutes from the department now. "Where is Evans?"

"She got called out by SWAT, an armed standoff."

Those situations often lasted hours. Schak had been on his own. "What about Sophie?"

"She's in the party house, texting me occasionally. She gave me the Skylar tip."

Jackson cringed at the idea of having a civilian involved in their sting. But if it had to be anyone, he would have picked Sophie. The reporter had proved to be quick minded with nerves of steel. "Did you see the judge about accessing Kelsey's account?"

"I sent signed docs to Facebook and Dragoo, but I can't get ahold of the tech guy."

"I'll find out what I can and get back to you."

Ten minutes later, he was at his desk, alone in the big building except for a few patrol personnel downstairs. He logged into Ashley Devonshire's Facebook page, uncomfortable with using a dead girl's social media account. No one had posted anything using her profile, and the tech guy had locked her account so it looked silent to her friends, but still, it was creepy. He keyed Kelsey Walker's name into the search bar, and the page loaded. The profile's last public post had been an hour earlier, the final exchange in the conversation with Skylar Norton. He clicked

Skylar's name to see the bigger photo on her home page. Yep, she fit the predator's physical type. But he couldn't access her personal information.

She'd been smart about not sharing those details of her life with everyone online, but if she was being targeted, it worked against her now. But was she? They didn't know who else Kelsey was chatting with privately. Skylar may have been unwilling to engage, and the perp could have moved on to someone else. They needed access to the account. And a lot more time. Had Sophie pushed to set up the party for tonight or had Kelsey? If Kelsey was their perp, and he had been the one to suggest an immediate party, then they were right about him being eager to find and extort his next victim. Jackson scrolled back through Kelsey's postings and saw an exchange with a woman named Sophie Lynn, who looked like a younger version of the reporter. Kelsey had suggested that evening for the party.

Dread growing in his gut, Jackson called Detective Dragoo on his work cell phone. It took seven rings, but the tech specialist finally answered. "Yes?"

"Jackson here. We need your help with the sexual predator case. Can you come in right now?"

"What's going on?"

"We think the predator might strike tonight. We have a warrant that gives us access to the profile we think he's using, and we need you to hack in so we can see private conversations."

"I can try, but these things take time."

"You're coming in?"

"I'll be there soon."

What if they were too late? Just because the perp hadn't been violent in the past didn't mean his deviant behavior wouldn't escalate. A young girl's life could be at stake. Should they have asked Dragoo to hack in without a warrant? Would he have done it?

Jackson searched their database of citizens who'd interacted with the police and only found one Norton. A male, too young to be Skylar's father, and currently in jail. He tried the online phone book and found ten pages of listings for people named Norton. He didn't have time to call all of them asking if they knew Skylar. *Crap!* Who would know how to find her? Someone at her school? A friend, of course. Jackson scrolled through her friends to see who was online. A girl named Beth was the first Eugene friend he came across. How to approach her—from Ashley's profile—without freaking her out? He didn't have time to be anything but direct. He keyed in a private message: *This is Detective Jackson. I need your help to find an online predator. Do you know Skylar Norton's phone number? Or where she lives? Or how I can contact her parents? This is very important.*

He studied the message, worried she would think he was a predator. Asking about Skylar's parents made him seem less so, but it wasn't enough. He added, *Call Sergeant Lammers at the Eugene Police Department to verify my identity*, and tacked on his boss's cell phone number.

After he hit Send, he repeated the message to another of Skylar's friends, then called Schak. "Anything new?"

"Not yet. Sophie hasn't spotted anyone matching the cop's description, and I haven't seen him outside the house. Did you find contact information for Skylar?"

"I'm working on it."

Schak's voice was tight. "If the perp lures her away from the party, instead of coming here, this could go badly."

Jackson feared that too. "You've seen Skylar's photo, right?"

"Yeah, but I'm a half block from the house, it's dark as hell, and these young girls all look the same to me."

"Do we know a patrol officer or two we can absolutely trust for backup?"

"Brad! My son. Why the hell didn't I think of him earlier?"

Jackson hadn't thought of him either. "Brad hasn't been on the force long, that's why. Get him out there, even if he's off duty. I'll call Lammers. I've been giving her number to teenage girls as a reference, so she'll soon be pissed off that we haven't notified her of this sting."

"It came together too quickly to do anything but respond. Plus, we still don't know if Kelsey Walker is anyone but who she claims to be. It's just a hunch. I'm hoping to hear from my contact at Facebook soon."

"I've got Dragoo coming in to hack into her account."

"Excellent news."

They hung up, and Jackson checked his monitor. One of the girls had responded to his message: *U R a cop?*

He typed back, *Yes. Please tell me how to reach Skylar*, then hit Return. He sent another message right away: *Do you know Kelsey Walker? Ever met her in person?*

After a few minutes, the girl responded: *The number you gave doesn't answer, but voice mail message matches. IDK Skylar's number or address but I know someone who might. I'll get back to you.*

IDK meant *I don't know.* He knew that one. Jackson messaged back: *Ask everyone you can think of. I need to know right now!*

He found another friend in Skylar's group who was online. Dustin. Was he really a high school boy with kinky hair and glasses? Could he trust him? Jackson copied and pasted the message he'd sent the girls and tried again.

While he waited for a response, he called Lammers. His boss picked up, sounding sleepy. "What's going on, Jackson?"

"Possibly an arrest. We found a Facebook profile that interacted with a sexual assault victim. We think it's our perp and that he's targeting another victim right now."

"So go get the bastard. Why are you calling me?"

"We need backup. I'm at the department monitoring the profile and trying to locate the girl's contact information. Schak needs you in the field."

"You can't get a patrol officer?" She sounded more worried than irritated now.

"The perp may be a cop, and the sting is going down in what could be his patrol area."

"For fuck's sake." A drawer slammed in the background. "I'll be out the door in three minutes. Where am I going?"

"A party near the UO." He gave her the address. "One more thing. The description of the cop matches Quince, and we can't reach him."

CHAPTER 36

Schak wished he'd pressured Dragoo to help them earlier. But he and Jackson were by-the-book investigators, and he'd worried that if they busted the perp based on information they'd obtained illegally, the pervert would beat the charges. But if they caught him in the act, and the girl could testify . . .

He had to quit thinking about the conviction process. What mattered was catching this guy. Schak shifted in his seat, trying to get comfortable. But his hips hurt from sitting too long, and his toes felt a little numb. He glanced over at the party house. A young couple came out the door, the girl a step ahead. For a fleeting second, they were under the porch light, and he focused on her. Shoulder-length hair, college-aged, and a little overweight. Probably not a potential victim. Schak rolled down his window a few inches anyway, as he'd been doing intermittently, to hear what he could. The girl tripped on the step going down, but the guy caught her and grabbed her ass as he helped her straighten up. They both laughed.

Schak hoped she got home safely. Thank god he'd been born male. Police work had shown him just how bad it could be for women. Social expectations pressured them to look pretty, wear stupid shoes, and hide how smart they were. Men encouraged them to drink, then took advantage of them when they did. Women didn't get to relax and be themselves until they were over forty and didn't give a shit about what men thought anymore. The revelation made him think about Tracy. Was that what was going on with his wife? Had she finally decided she didn't need him— unless he met her terms? He'd been a good husband. Faithful, supportive, and financially responsible. Hell, he even took her dancing sometimes. So he drank a little after work. How could that be a deal breaker?

The pain in his hips and knees drove him to get out of the car and stretch for a moment. He needed to pee too, but that would have to wait. He should have skipped the coffee. *You should have skipped the bourbon too,* his conscience echoed. Schak bent over to stretch his spine, reaching for his toes and not coming close. He heard a car, scrambled to climb into his Impala, and scrunched down in the seat. When he scooted back up, he glanced down the street at the vehicle. Older-model dark-colored sedan, like a detective or undercover officer would drive. Or a fake cop? *Damn.* If Evans were here, she could follow while he watched the house. But if it was the perp, the driver would stay in the area.

He called Brad again. This time his son answered. "Hey, Dad. Are we still cutting wood this weekend?"

"I'm on a stakeout, and I need you as backup." He'd left a message earlier, but his son was bad about accessing his voice mail. No point in mentioning that now.

"I'm not on duty." Brad's tone shifted. "But you sound a little stressed, so I'll get my weapon and get out there."

"Thanks, son." Schak gave him the address. "Watch for a dark sedan, like an undercover vehicle. Mine is parked across the street and halfway down the block, but the other one is on the move."

"You're watching a police officer?" Brad sounded stunned. "Is that why you called me instead of someone on duty?"

"Yes. But he could be a fake cop. Are you in your car yet?" Schak heard the engine start as he spoke.

"I'm on my way. What are my orders?"

"Don't let him out of your sight, and stay in touch." Schak realized Brad needed to know more. "If you see him with a young girl, be ready to move in."

"A sexual predator? Good god."

"He may not be in that sedan. If you don't spot it, keep circling. Our description is mid- or late thirties, six-foot, and good looking."

"You know I'm not in uniform or in my patrol car, right? I won't have a radio."

"I know." A damn shame. But once they had the guy, they could call in patrol backup. "Keep in touch." Schak hung up, leaving his earpiece in. Cell phones had altered the function of his job and made it so much easier. The internet, on the other hand, was a mixed bag.

Six minutes passed with no movement outside the house and no contact with his team. Finally, Sophie texted him: *I haven't met Kelsey. I don't think she/he is at the party.*

That only confirmed their suspicions. If Kelsey were a young woman, she would be at the party she had instigated. He wanted to text back, but it wasn't really in his skill set. His fingers were too damn big, and he hated the process on principal. Yet, he knew it was only a matter of time before he forced himself to learn.

Lammers called a few minutes later. "I'm here, but there's nowhere to park in sight of the house."

Jackson had called in their boss? "Close by is good enough. Keep an eye out for a dark sedan. One cruised past the house about ten minutes ago, but I haven't seen it again."

"Jackson says we're looking for a guy who matches Quince. Have you heard from Quince?" Her deep voice sounded tense.

"No, and he's supposed to be watching the profile."

"Something is going on with him. I got a call recently from the Portland PD, where he'd applied for a job. But you can't repeat it to anyone."

That threw him. Was Quince relocating to get away from his crime scenes or to deal with a personal crisis? "I'm stumped, but we'll know soon enough."

"I'm parked on High Street for the moment, but I'll get moving again soon."

"My son, Officer Brad Schakowski, is with us too. He's in civilian clothes and his personal vehicle, a blue Bronco."

"Good. Between the three of us, we should have him boxed in."

"I hope so." Schak clicked off. The additional backup didn't reassure him the way it should have. Too much time had passed, and he had a growing dread that their perp had outmaneuvered them.

CHAPTER 37

Jackson paced the open area behind his cube and racked his brain for other ways to track Skylar Norton's contact information. He'd googled her and found one mention on the *Willamette News* website from when she'd participated in a fund-raiser for her high school, which he now knew was Spencer. Not Riverside, like two of the victims, but a school in South Eugene with students from middle- and upper-class families. The school office wasn't open, and the newspaper hadn't mentioned her parents' names, so the article hadn't been much help. He rushed back to his computer to check the Facebook chat box he had open. Nothing yet. The Kelsey profile was silent too. Feeling useless, he searched for the school's principal, a name he knew because Katie had attended Spencer. If he could contact the principal, she might be able to access the school's records.

Did Katie know Skylar? It didn't matter. His daughter was unconscious in the ER after a miscarriage. He didn't even want her to know he was working instead of sitting by her side, waiting for her to wake up. She'd never mentioned Skylar anyway. It was a big school with nearly fifteen hundred students.

A soft ping made him glance at the dialogue box. Beth was back with a message. After giving him Skylar's number, she wrote: *She lives on High Street between 39th and 40th, but Jess doesn't know the address. A green, 2-story house.*

Jackson quickly keyed back: *Parents names?*

Beth: *IDK*

Jackson called Skylar's cell phone. It rang eight times, then went to voice mail. He left her a message, stressing the importance of a return call. At the last minute, he added, "Don't go anywhere with a stranger, no matter what he looks like or what he says." Intense enough to make her cautious but vague enough to keep the department off the hook in case they were wrong.

Now what? He couldn't stay at his desk. The Kelsey profile had been inactive for hours, and he hadn't accomplished anything. Schak already had the backup he needed. Jackson strode across the building to the tech area. Dragoo was hunched over a keyboard, glancing at his monitor occasionally.

"Any luck getting into the profile?"

"Not yet." Dragoo looked up and grimaced. "Facebook has decent safeguards, and this profile has little to work with."

Jackson made a decision. "I'm driving over to the home of the potential victim. Call me if you come up with anything." He started to walk away, then turned back. "Call Schak too. He's watching a party house where they all could be."

• • •

Snow fell as he drove up Willamette Street, a now empty thoroughfare that had been clogged with traffic a few hours earlier. He called Schak, nervous about leaving his computer duties. "What's the update?"

"People are coming outside. Some are leaving, and others are just standing in the snow like drunk fools. But I don't see our perp or our victim. Did you find her contact info?"

"Yeah, and I called, but she doesn't answer. So I'm driving up to Skylar's house."

"What's the location?"

Jackson gave him the cross streets and description. "No address, sorry. Are you coming out?"

"I'm staying here until everyone has gone home. Then I'll knock on the door and look into every bedroom if I can."

"I'll talk to the Norton family, then we'll regroup. It seems like our perp may have backed off tonight."

"I hope he didn't spot me."

"He may have just had trouble luring a victim out in this weather." Jackson turned left on Thirty-Ninth. "I'm almost there. Call me if anything changes."

He hung up and turned right on High Street. About half the houses on the block were two stories, and in the dark, they all looked brown. Did he have to get out and look at names on mailboxes? He rolled down his window for better visibility, and snowflakes drifted in. He searched the left side of the street first, driving in the wrong lane. The main lights were out in most houses, with just an upstairs lamp or a small glow from a back room. Nothing moved on the street. Not a car, not a walker, not a stray cat. Snow drifted down, wrapping the neighborhood in an eerie silence.

Jackson cruised slowly, ignoring the ranch styles and the split-levels, watching for the big two-story homes. That one was definitely beige, but sometimes beige looked like pale green to him. Had she meant sage or forest green? He stopped the car, jumped out, and checked the mailbox. Not the Nortons. He turned back to his car and spotted something unusual farther up the street. A dark lump on the lawn of another house. A sleeping dog? He jumped into his car and rolled forward. The home connected to the yard was a two-story. When he reached the edge of the lawn, the shape came into focus. A person lying across the walkway. *Oh no.* The other victims had been dropped in their parents' front yards after the assault. Goddammit, they'd been too late.

Heart hammering, he slammed his car into park and shut it down, leaving it in the street. Jackson ran to the body in the grass and kneeled down. A teenage girl, slim and lifeless. He touched her neck. Dear god, she was cold. He grabbed his phone and dialed 911. "Jackson here. I've got a young girl with hypothermia. High Street between Thirty-Ninth and Fortieth." Keeping the line open, he ran for the trunk of his car. Inside were a tarp and a blanket, as well as other emergency supplies. He grabbed the blanket, slammed the trunk, and ran back to the girl.

A porch light came on, and the front door opened.

To the dispatcher, Jackson said, "I'm taking her down the hill. She's not injured, just freezing. I'll meet the ambulance at the Woodfield Station shopping center."

Someone ran toward him on the sidewalk. "Skylar?" Then full panic. "Skylar!"

The man grabbed his arm. "What's going on?"

"I'm EPD. She's freezing, so I'm taking her to the ER. Open the back door of my car!" Jackson threw the blanket over the girl, scooped her up, and ran for his vehicle.

CHAPTER 38

Wednesday, November 26, 7:50 a.m.

Jackson stood in the conference room, chugging coffee and waiting for the others to show. The caffeine made him sweat, but the weight in his legs and eyelids didn't change. He'd been up until three that morning talking to Skylar's parents in the ER lobby, then conferring with Schak and Lammers near the party house, while the snow blanketed everything around them. Then he'd gone back to the hospital to take Katie home. She'd been sleeping when he left that morning, and Benjie was still with Kera. In about two hours, she would bring the boys and meet him at the juvenile court for the custody hearing. Of all days to be this tired and full of self-doubt. He wanted the judge to see him at his best. But the task force had to regroup and form a new plan for catching the predator.

Quince walked in first, looking as tired as Jackson felt.

"Where the hell were you last night?"

Quince slumped into a chair. "I'm sorry, but I have a second job now. I'm a part-time TSA agent at the airport."

Relief hit Jackson hard. Quince wasn't their perp. "But why?"

"My mother lost her job two months ago and is broke, and my girlfriend is having health issues and can't work. Suddenly, a lot of people depend on me financially, and this position just doesn't pay enough by itself."

Compassion first. "I'm sorry to hear all that." *Now the reality check.* "But you should have told me. Or Lammers. We needed you last night. We lost the perp, and a girl was not only assaulted, but she almost froze to death too."

"Oh shit." Quince covered his face. "I'm so sorry."

Jackson let him off the hook. "The sting came together at the last minute, and it could have gone badly, even with your help. But we had to call Lammers out for backup, so I'm sure she'll have something to say about it."

"Right after this meeting." The boss strode in, looking alert despite her late night. "How is Skylar Norton doing?"

"I was with her parents when a nurse reassured them she would survive."

They were all quiet for a moment. Schak strode in and dropped his carryall on the table. "What a clusterfuck that turned out to be." He slumped into a chair, looking haggard.

Evans came in behind him. "The Kelsey Walker profile is gone. Deleted. I checked first thing this morning."

Schak let out a string of curses—something they all tried not to do, especially in the building. Except for Lammers. She did and said whatever she wanted.

He caught his partner's gaze. "Schak, this is your case. What do you want to do next?"

"I'm going back to Cranston with another subpoena. A girl almost died last night after chatting with the Kelsey profile. I want to find out everything we can about that account."

"I thought Facebook was going to send a location."

"They did. Kelsey's page was created at the library. But there has to be more. If the guy ever used a credit card on the site or uploaded a photo from his cell phone—that information is still out there. We also need to dig into the site where he posted the video of Ashley." Schak's voice became loud and passionate. "We need to sit here in this conference room and write subpoenas until it's time for Danny's funeral service."

Jackson patted his friend's shoulder. "I'm sorry, but I can't make the service. I have a custody hearing for Benjie, and now I have a challenger. If I'm not there, I'll lose."

Schak spun toward him. "Who else wants Benjie?"

His teammates had all become fond of the boy during an earlier investigation. "A woman named Caprice Arlen. She claims to be his aunt."

"I'll testify to how quickly he bonded to you," Evans offered.

"Thanks, but his social service manager will be there to recommend me." Jackson looked around. "Let's get focused." He'd decided to run the meeting. Now that the cases had merged, Schak needed to step back again because of his emotional involvement. Which reminded him: Lammers didn't know the cases had merged and that he was still investigating Thompson's death. He would explain when it came up.

"What went wrong last night?" Evans asked. "And again, I'm sorry I wasn't available."

Schak shook his head, the circles under his eyes even darker this morning. He hadn't shaved either. "The perp never showed at the party. Plus, he used a private chat to find out Skylar's plans, then picked her up when she left a friend's house."

"He used chloroform this time," Jackson added. "The hospital found traces. So he's becoming more aggressive."

"Have the parents received a blackmail text?" Evans asked, standing next to the whiteboard.

"Not yet. But the last time he waited until the next morning, so it could still be coming," Schak said. "We still have a chance to grab him during the money drop."

"If he shut down the profile, he's not going to risk a blackmail scheme," Evans argued.

Lammers spoke up. "Are we certain the person behind that profile is our guy?"

Jackson was confident. "Dragoo accessed the account and saw some of the exchanges with Skylar and another girl right before the predator shut it down."

"How did you find the profile?" the boss probed.

Jackson tried to finesse the fact that he had continued working Thompson's case after she'd ordered him not to. "We found another victim from a few weeks ago. The perp claimed to have a video, but he couldn't produce proof of it, so the parents didn't pay the blackmail."

"They didn't report it either?"

"The perp also said he had proof that the daughter smoked the mother's medical marijuana, so she was afraid to be arrested and fired."

Lammers tapped a pen on the table. "So the blackmailer failed to collect a payment two weeks ago, then failed to collect again last week with Ashley's parents." The sergeant looked at Jackson. "He seems desperate and escalating. He may try something more direct."

"Like what? Rob a bank?" Schak scowled.

"Or straight blackmail," Jackson said. "He seems to know things about the parents. We need to figure out where he's getting his information."

"I thought it might be Riverside school," Schak said. "But I checked the list of employees, and no one has any criminal history. But now we have Grace, who attends Sheldon, and Skylar goes to Spencer, so maybe he works for the school district."

"Good thought." Lammers was animated, enjoying herself. "Let's see if we can get a complete list of employees who have access to the district's computers, then cross-check them with criminal files."

"And everything else we know about him," Schak added. "School districts usually run background checks."

"Teachers sometimes sexually molest their students anyway," Evans argued. "So he might not have a criminal background."

"What other angles can we work?" Lammers seemed to have taken over the meeting.

"I can do more follow-up on the one blackmail payment he successfully collected," Schak said. "He used Mobile Source and one of its clients. So I think he lives or works in the area around the drop. We can correlate that location with school employees."

Jackson had a thought. "If he's using the library computers, maybe we can set up some flags in their system. I'll call and ask."

"What else do I need to know?" the boss asked.

Jackson had to tell her. "Officer Thompson knew about Grace Marston's assault. Grace interacted with Kelsey Walker right before she was attacked. That's how we found the profile."

Lammers was silent, her expression unreadable.

Schak jumped in. "What if Danny was investigating these assaults on his own?"

Lammers turned slowly toward Schak. "You're saying that Dan Thompson's murder might be connected to the rape-and-blackmail crimes?"

"We think so." Schak grimaced. "Maybe the perp killed Danny to protect himself."

"For fuck's sake." Lammers stared at Jackson now. "How does that explain Pete Scully's death?"

"He was framed. I think the killer shot him while he slept."

"The Walsh twins had nothing to do with Thompson's death? And neither did the drifter?" Lammers seemed shell-shocked.

"It looks that way."

"Then we start over." The boss stood. "But first, we have a funeral service to attend."

CHAPTER 39

On the way out of the building, Jackson said, "I'm sorry for your loss, and I'm sorry about the bad timing of my court hearing."

Schak didn't need an apology. "Don't worry, the rest of the department will be there. Besides, you broke open the case. That's the best way to honor Danny."

Jackson pulled something from his pocket and handed it to him. "I found this in your cousin's truck. I listened to a few files, and most of them seemed personal. Maybe you should have it."

Schak slipped the recorder into his pocket. How much would it hurt to listen to Danny's voice? "Thanks. Good luck in court."

They parted ways in the parking lot, and Schak hurried to his car. He still had to swing by and pick up Kurt for the service. His cousin had contacted him early that morning and asked for a ride. Aunt Donna had been called in to perform a heart transplant surgery at a nearby hospital and wouldn't make the service either.

Schak drove across town, grateful for the unexpected blue sky. Danny deserved a glorious memorial with bright sunshine to reflect his life of service. Thinking about Danny hurt like hell. It was so hard to accept that he was gone. They would never camp and fish together again. Or attend UO football games, drinking in the parking lot with the rest of the tailgaters. Maybe he would start to spend more time with Kurt. He and Danny had tried to include him, but the wheelchair made things challenging, and Kurt didn't care for sports.

He turned on Lincoln Street and started up the hill. Hoping to make himself feel better, Schak reached into his pocket for the recorder Jackson had given him and played the first file. Instead, hearing Danny's voice almost made him cry. It was just a list of things to do, with an occasional humorous comment, such as "See eye doctor for glasses. Squinting ruins my handsome face." God, he would miss him.

Schak waited until the emotional moment passed, then listened to another file. "Find out what medicine Kurt is taking. It's helping him get around better, but the side effects are awful."

That was news to him. Kurt had always been able to stand and take a few steps, but the pain was unbearable. Schak had never seen him walk more than a few feet. He turned on Twenty-Fourth and realized he was passing the location of the blackmail money drop. Too bad that turned into a dead end.

He listened to several more of Danny's mundane messages, then one caught his attention. "Confront Kurt with the list of my username and password violations."

What was that about? As a computer specialist with the county, Kurt had access to employee databases, but what did he have to gain by logging into police files? Schak drove a half block and parked in front of Kurt's small house. His aunt had recently helped his cousin buy it so he could be more autonomous.

Schak hurried up the walkway and rang the doorbell. Kurt didn't respond, so he rang again then opened the door a crack. "Kurt, you ready?"

He stepped inside. They were family, and that was how it had always been with their mothers and their homes. "Kurt, let's go. We don't want to be late for Danny's funeral." In his head, he heard Aunt Donna teasing Danny about being late to his own funeral. Schak fought the grief that threatened to engulf him. Kurt's wheelchair was by the door leading from the kitchen into the garage, but he didn't see his cousin. He stepped into the short hallway and called out again.

From the garage, Kurt called back, "I'll be right in."

What was he doing out there? Schak started in that direction, then froze. A bedroom door was ajar, and he stepped toward it. Something had caught his eye. The bed. It was shoved into a corner and covered with only a dirty white sheet. Like the background in Ashley's assault video. *No!* It had to be coincidence. This was just a spare bedroom, like thousands of others. Schak pushed open the door and looked around. Nothing else was in the room except a small dresser against the wall near the door. Instinctively, he stepped toward the closet and jerked open the bifold doors. A blue patrol uniform hung in the back. Queasy dread made his knees buckle a little. *Oh, fuck, no.* But how? Kurt couldn't even walk.

He heard the sound of Kurt's wheelchair coming. Schak stepped away from the closet.

His cousin rolled into the bedroom. "What are you doing in here?" His handsome face was unsmiling.

"You can walk now, can't you?" Schak felt the anger in his voice and didn't care.

"A little bit. I've been taking a gene therapy for a year now, and it's working." Kurt sounded calm, but his eyes flashed with fear. "I still need the wheelchair."

"Why keep your progress a secret?"

"Because I don't trust it. I keep thinking I'll slip back."

Schak thought about the girls who'd been assaulted. They'd been abducted first and transported to the perp's house. "Is your car in the garage?"

"Yes, why?"

"What were you doing out there?"

"Just cleaning it out. Why all the questions?"

"Why did you call me for a ride?"

"It's Danny's funeral service." Kurt's voice cracked with emotion. "Mom had to get ready for an important last-minute surgery, and I didn't want to go alone. We should leave now."

"Why do you have a cop's uniform in your closet?"

"I bought it for a Halloween party a long time ago. Because my brother and my cousin are police officers. Because I wanted to be one too. What's the big deal? Come on, let's go."

Shaking with anger, Schak yelled, "Stand up! I want to see you walk."

"Why are you being like this?" Kurt rolled away from him.

The truth was obvious and deeply painful. He'd lost another cousin. "You're lying! Ashley Devonshire was sexually assaulted in this room. You videotaped it and blackmailed her parents." Schak lurched toward him, grabbed the lapels of his suit, and pulled him to his feet. "What the fuck is wrong with you?"

"Get off me!" Kurt jerked free and took a swing at him.

Schak blocked it, rage taking over. He punched Kurt in the gut to stun the taller man, then followed up with a shot to his face. "You fucking pervert!"

Blood ran from his cousin's nose, but Kurt didn't cry out. He charged Schak, head down, and slammed into his chest. Schak bounced into the wall, but brought a fist up under Kurt's chin. He pummeled his cousin's head until he dropped to his knees.

Schak knocked him to the ground and straddled him. "Tell me why you did it."

"Just let it go." Kurt's face had begun to swell, and his eyes filled with tears.

Schak grabbed a handful of hair and slammed Kurt's head into the floor. "Why? The money? Sexual jollies? Was it worth it? Your last victim killed herself!"

His cousin cried out, "I didn't know she died. I'm so sorry."

Schak wasn't moved by his pain. It meant nothing compared to the hole that had just been ripped in his heart. "Why the blackmail? Aunt Donna has always taken care of you. What did you need the money for?"

"The medication is expensive and not covered by insurance." Kurt's voice was loud, raw, and defensive. "Mom lost a malpractice suit and couldn't pay for it anymore."

It hurt to think about. "But rape? So you could afford the pills that helped you walk?"

"It wasn't rape. Just a little finger fucking. No one got hurt."

"A girl killed herself!"

"That wasn't supposed to happen."

Sick to his stomach, Schak stood and reached for the cuffs he always carried in his work suit. "Get up. I'm taking you in."

"Please don't. I'll stop, I promise. I'm not a real threat to anyone." Kurt struggled to his feet, wiping blood from his face.

Was he serious? Did Kurt not realize he was a criminal? How could he and Danny be brothers? Even half brothers? *Danny!* A realization hit Schak with a force that felt physical. Danny had figured it out. Rage crushed his brain and distorted his vision. "You killed your own brother to keep from going to jail? You worthless piece of shit!" Schak slammed his fist into Kurt's mouth. Kurt cried out and fell, landing on his wheelchair.

Holding his chin, Kurt shouted, "What are you talking about? I thought a homeless man killed Danny." His cousin looked stunned.

"Danny knew about two of the assaults. He confronted you, didn't he?"

"No." Something shifted in his eyes. "I would never hurt Danny."

"But he hurt you all those years ago and put you in a wheelchair."

"That was an accident, and I'm getting better." Kurt clasped his hands together, begging. "You've got to believe me. I didn't kill Danny, and I can't believe you think I would."

"Liar!" Schak spun him around and cuffed him. "You'll get the death penalty for killing a police officer. But you're already dead to me."

"I didn't kill him!"

"Then who did?"

Kurt began to weep. "Oh god. I think I know."

CHAPTER 40

Jackson walked into the court at the juvenile justice center, and his body tensed. The last time he'd been in this room, a judge had determined that Katie needed counseling for her drinking, and he'd had to recount the whole scenario of how her mother died. This time would be different, he told himself. The guardianship hearing he'd already had for Benjie had taken place in the judge's office, and it had been brief.

Jackson spotted Kera in the back row and took a seat next to her. Benjie climbed out of her lap and into his, then kissed his face. "I missed you, Daddy."

"I missed you too." Jackson leaned over and kissed Kera. "Thanks for taking such good care of the boys." He tousled Micah's hair so Kera's grandson didn't feel left out. If he and Kera were going to move in together, he had to start treating Micah more like a son.

"You should sit up front with your lawyer and your primary witness," Kera whispered.

"I know. I was just saying hi." Jackson tried to set Benjie back on the seat, but the boy clung to him. A familiar feeling.

He carried him to the front and sat down next to Mariah Martin, the social worker who'd come to the original crime scene. Benjie whispered in his ear, "I don't want to go with her."

"Don't worry. You won't." What if he lost this petition? What if they took Benjie out of his arms and sent him home with a stranger? Worry churned in Jackson's stomach.

Next to him, the social worker patted his leg. "We've got this."

Jackson tried to relax, but he knew judges tended to side with biological family members. Some people were focused on genetics. Jackson couldn't help but think about the man who'd sired Benjie, or thought he had. He'd become so obsessed with getting his son back that he'd resorted to outrageous criminal behavior. Some people would do anything to protect and keep their children. Jackson grew more worried. The other petitioner was a woman. Judges liked to award custody to women.

A moment later, the judge came in, and they all stood while she settled into her elevated seat. A stout woman with a buzz cut like Schak's, Judge Holt called the room to order and promised to keep the hearing short.

"I already spoke with Mr. Jackson when he applied for guardianship," the judge said, "so I'd like to hear from the other petitioner first. Caprice Arlen, are you present?"

A woman on the opposite bench stood. She was fifty-something and wore a plain brown dress and a white hairnet-like thing. Was that a religious preference?

"What's your relationship to the child, Benjie Caiden?" the judge asked.

"I'm his great-aunt. He's my sister's grandchild. But she's dead, Your Honor."

"Do you have other children in your home?"

"No, I wasn't blessed." A solemn voice.

"Who else lives with you? A husband or any other family?"

"Just me. My husband passed away last year."

Jackson felt sorry for her, but she wasn't right for Benjie.

The judge continued. "Why didn't you come forward when Mr. Jackson was looking for family members?"

"I didn't hear about the child until recently."

"You mean when the court notified you of your sister's will?"

Thank god. Judge Holt thought the woman was after Benjie's small inheritance. Jackson would gladly give it to Arlen to make her go away. His phone rang, and he slipped it from his pocket. *Jasmine Parker.* He silenced the cell and rejected the call, even though he really wanted to know what she had for him. He glanced at the judge, who was still asking questions, set Benjie next to him, and texted Parker: *What have you got?*

The social worker gave him a dirty look. Jackson tuned back in to the proceedings. A moment later, the judge asked if his family situation was the same. Jackson stood. "Yes, your honor. But my longtime partner and I are planning to move in together. She has a young child, and we want to raise the boys as brothers."

"What's her name and what does she do? Or *his* name, if that's the case."

Jackson held back a smile. Eugene was so politically correct. "Kera Kollmorgan. She's a part-time nurse."

The judge turned to the social worker and asked her in which home she thought Benjie should be placed. As Martin responded, his phone buzzed in his pocket. Jackson slipped it out. Jasmine had texted: *Dr. Donna Thompson wrote the Rx you asked about. The date matches a community outreach program for the homeless.*

Dan Thompson's mother? A cold chill ran through his chest. The victim's mother was connected to the drifter. It couldn't be coincidence. The earlier thought echoed in his head. *Some people would do anything to protect their children.* But Dan Thompson *was* her child. A more heinous thought gripped him. Danny wasn't her only child. He had a brother. Why would Donna need to protect her other son? Then it hit him. Officer Thompson might have known something incriminating about his sibling. What was his name? Jackson pulled out his case notes and flipped through them. Kurt. And if Dan had threatened to put Kurt in jail, their mother might have protected her weaker child by silencing Dan. If he hadn't seen worse, it would be hard to believe. Schak wouldn't want to hear it at all.

Still, Jackson had to find Donna Thompson immediately.

He glanced up and heard the judge say: "Full custody of Benjie Caiden is awarded to Wade Jackson."

Thank god. Now he had to adopt the boy and give him the Jackson name. He squeezed Benjie. "We won. You get to stay with me."

Benjie let out a "Boo-yah!" and Jackson almost smiled. The boy had been watching basketball with Katie, who'd gotten her love of sports from her mother.

Jackson jumped to his feet and thanked Martin and his lawyer, who would be well paid for sitting there and saying nothing. He hurried back to Kera. "We just got a huge breakthrough on this case, and I have to go."

"Good news all the way around." She tried to look happy.

"We'll make an arrest today. Probably several. And I'll be home all day tomorrow for Thanksgiving."

"Congratulations on becoming a father again."

He handed Benjie over, kissed her, and bolted from the courtroom.

CHAPTER 41

In his car, Jackson called Schak. "Hey, partner. How's the service?" He had to ease into this slowly.

"I'm not there. I'm at the department. How did your custody case go?" Schak's voice was strangely quiet.

"I won." Jackson pulled onto the road. "Why are you at the department?" Something was going on.

"I arrested the sexual predator. He confessed when I confronted him."

Holy shit! "Who is it?"

"Kurt Thompson, my cousin. Danny's half brother."

It all fell into place. "I'm so sorry. You must be devastated."

"Yeah, it's been a shitty week for my family."

Jackson had to tell him, and there was no gentle way. "I'm afraid it's worse than you think."

"You mean my aunt?"

"You know?"

"It's just suspicion so far, but yeah." Schak's voice was dead-pan. His partner was holding in his emotions.

"We may have something solid," Jackson offered. "Donna Thompson wrote the prescription we found in Pete Scully's rucksack."

"So she killed the drifter too?" Schak's voice cracked. "Kurt knows something about Donna's involvement, but he's still protecting her."

"Let's bring her in and pit them against each other."

Schak was silent for a long moment. "My aunt never forgave Danny for accidentally shooting Kurt. She pretended to, maybe even wanted to. But she never treated them the same after the accident. She even sent Danny to live with us for a while."

"Do you know where she is?"

"She has a surgery, a heart transplant. So she's probably at the hospital."

"I'll head over there now." Jackson hoped she hadn't started the surgery yet. But if so, they would be there when she completed it. Her crimes were potentially horrendous.

"I'll meet you there."

"You don't have to. I'll get Evans to come out."

"No, she's at Danny's service. And I want to be present when you arrest Donna. Maybe I can get her to confess or at least admit something we can use."

"What about Kurt?"

"I'll leave him in the hole."

• • •

Twenty minutes later, Jackson charged into the main lobby of the new hospital, struck again by how spacious and upscale the building was. He gave his name and showed his badge to the young woman behind the circular reception desk. "I need to speak with Dr. Donna Thompson immediately."

"I'll see if I can locate her in the system." The young woman keyed in some information, her nails making a loud clicking sound in the massive, silent lobby. "Dr. Thompson has a surgery this afternoon, so she's in the hospital somewhere. Probably in the cardiothoracic institute next door." She pointed at a hallway to his right. "Down that hall."

"Will you page her?" Tracking down a doctor in this massive complex would waste his time. "Don't mention my name. Just tell her it's important to come to this reception desk."

"I'll try."

Jackson stepped back and checked his phone. Nothing new had come in. He started to doubt his case against the doctor. All they had was a prescription written months ago at a community outreach program. He still had to question her. Considering what he would accuse her of, the emotional element should work in his favor, maybe even break her down. Unless she was a sociopath with little empathy for others. Many high achievers were.

Hurried footsteps behind him. He glanced over and saw Schak—still in the black suit he'd worn with the intention of attending a funeral. Poor guy had missed the department's tribute to his cousin, a fallen officer.

"Is she here?" Schak's voice and face were filled with anxiety.

"Yes, they're paging her."

The receptionist called out, "Excuse me."

Jackson turned back to her.

"The scheduler at the institute says Dr. Thompson isn't available. She's traveling with the donated heart to Bend and will be part of the team that transplants it into a new patient." The receptionist gave a small smile. "It's a miraculous day for someone and their family."

Oh no. Jackson was torn. He didn't want to interrupt a process that could save someone's life. But he couldn't let a killer leave town. If she figured out they wanted to question her, she might disappear. He turned to Schak. "Do we intercept her?"

"Hell yes. Another doctor can do the surgery. I want answers now."

The receptionist cut in. "You'll have to wait. The helicopter is on the pad, so she's leaving."

Schak lurched toward the desk. "How do we get up there?"

The receptionist's eyes went wide. "Take the elevators in the Emergency Department."

Schak bolted for the hall on the right, and Jackson rushed after him. At the intersection, they turned left and ran toward the emergency area. Jackson reached the admitting desk first. "Where are the elevators to the roof?" He showed his badge. "I need to get up there now."

The man in blue scrubs didn't move, but confusion spread over his face. "The team is taking a donor heart to a patient in Bend. We can't interrupt that."

"We have to," Schak said. "Dr. Thompson is wanted for murder."

The desk attendant blinked, looked them over thoroughly, then said, "Follow me."

They went back into the same maze of hallways Jackson had traveled the night before with Katie, then Skylar. Most of the doctors and nurses didn't even look up from their tasks. Jackson hoped this was his last trip here. He'd spent far more than his share of time in hospitals.

They stopped in front of a set of steel doors. The attendant hit a red button, the doors opened, and they stepped into an oversize elevator, designed for a gurney and several people. The ride to the roof took only a moment, and they stepped out. Cold wind whipped Jackson's pant legs and made his eyes water.

Two people bundled in heavy coats over blue scrubs climbed into the helicopter in the center of the landing pad. Jackson called out, "Wait!" and ran toward them.

The woman glanced back, then shouted something at the pilot.

The rotors came to life, filling the quiet day with a whooping sound. Jackson shuddered, and his pace slowed instinctively. The blades were on top of the helicopter, he told himself. It was safe to approach.

Inside the chopper, Donna Thompson gestured and shouted at the pilot.

The pilot turned to face her and shook his head.

Jackson couldn't hear what they were saying, but she looked furious. After a brief shouting match, the blades began to slow. A minute later, their suspect stepped out of the helicopter.

"Can this wait?" she snapped. "I have a heart transplant to perform. A life is on the line."

The irony was overwhelming. "Other lives have been lost, and we'd like to talk to you about them."

CHAPTER 42

Schak sat across from his aunt in the windowless room, a scenario he would have never predicted. His whole body ached with tension.

"I'm not answering questions without my lawyer," Donna stated.

He leaned over the table. "You haven't been charged or read your rights. This is the only moment when you get to tell us anything, and we can't use it against you in court." A half-truth.

"I have nothing to say."

"What about the prescription you wrote for Pete Scully? Why not explain that?" Schak gestured around. "There's no camera in here, and my recorder is turned off." He hoped she would buy it. Schak tapped the device on the table. "It's just you and me. Help me understand why you're connected to a vagrant."

"I'm not connected to him. Danny asked me to participate in one of those community outreach fairs for the homeless, and I wrote scripts for several people. So what?"

At least she was talking. Jackson would come in any moment to confront her with Kurt's betrayal—real or fictitious—whatever they needed to make it work. Evans was watching both interrogations on the monitors. "A gray Lexus was spotted a block away from Danny's body that night. We're pulling security video now. If you got in or out of that car, it'll be on the footage, placing you at the murder scene."

Donna's artificially smooth skin seemed to tighten even more. "So what if I came out there to meet Danny? I wanted to see him."

Yes! She had admitted to being at the crime scene. "Did you get in his truck?"

"Yes, we had a drink. So?"

Jackson breezed into the room but didn't sit. "Mrs. Thompson," he said, leaning on the table with both hands. "Your son Kurt claims you killed Danny. Kurt has already confessed to sexual assault and blackmail, so there's no need to protect him anymore. You need to tell us everything and make the best deal you can."

Donna, looking thin under a loose white doctor's coat, shook her head. "Kurt didn't betray me."

"One of you will get the death penalty for Danny's murder, and Kurt decided to save himself."

"I want to see Kurt. Right now."

Schak repressed a smile. She was playing right into their setup. He looked at Jackson. "I don't think we should let them confer."

Jackson shrugged. "I'm curious to see what kind of story they come up with." Jackson stepped toward the door. "I'll get Kurt, and he can tell you himself that he spilled everything he knows."

Donna made a low-pitched sound, displaying her disgust. "Kurt doesn't know anything. He's a sweet boy with a talent for computers, but otherwise not all that bright."

Schak stepped out of the room and waited while Jackson moved Kurt into the small space with Donna, came out, and closed the door.

"This could backfire," Schak warned. "Those two have always been close. And Donna has protected and coddled Kurt from the moment he was born."

Jackson turned for the stairs. "But now that he knows his mother killed Danny, all the old patterns go out the window."

Schak followed him up to the conference room, and they stood next to Evans in front of the monitors.

Evans laughed. "She just slapped him, so this is going to be good."

"Shhh." They all went quiet, needing to hear every word.

On the monitor Donna screeched, "What did you tell them?"

Kurt stepped away and rubbed his face. "Just what I saw that night when you came home. I was there, in the family room. I heard you come in, so I got up and walked into the hall. You had blood on your face."

Donna's brow creased. "Why didn't you talk to me? I didn't even see you."

"I know. You looked upset and went straight to the shower, so I left."

"And you told the detectives that?"

"I had to," Kurt whined. "Rob thought I killed Danny. He was going to charge me with aggravated murder."

"You think I killed your brother?"

"I don't know what to think. Whose blood was on your face?"

"That drifter's. I saw him kill Danny, so I got justice."

"No, you paid him to do it. Why?" Kurt's eyes were pinpoints of pain.

"To protect you, as always!" She stepped in close to her son and lowered her voice.

. . .

Donna couldn't believe Rob, the fat little fuck, had somehow figured out her role in Danny's death. Her alleged role, she corrected. They had nothing on her but speculation. She'd been careful. Except for leaving the damn cash in the drifter's pack. But at the time, she'd been a little rattled. Scully had been late, and Danny had almost passed out before the bum had shown up to do the stabbing. Later, as she waited for him to settle into the sleeping bag, snow had really started coming down, making her rush the job at the last minute. Crawling into that space in the dark had unnerved her, even with all the camping she'd done in primitive settings. So she'd moved quickly to shoot him, fake the suicide, and get the hell out—forgetting to take back the cash. *Damn.* Had that little mistake put them onto her?

She couldn't believe it had come to this. The plan had seemed foolproof—and meant to be. Scully, the drifter, had contacted her asking for a different prescription, right after Danny confronted her about Kurt's problem. The timing was serendipitous, and she'd known exactly how to handle the issue. But Kurt was never supposed to know. Why had he been in her house? Why hadn't he confronted her?

Watching Danny die had bothered her more than she'd expected. Yet, afterward, she'd felt mostly relief. She loved Danny, but she hated Danny. He'd been forced on her by her first husband, a man she'd grown to hate. But she'd tried to love her son. Then Danny had taken Kurt's wholeness when he'd shot her little one all those years ago. Heartbreaking! With his looks and charm, Kurt could have been a politician or an actor. But no. Danny had robbed him of that. Then just as Kurt was getting better as a result of taking a new miracle drug, Danny had threatened to take what was left of Kurt's life and freedom after he'd discovered his unsavory activities. She couldn't let him. Kurt deserved a chance to really live. She could have put a stop to Kurt's deviancy, if Danny had given her a chance. But he was so self-righteous.

Focus! She had to dig out of this. She would get the best defense lawyer she could afford. She would also file a lawsuit against the police department for harassment. Because they would never prove their case. Never! This would all work out. She might lose her job and reputation here in Eugene, but the rest of the world needed doctors. And she needed to continue making life-and-death decisions. It was how she thrived. But she had to get Kurt back on her side. "Danny confronted me about your sexual escapades and blackmail schemes. If you hadn't worn the damn cop uniform and used his password to access files, he might have never suspected you."

"Was he going to turn me in?"

"Of course. But none of that matters now. We need a cohesive story." She grabbed her son's hands and squeezed hard, her voice low and pleading. "You need to tell them you were mistaken about the night you saw the blood on my face. Say it was Thursday, and I'll say it came from a trauma case in the ER."

"It's too late." Kurt moved toward the door. "You killed Danny, and it's all fucked up now. I can't help you. Only myself." He pounded on the door and yelled to be let out.

CHAPTER 43

Wednesday, November 26, 3:45 p.m.

Schak slumped into a chair in the conference room. His body felt as if he'd been beaten with a bat, and his heart had shriveled to a black hole. His entire second family—gone. He would never spend another moment, outside of court, with any of them. Kurt and Donna had turned out to be strangers—people he didn't even know.

Donna's lawyer had arrived before they could pressure her into a plea deal, and she'd stopped talking except to say she'd been home all Friday evening. He and Jackson had consulted with the district attorney, who said it was too soon to charge her with murder. The video of her confession to Kurt would likely be suppressed by a judge, but Kurt would testify against her. The DA's office had produced a subpoena, so they were able to collect a DNA swab before they were forced to let Donna go. At least they had her forensic evidence to compare with everything at both crime scenes.

The rest of the team filed in, looking glum. Evans started to say something to him, but Schak held up his hand. "No sympathy, please. Let's just get this done." Schak wanted to go see his wife and son, to know that he still had a family.

"Tomorrow's Thanksgiving, and I want you all to take the day off," Lammers said. "I know we have a lot of work ahead to build a case against Donna Thompson, but we can wait until Friday to start."

"At least Kurt took a deal." Evans turned to Schak. "Why did he need the money?" Her voice had a pained quality he'd never heard before.

"Expensive gene therapy treatment that was helping him walk."

"So he regained the use of his legs and decided to become a rapist." Evans shook her head in disgust.

"Kurt says he didn't rape them, that it was all manual."

"Kurt's a misogynistic soulless idiot." Contempt oozed from every pore in Evans' face. "But he confessed, so he's going to prison, and we don't have to talk about him." Evans flashed a small smile. "Speaking of idiots. Gene Burns was arrested again last night. He hit Trisha, and this time there's a witness."

Jackson said, "Good to hear," but nobody else seemed to care.

"What do we have left to talk about?" Schak asked. "I'm ready to get out of here."

"We need a plan for Friday," Lammers said. "We have to take Donna Thompson's photo to every business near the crime scene and to every homeless person in the camp. We need at least one eyewitness who saw her in the area."

The video footage from the business district hadn't caught the car. And Donna had changed her story about meeting Danny that night, claiming it was the night before at a different home-less camp. Jurors wouldn't buy her lame confusion if they had an eyewitness contradicting it.

"Jacob Walsh saw her," Jackson reminded them. "I'll take a picture to him and get it confirmed. I also need to follow up on my promise to buy him a unit in Opportunity Village."

"I want to split that cost with you," Schak offered, surprising himself. "And I'll go with you when you talk to the chief. We need to change some attitudes around here." Starting with his own. He'd been too quick to think a street person was capable of mur-der and too slow to see the truth about his own family.

"We need to find the clothes Donna Thompson wore that night," Jackson said. "Even if we have to search every trash can in the area." He hit the table for emphasis. "She was there! She sat in his car and got him high on alcohol and benzos, then dragged him to the brush where Scully stabbed him. We need a search warrant for her home immediately."

"I've got the paperwork," Lammers said. "Evans and I are going out there right after this meeting, and I'll call in search teams to check trash cans. We'll nail her, I promise."

Jackson looked surprised, relieved, and irritated all at once. "I can do it. This is my case."

"Go home and celebrate your new family member," Lammers said. "You've put in your share of time."

Jackson didn't argue. Schak stood too. "I'm going home. I need to find my wife and hug her, then sleep for ten hours." *And attend an AA meeting tomorrow*, he thought. Did they have them on Thanksgiving? Probably not. Maybe he'd go tonight and ask Tracy to go with him. The first step toward bringing her home.

• • •

4:15 p.m.

As she gathered her personal items into a box, Sophie's desk phone rang. *Oh boy.* The dreaded internal call. She answered with her usual chipper greeting.

"Chet Harris. Will you please come to my office?"

This was it. The official *You don't work here anymore.*

Sophie trudged downstairs to the management suite. She wasn't even nervous. She'd known this was coming for so long that it would be a relief to finally have it over with.

She stepped into his office and sat down, intending to beat him to the punch. "I'm sorry, but I can't cover Springfield cultural events. I'd rather quit. So put me back on crime and courts, or I'll turn in my resignation."

"That's why I called you in, to put you back on your beat."

WTF? "Wow. I'm surprised, but incredibly grateful. Can I ask why?"

"Your story on the eco-terrorist won the grand prize in the Northwest Journalism awards, and we realized we'd acted too hastily." Total deadpan. No shame, no apology.

Sophie bit her tongue.

"Congratulations, by the way." The boss gave her an odd smile.

"Thanks." Sophie stood. "I'd better get back to work. There's a dead body that needs explaining." She walked out before he could get in the last word.

• • •

5:07 p.m.

Jackson's phone rang on the way home, and it was Kera. "Hey, everything all right? You looked worried when you ran out of the courtroom earlier, and I haven't heard from you."

"I'm exhausted but good. We arrested the sexual predator and identified the killer, so it was a productive day. What about you?"

"I found a rental for us."

"Nice. Where is it?"

"Off Videra. With a nice view. Do you have time to see it?"

"Right now?"

"I made an appointment, and I'm on my way there. The rental office is closed tomorrow, and I didn't want to wait until Friday. All the kids are with me."

"Katie too?"

"Yep. She wanted to see the house."

"Give me the address, and I'll meet you there."

Kera rattled it off and hung up.

Excitement mixed with a little dread as Jackson drove out to the location. They were really going to do this and converge into one house. *It will be great*, he told himself. They were a family, so they might as well give each other their full support.

One look at the house, and he loved it. Modern lines, tall windows, and a stunning view of the Cascades. Not to mention the three-car garage that would hold all his vehicles and tools.

He parked next to Kera's car and climbed out. She and the boys were in the house, but Katie had waited for him in the driveway.

"Hey, Dad." She held open her arms.

His heart lurched. His daughter hadn't initiated a hug since her mother was killed. Jackson stepped forward and pulled her in for a long squeeze. God, it felt good to have her back.

She pulled away so she could look at him. "In the hospital I started thinking about the baby and feeling responsible for her death."

Her? They'd lost a baby girl? Jackson didn't ask. "It's not your fault. Don't ever think that."

"That's what the nurse said. But still, I could have done a lot better. I know that."

"You have to forgive yourself."

She blinked back tears. "I know. And I have to forgive you. Because Mom's death wasn't your fault."

Jackson fought back tears. "Thank you. I needed to hear that."

Katie shuffled her feet in the thin layer of snow. "I need to really let Kera into my life too. She's pretty amazing."

"We're lucky to have her." His heart was about to burst with joy. "Shall we go in and see the house?"

"I still want to paint my room black."

He pretended not to hear.

ABOUT THE AUTHOR

 L.J. Sellers writes the best-selling Detective Jackson mystery/thriller series—a two-time Readers' Favorite Award winner—the Agent Dallas series, and provocative stand-alone thrillers. Her sixteen novels have been highly praised by reviewers, and she's one of the highest-rated crime fiction authors on Amazon.com.

Sellers resides in Eugene, Oregon, where many of her novels are set, and is a Grand Neal Award–winning journalist. She's also the founder of Housing Help, a charity dedicated to keeping families from becoming homeless. When she is not plotting murders or working with her foundation, Sellers enjoys standup comedy, cycling, social networking, and mystery conferences. She's also been known to jump out of airplanes.